WRITE FOR ME, MARQUESS

A Very Fine Muddle
Book Five

Kate Archer

ARE YOU SIGNED UP FOR DRAGONBLADE'S BLOG?

You'll get the latest news and information on exclusive giveaways, exclusive excerpts, coming releases, sales, free books, cover reveals and more.

Check out our complete list of authors, too!

No spam, no junk. That's a promise!

Sign Up Here

www.dragonbladepublishing.com

Dearest Reader;

Thank you for your support of a small press. At Dragonblade Publishing, we strive to bring you the highest quality Historical Romance from some of the best authors in the business. Without your support, there is no 'us', so we sincerely hope you adore these stories and find some new favorite authors along the way.

Happy Reading!

CEO, Dragonblade Publishing

Additional Dragonblade books by Author Kate Archer

A Very Fine Muddle
Romance Me, Viscount (Book 1)
Be Daring, Duke (Book 2)
Stand With Me, Earl (Book 3)
Sweep Me Up, Baron (Book 4)
Write for Me, Marquess (Book 5)

A Series of Worthy Young Ladies
The Meddler (Book 1)
The Sprinter (Book 2)
The Undaunted (Book 3)
The Champion (Book 4)
The Jilter (Book 5)
The Regal (Book 6)

The Dukes' Pact Series
The Viscount's Sinful Bargain (Book 1)
The Marquess' Daring Wager (Book 2)
The Lord's Desperate Pledge (Book 3)
The Baron's Dangerous Contract (Book 4)
The Peer's Roguish Word (Book 5)
The Earl's Iron Warrant (Book 6)

PROLOGUE

THE BENNINGTON FAMILY'S unique style of courtship had not been lost on the *ton*.

At first, it must seem an anomaly that Lady Beatrice had a full coterie of gentlemen dying of love for her, only to turn round and marry the viscount, who nobody thought was in love with her, including the viscount.

Then had come Lady Rosalind. Still, it was only seen as a coincidence to note the circumstance of that daughter also taking an unusual route to the altar. One generally did not view a kidnapping as the ideal mode.

But then a pattern had begun to emerge when Lady Viola came on the scene. Really, it was hard to ignore that she'd somehow caused her young gentleman to engage himself for three duels on the same morning.

By the time Lady Cordelia made her curtsy, all were braced for whatever would transpire. It was well they did brace themselves, as it would have been very hard to predict discovering her on the stairs with Lord Harveston, the two of them having recently set fire to the Duke of Castleton's house.

As if the ladies themselves were not original enough, there was Miss Eloise Mayton to consider. She had acted as aunt and chaperone to all of the earl's daughters and few in society were certain what to make of her.

For some, she was the eccentric spinster dressed in widow's

weeds, though she was the widow of precisely nobody and seemed exceedingly cheerful for one allegedly swimming in the depths of grief. One deep in mourning was not generally seen delightedly trouncing another at cards, or charging at a sideboard and filling a plate with gusto.

For others of the *ton*, Miss Mayton was an unrepentant fibber and preposterous storyteller. After all, were they really supposed to believe that all those fellows on the continent had died of love for her? Whether it was flinging themselves off a mountaintop, a hanging, an impalement, or inflicting a deadly blow, it was all too absurd.

For still others, Miss Mayton was amusing, as they never did know what she'd say next.

But to her charges themselves, Eloise Mayton was their dear aunt. There was nothing they could not confide in her, there was nothing they could ever do that would meet with disapproval. Miss Mayton was always ready to admire and support her girls in whatever idea they had. Even if it turned out to be, as the Benningtons' butler was forever pointing out—a shockingly bad idea.

Now, the new season was ready to begin. The talk flew from drawing room to drawing room—another Bennington girl was coming to Town.

Lady Juliet, blessedly the last of the Bennington ladies, was on her way. It was said she marked herself a poetess and was determined to locate her poet.

The *ton* could not guess where it would go. But then, nobody ever had any luck predicting how a Bennington would proceed to church. She was likely to get there somehow, but she was unlikely to take the well-worn path through the front doors.

CHAPTER ONE

The Angel at Basingstoke, 1806

JULIET WAS ENORMOUSLY satisfied with the trip to Town so far. They had reached Basingstoke in only nine days, which was remarkably slow for the usual traveler, but lightning fast for a Bennington caravan.

There had been the inevitable delays, as there always were.

So many vistas to stop to admire, and then so many odes to write about them. Of course, when one wished to admire a vista, one must descend one's carriage to properly pay homage to Mother Nature in all her glory.

Where a person of a more pedestrian outlook might simply notice that the sun was up, a poetess such as Lady Juliet Bennington credited herself with perceiving that the wondrous orb had made its majestic rise to shower the world with warmth once more.

That wondrous orb had been their companion all day long and now it sunk slowly on the horizon to take its rest. They had just arrived to The Angel as the orb waved its final adieu.

Juliet and Miss Mayton had been escorted inside the inn while the earl and his butler made arrangements about the horses. As they waited in the foyer, Juliet heard a conversation that shook her to her bones.

"I tell ya," one man said to another, they both appearing

somewhat worse for wear in both drink and attire, "Marvelous Marvin ain't never let me down."

"Bosh," the other said. "That rooster is on his last legs, anybody can see it. He'll be killed in under a minute."

"You'll eat your words for dinner, Cresher. In one hour's time, the ring's set up in the far stables and you'll eat those very words."

Mr. Cresher, as that was his supposed name, retorted, "And you will be eatin' old Marvin for dinner!"

The men moved off. Juliet stared at her aunt. "What cruelty is this?" she whispered.

Miss Mayton nodded sadly. "Cockfighting, I'll never understand it. But then, Lord Darden says men will lay bets on practically anything. He had to stop the betting at his club after Lord Dunston lost a thousand pounds betting wrong that Mr. Cahill would arrive wearing a blue waistcoat. Lord Dunston's father was very put out about it."

"But Aunt, think of dear Marvelous Marvin!" Juliet said. "Anybody can tell he is not up for fighting. I suppose that awful man has made that poor bird fight no end of matches. It is too terrible to think of."

"Oh dear," Miss Mayton said.

"My thoughts exactly," Juliet answered. "We must rescue this Marvin from what can only be certain death!"

"Well now, your father…the earl has really been very good about…the goat, the parrot, then the other parrot, the dogs, and the cats we've rescued during other relocations to Town. But I am not entirely certain how he would view a rooster?"

"I feel, and I am really confident about it, that Papa will learn to love Marvin."

If Miss Mayton had thought to turn her charge away from the idea, she did seem swayed by Juliet's confidence about it.

"If you are certain, then I suppose—"

"Let us get settled into our rooms, and then we will snatch Marvin from the jaws of death."

"I do not suppose we ought to inform the earl ahead of time?"

"Goodness no," Juliet said, "we never like to trouble him."

Just then, the earl came into the inn, looking very jolly indeed. "You will not believe it, my dear girl. We are to have a poet as our guest at dinner. The fellow set to talking to me about my new carriage springs and, well one thing led to another. I've told him all about your odes!"

"Oh Papa, you are such a dear," Juliet said. "Is he handsome? Could he be *my* poet?"

She was determined to find her poet so they might read to each other their creations for all of their days. She had no care for her poet's circumstances, he might live in a garret and she would be perfectly satisfied with her accommodations. Poetry was everything.

Juliet thought it would be very typical of the fates to send her poet rushing to her side so quickly.

"I am afraid not," the earl said. "He is a bit too old and I believe him to be married."

Juliet was cast down to hear it.

"But only consider, my dear," Miss Mayton said, "there is every chance that this poet knows all the other poets."

"That is so true," Juliet said, considering. "And just think, if he were to hear one of my odes, then when he was meeting with all his poet friends in some dark and cramped tavern where they all exchanged their poignant ideas, he would be very likely to mention it."

"I do not see how he could fail to do so," Miss Mayton said.

"I suppose my poet would hear it and be determined to be introduced to the poetess who had composed the ode," Juliet said, already envisioning how it might come about.

"Nothing more likely, in my view," Miss Mayton said.

"I know nothing about dark and cramped taverns filled with the poignant ideas of poets, but I like this particular fellow exceedingly," the earl said. "I think we will have a very genial dinner."

With that happy note, they were shown to their rooms.

While Juliet was of course delighted that they would meet with a poet at dinner, even if he was not to be *her* poet, she found her thoughts far more consumed with Marvelous Marvin.

They hurried to their room, as she and Miss Mayton would share a bedchamber, while their maids, Lynette and Fleur, would be in an adjoining room.

"Where is Fleur?" Miss Mayton asked, as Lynette set about unpacking what they would need for the night.

Lynette sniffed, and it did not surprise Juliet one jot. Fleur was always trying to lord it over Lynette and Lynette was always fighting her off. The two maids had been locked in battle for as long as Juliet had been old enough to notice it.

"She has taken your nightdress, Miss Mayton," Lynette said, "and she claims she is 'le préparer pour la nuit.'"

"Preparing it for the night? That is new, I wonder what she is doing?" Miss Mayton said.

Lynette threw Juliet's own nightdress on her bed. "Holding it up to the light of a candle, Miss Mayton. Meaning, nothing at all!"

"We have little time to discuss it," Juliet said. "Now Lynette, Fleur will end sorry that she was not here helping you, as we are going to forget the unpacking and set off on an adventure."

"Adventure?" Lynette asked, looking suspicious.

"Now," Juliet said, "we'll need weapons of some sort. Oh, I know, we will bring our parasols."

"Weapons!" Lynette said.

"And candles to guide our way. Let us hurry," Juliet said, handing them out. "Marvin's fate hangs in the balance!"

Juliet led them down the stairs as Lynette muttered, "And who is Marvin? Why should Marvin need rescuing? Why should we be the ones doing it, I would like to know."

Neither Juliet nor Miss Mayton answered the maid, as they both knew well enough what her opinion would be.

They briefly stopped to inquire of the innkeeper the most pleasant way to take a stroll. The innkeeper pointed out it was dark and not particularly conducive to strolling. Juliet pointed out that they *had* brought candles.

Seeing no answer to that, the innkeeper had told them to go left toward the center of the village. They departed the inn, went right, and headed toward the back stables.

They could see already that men were lighting their way toward that location. Juliet thought they looked very shifty while they did it, though she could not see their faces.

She could not think the innkeeper was aware of the activity. She guessed it was all being run by somebody associated with the inn, who would know when the back stables were not needed for horses and would be empty.

"Do not worry, Marvin," Juliet said quietly. "We are on our way."

"Who are all those men?" Lynette whispered. "Why do we follow them? Is one of them this Marvin fellow?"

"They're all heading that direction on account of Marvin," Miss Mayton said. "Now, Lynette, I am sure Fleur would not be behaving as if she did not have cool and calm wits about her."

Lynette sniffed. "My wits and cool and calm enough, Miss Mayton."

They had reached the doors and found the stables cleared of hay underfoot and well-lit. As was to be expected, the arrival of three ladies did not go unnoticed.

Juliet was certain there was only one way forward in such a matter. One must sally forth in all confidence.

She strode through the doors, while Miss Mayton and Lynette hurried behind her.

"Where is Marvin?" she shouted in a stern tone.

The men froze, none of them quite knowing what to do. Then, several of them pointed in the same direction.

There he was. Of course that was Marvin. He was caged next to the man they had heard speaking at the inn. He was also, now that Juliet had time to look about her, the only rooster in the barn.

Marvin was, just as had been predicted, a rather scraggily and worn-out specimen. Despite his rundown appearance, his bright eyes gazed at her with interest and he made a little crow.

Yes, indeed. Marvin's outward shell was not very prepossessing, but Juliet could see well enough that there was a willing spirit inside that bedraggled body.

Juliet drew her parasol to allow all in the barn know she was ready to use it if necessary. She approached the man and said, "You! How could you? Anyone can see that Marvin is not up for fighting!"

The man heatedly whispered back, "Don't say such things! You'll influence the betting."

"Influence the betting?" her tone incredulous. "You really believe there will be betting?"

"There has already been betting," the man said. "We just wait for the challenger to arrive."

"Do not be ridiculous, you torturer of Marvin," Juliet said, feeling in nearly a fury. "Here is two pounds, Marvin is coming with me to live his last days in luxury, and if you resist I will tell the innkeeper what you have been doing here."

At the mention of the innkeeper being informed, several of the men slipped out the door. The owner of Marvin blanched.

"Yes, I see how it is," Juliet said. "The poor innkeeper knows nothing about it. Now, you terrible person, I would advise that you go home and think long and hard about your treatment of animals. Do you think St. Francis cannot see you? Do you imagine he hasn't told God what you've been doing?"

The owner of Marvin glanced furtively toward the heavens. Juliet did not know if St. Francis made it a habit to search the world for cockfights, but she did think it was rather inspired to claim it must be so.

"Lynette," Juliet said, "I will carry one side of the cage and you the other. It is time Marvin was treated well, for once in his life."

With that, they strode from the barn with Marvin's cage

between them, as Miss Mayton lit their way forward.

They were not followed, though there was plenty of muttering heard behind them.

Juliet had hoped to get Marvin above stairs without running into anybody, but of course the innkeeper was always lurking around downstairs.

He hurried to them. "Lady Juliet?" he asked, staring down at Marvin.

"There is nothing at all to be concerned about," Juliet said smoothly. "This is Marvin. He is going to our room. Do be so good as to send a likely dinner for a rooster. A good dinner, as I fear he has not had many."

Miss Mayton nodded. "You may put it on the earl's bill. Seeds, nuts, fruit…oh, and a salad with no dressing. Worms if you have them. And I suppose the hay at the bottom of the cage might be changed."

The innkeeper stared rather uncomprehendingly at Marvin. "But…you just went for a stroll!"

"And we have found Marvin on our stroll," Juliet said. "Do be so good as to accommodate us."

"Very well, of course, ladies," the innkeeper said, looking toward Lynette.

Lynette only nodded sagely.

"Shall I tell the earl that you have arrived back from your stroll with…the rooster?"

"His name is Marvin, and goodness no, we never trouble the earl," Juliet said.

And so, they relocated Marvin to their bedchamber.

In the hour before dinner, Juliet sat by his cage and had a long chat with Marvin. Seeing his rather docile nature, she was incredulous that anybody could think he'd be any good at fighting. She became so bold as to let him out of his cage.

He was an absolute darling! Seeming to know he'd been rescued, he promptly located himself on Juliet's lap, shook his feathers and settled himself.

If there had been anything to discompose the rooster, it was only when a boy knocked and came in with a basket of fresh hay for his cage and a plate filled with everything they'd asked for, except the worms.

Marvin had leapt from Juliet's lap and stared at the boy. Then he crowed, puffed out his feathers, and reached one claw out threateningly.

Naturally, that was to be expected. Marvin had been badly used by men, and now he found he did not prefer them.

⊱⊰

RUPERT DONCASTER, MARQUESS of Hamill and son of the Duke and Duchess of Castleton, handed several pistols to the Duke of Conbatten and Marquess of Rowndale. They were all three members of the Queen's Knights, as had been their fathers.

Very few of the *ton* knew of the operation, which had the sole purpose of taking down the worst criminals in England. Conbatten's wife, Lady Rosalind, knew, but then she was an original lady and quite approved of waving her duke off to his late-night activities.

During those nighttime activities, the Knights did not concern themselves with pickpockets or gin-soaked thieves grabbing an apple from a cart. They did not bother a lady making a living in any unorthodox manner. They did not interrupt brawls or insert themselves into shady dealings between merchants.

They did not chase after orphaned boys always up to trouble, but for the occasions when they rounded up a dozen and put them into a school in the country.

They did not even concern themselves with highwaymen, as long as the attacks were not frequent and nobody was hurt. Many a highwayman only ventured it once, and out of desperation. A farmer at the brink of insolvency might try it, as might a grocer without funds to restock. If Lord and Lady So-And-So lost a few jewels and coins, it was not the crime of the century.

The Knights were solely set on taking down violent or particularly problematic criminals—the rapists and murderers, and those masterminds who did not steal a handkerchief or housebreak, but controlled fifty boys who did.

They barreled toward the Rats' Castle, a warren of preferred locations for criminals to hide among their poor neighbors.

The inhabitants of the Castle's environs would be well used to seeing Rupert's carriage. It was built like no other, having been reinforced with iron, pulled with a team of six horses, and carrying two well-armed fellows on either side, riding the foot irons.

Inside the carriage, there were compartments in every conceivable location housing weapons.

The carriage was driven by Rupert's coachman, Davis, who was himself reinforced with iron. The fellow never smiled, but then he never flinched either.

They made their way deeper into the Castle. Windows went dark as candles were snuffed out, gin shops shut, brawls ended, scantily dressed ladies slipped deeper into shadows, and the news was whispered down the narrow lanes.

All the inhabitants knew who they were, and why they had come. Even the most hardened criminals would pull down their hat and hope to escape notice.

As they had done so many times before, Davis stopped the coach when the lanes narrowed and he could drive no further. They had in their possession a detailed map of the Rats' Castle and they all knew it like the backs of their hands.

They would slip down the warren of alleys to a certain abode currently occupied by one Lester Jacobs. He had come in from Hampshire, after having poisoned his wife and then realizing that murder was not as easy to get away with as he'd thought.

The fellow was wanted for the crime and had worked to disappear, but his daughter had given him away. He'd written her to send money, not comprehending that after murdering her mother, said daughter would be more inclined to see him hang than finance his escape.

Rupert slipped out first. It would be him who broke down Jacobs' door, while Conbatten and Rowndale covered the exits.

He always did like breaking down a door—there was something athletic and active about it.

Though, he sometimes lamented at the state of doors in the Castle. Most were so worn out and thin that he suspected a child could break through them.

Mr. Jacobs's set of apartments was no different, and as was the case with all men who'd done something so singularly stupid as to poison a wife, Jacobs did not put up much of a fight.

After a womanly scream and halfhearted attempt to get out the window, Mr. Jacobs was promptly tied up, gagged, dragged down the stairs and through the alleyways to be thrown into the carriage.

As they made their retreat out of the Castle, Rupert said, "Conbatten, you really ought to come out on a run with me on the morrow. This time of year is glorious."

"Run where and run why," Conbatten said languidly.

"Around the park, right at sunup. I go barefoot and run on the grass. It's terrific to increase your wind."

"At sunrise, I will be in bed with my duchess," Conbatten said. "Well after sunrise, we will breakfast in bed. Then we will bathe together, the water being precisely heated to ninety-eight degrees, with a glass of chilled champagne."

Rupert sighed. "Rowndale? What about you?"

"I will just be abed," Rowndale said.

Rupert never could understand why men did not wish to be up and out of the house at sunup. He was ready to leap up as soon as his eyes opened.

"You have entirely too much energy, Hamill," Conbatten said. "You need a wife, marriage will settle you."

"The last time we talked about that," Rupert said, "you counseled that I was too young for it."

"That was two years ago. You are no longer too young for it. Time does have a way of marching on," Conbatten said drily.

Rupert sat back, ignoring Mr. Jacobs's various attempts to talk through his gag.

A wife?

Yes, why not? He had thought of it from time to time, though he had not so far met a lady he would wish to spend eternity with. Why should he not think of it? As far as he could see from his own duke and duchess, marriage was very congenial. His parents had a cracking time together.

And who knows? He might be able to find a wife whose temperament was similar to his own. Some lady who would wish to leap out of bed and start the day as soon as the sun was on the horizon and who thought a library was where vitality went to die.

Yes, he really must find such a lady. He imagined his parents' similarities were why they got on so well—they both liked to be doing something and that something was usually the same thing.

My God, even intellectual Harveston had managed to find himself a wife. A Bennington, just as Conbatten had. For that matter, Baderston had married a Bennington too.

The Earl of Westmont had a whole slew of daughters ranging round. Though, he was not certain if Lady Cordelia had been the last of them.

"I do not suppose there are any more Bennington ladies on the way?" Rupert asked.

Conbatten smiled. "Lady Juliet."

"And? What is she like?"

"Find out for yourself."

He might just do that.

CHAPTER TWO

J ULIET AND MISS Mayton had left Lynette and Fleur to look after Marvin.

Though Lynette had been decidedly against the whole rescue operation, she'd since taken the opportunity of using it to lord over Fleur.

Just before closing the door, Juliet heard Lynette say, "While you were pointlessly staring at Miss Mayton's nightdress to avoid working, we were out on an adventure, saving Marvin from certain death. Cool and calm wits were required."

The innkeeper escorted them to the dining room, glancing several times at the stairs as if he feared Marvin would come flying down them.

The earl was already there, standing by the mantel next to a man of early middle age with a receding hairline, ruddy cheeks, and a distinctive Roman nose.

"Ah, here they are," the earl said. "Mr. Wordsworth, this is my daughter, Lady Juliet, and this is my esteemed cousin, Miss Eloise Mayton."

Juliet was very surprised. She had not thought to ask her father who the poet he'd met was, once she'd been apprised that he could not be *her* poet.

Goodness, while she supposed Mr. Wordsworth had some sort of talent, what she'd heard of his poems had illuminated where he was going wrong. They were simply too long. She, herself, refused to go on past four lines. Really, if one could not capture a moment in four lines, what was one doing?

She had curtsied to the gentleman, as did Miss Mayton.

"Very pleased to make your acquaintance," Mr. Wordsworth said. "Lady Juliet, the earl tells me you are also a poet?"

Juliet nodded. "Indeed, though I prefer being named a poetess."

"Ah. I see. And Miss Mayton, I was not aware that you were in mourning. My sincere condolences."

Juliet was not surprised he'd made the mistake. Her aunt had taken to wearing widow's weeds as a touching tribute to all the gentlemen who had loved her when she'd lived on the continent. They'd all died tragically from one cause or another. It was an original way to honor them in death, and so of course Mr. Wordsworth would assume the rather pedestrian circumstance of simply having a dead husband.

The waiters had shown them to the table and they took their respective seats.

"I have suffered some terrible tragedies, Mr. Wordsworth," Miss Mayton said nodding.

"As one must have, to lose a husband."

Miss Mayton took a sip of her wine and said, "Imagine if it were four that have perished."

Mr. Wordsworth looked a bit alarmed to hear it. "Four?" he said, almost in a whisper.

Juliet said, "Our dear Miss Mayton was nearly married four times while she lived on the continent. Sadly, they all died by their own hand."

Now Mr. Wordsworth looked *entirely* alarmed.

"But then," Miss Mayton said, "now is not the time for sad reflections. I do not suppose reminisces will get poor Hans out of the ravine, or magically mend Gregorio's deadly blow, or unhang dear Phillipe. And goodness knows it can do nothing about my Transylvanian duke's impalement."

Mr. Wordworth's hand shook as he raised his glass of wine

and promptly drained it.

"Miss Mayton is right, I believe," the earl said hurriedly. "Now is not the time for sad reflections."

Miss Mayton nodded sagely. As the soup came round, she said, "Mr. Wordsworth, we do like to have a jolly evening when we stay at an inn. I propose that after dinner, I read a bit from the latest novel we are engaged in."

"Oh," the earl said with real enthusiasm, "you shall enjoy that exceedingly, Mr. Wordsworth. Our Miss Mayton always does find the most riveting stories."

"Richard Roydon is our favored author," Miss Mayton put in.

Mr. Wordsworth said, "That sounds most genial. I am always interested in being introduced to authors I do not yet know."

"Then after that," Miss Mayton said, "we shall have a little bit of a poetry reading. Juliet will read one of her own and I do hope we can press Mr. Wordsworth to delight us with something that he has composed."

Mr. Wordsworth looked entirely pleased. "Well, I would not usually…but if it is the plan for the evening…"

The dinner went on most pleasantly. Juliet was gratified that there had been no mention of Marvin. The morning would be time enough to acquaint her father with the rooster's sad circumstances.

Rather, she spent her time occupied with considering which of her most recent odes she would recite for Mr. Wordsworth. She wished it to be something that he might repeat within hearing of her poet, and that her poet would be instantly struck by it and demand to know the authoress.

As the dishes were cleared, port was brought in for the gentlemen and a tea service for the ladies.

Miss Mayton had retrieved her book and said, "Mr. Wordsworth, we are just starting this book, so I will not even need to catch you up. It is *The Ghastly Goings-on of Gallowing Glen*. All we know by the description is that the gentle governess is caring for the duke's children by a lake for the summer. He is a widower and hopelessly in love with the gentle governess, but is there a difficult problem that might stop them coming together?"

"Gracious, I hope not," Mr. Wordsworth said.

Juliet said, "But there always is, Mr. Wordsworth. There always is."

"Chapter one," Miss Mayton said, thumbing the pages.

The gentle governess, being a rather practical gentle governess, had not taken the duke's warnings seriously. He'd said his dead duchess was a stubborn sort of lady who refused to entirely depart the world. He'd said that seven governesses before her had been frightened by her spirit and then disappeared mysteriously. He was, quite naturally, hopeful that those governesses had all just run off into the night, accidentally leaving all their belongings behind. After all, a governess's bonnet or shoe might wash up on the lakeshore entirely by happenstance.

The gentle governess had done her best to ignore it when books flew off shelves of their own accord, or her blankets attempted to smother her at night, or even when she heard the same whisper over and over—get out!

She did so love the children, and she was beginning to love the duke too. She would not for the world abandon them over books flying, smothering blankets, and ghostly whispers.

On this particular night, the children were abed and the duke and his gentle governess were having their dinner.

The lakeside cottage being so much less formal than the duke's great estate, it seemed very regular that they would dine together and it was becoming a habit.

The butler dodged silverware flung round by an unseen hand as he brought the duke a platter of sliced beef.

A carving knife suddenly launched itself from the sideboard, directed at the gentle governess's heart. She leaned to the left and it impaled itself into the wall. Dabbing her lips with a napkin, she continued on with her soup.

"You do not run!" the duke cried. "This has been the precise moment when the other seven governesses went screaming from the house. A carving knife flies at them and they are seen

no more."

The gentle governess sniffed. "They do not sound as if they were very well-trained governesses," she said. "A governess's duty is to be gentle, but to have nerves of iron. Children require such a temperament."

A large fork flew in her direction and she leaned right, it landing nearby the recently flying carving knife.

"Gad! You are marvelous, gentle governess!"

The gentle governess looked about her, hoping to discover the spirit of the dead duchess. "I have never been driven out of anywhere," she said loudly, "and I will surely not be driven from this place."

They could not be certain if the dead duchess had heard these defiant words, but as a China cabinet tipped over and smashed the other end of the table, they thought she might have.

Miss Mayton laid down her book. "Now we are left to wonder if the gentle governess can prevail over the spirit of an angry duchess."

Mr. Wordsworth appeared entirely stunned, which did not surprise Juliet in the slightest. So many novels did not have the same excitement and twists and turns that Mr. Roydon's did. It must be an unexpected delight to discover such an author.

"That was very…surprising," he said.

"As always," the earl said, "I am on tenterhooks over it. I never do know where these tales are going."

"It is the genius of the writing," Miss Mayton said. "Now, I suppose we would like to hear some poetry from Juliet?"

Juliet stood, so that she might be properly heard. "This one is called *Ode to Rocks on the Road.*"

Our carriage rumbles, crunching stones
As if to pulverize very old bones
I wonder how many carriages they have seen
And who they were, mayhap even the queen?

Juliet curtsied. Miss Mayton and the earl clapped enthusiastically. Mr. Wordsworth said, "Oh I see! It is over," and then clapped himself.

Juliet could not be too surprised. What she had heard of Wordsworth so far had told her he was not capable of brevity. Of course, not everybody was.

"Now, Mr. Wordsworth," Miss Mayton said, "I challenge you to move us so poignantly."

"Ah poignantly, yes I see, well there is something I have worked on…it is to be published next year."

"We are your willing audience, Mr. Wordsworth," the earl said, pouring himself a second glass of port.

Mr. Wordsworth nodded, seeming encouraged. "Yes, all right. I will begin."

He cleared his throat. "There was a time when meadow, grove, and stream, the earth and every common sight to me did seem appareled in celestial light…"

And so went on one of the longest quarter hours of Juliet's life.

Poor Mr. Wordsworth. She could have summed up the whole idea in four lines.

❧❧❧⧓⧓⧓

RUPERT WAS NOT very used to having the London house so full. In prior years, his mother and father might come for a few weeks of the season, but they never did stay for the whole of it. There were too many interesting things to do on the estate and they both began to feel cooped up when they were in Town.

But for his sister, Theodora, this would be her first year out in society. They had all come and would stay for the entirety.

He could not say he minded. His parents were jolly enough and he even got on well with Theodora, though they did not share many interests between them.

In any case, he was determined to help his sister through her season and now he had himself decided he ought to marry. It was bound to be busy, which was just how he liked it.

He found Theodora in the library, which was no surprise at all. She was scanning the books on shelves.

"You'll never guess, Theo," he said, bounding in. "I've decided to marry."

Theodora turned on her heel, book in hand. "Marry who?"

"I have no idea, I've just decided to do it. I don't know if it will take a week or five years, but I've firmly decided that I wish to have my lady by my side. Now, I'm telling *you*, but I do not wish to tell mother and father of it until I have settled on a lady. And, well, that a lady has settled on me."

"I see, so you have waited to dazzle the *ton* over news that Lord Hamill, future Duke of Castleton, has decided to wed just when it is my season?"

"That is no matter—the matrons in this town decided long ago that I ought to marry. In any case, I was not planning on making an announcement about it. And, if I *did* find my lady, we could both marry in the same season, do not you think?" Rupert said, having not imagined that would be difficult.

Theodora shrugged. "I suppose so. Though, I am not determined to marry this season anyway. If I do, then I do. If I do not, then I do not."

"Well, if you have any idea of marrying, you ought to get out of father's library, you will not find any likely fellows lurking here."

Theodora laughed. "And if *you* plan on marrying, you had better get off your horse or out of the boxing ring or stop running round the park barefoot. You will not find any likely lady in those places."

"I also dance, I like to dance. The ladies like it too," Rupert said.

"I see, so you will dance at Almack's, spin round, point, and pick one."

"Certainly not," Rupert said. "I must talk to the lady to ensure she is suitable. Then of course, I do hope to be struck by somebody very pretty."

"Suitable? By suitable, I presume you mean someone who cannot sit down, as you cannot? You will not find such a lady."

"You do not know that. In any case, Conbatten has told me that another Bennington is poised to arrive—Lady Juliet. *She* might be an energetic lady."

"I do like the Benningtons," Theodora said thoughtfully. "At least, I like Cordelia very much, as she's the only one I have met. Of course, I must think a very genial lady is likely to have genial sisters."

"That is just what I think. I've met all of the elder sisters and like them very well. And, all of them have gone to Almack's during their seasons so I imagine Lady Juliet will too."

"We will we go for certain, then? You have the vouchers and tickets?"

"All squared away. Mama might seem an easygoing sort of person, but if I had shirked my duty there, she'd be right cross."

"Then we will see precisely how genial this Lady Juliet turns out to be," Theodora said.

Yes, we would. He really had a very good feeling about it.

→»»×«««←

THE MORNING IN Basingstoke had dawned bright. Or, as Juliet said to Miss Mayton over breakfast—"The orb comes to us once more, never forsaking her grateful children."

They had since prepared to depart. Luggage had been stowed and now Juliet and Miss Mayton carried Marvin's cage between them.

They sailed by the wide-eyed innkeeper and into the yard.

The earl, as was to be expected, was taken aback by the sight.

"Papa, this is Marvelous Marvin. He was near certain death

last evening, but do not worry! We remedied the situation."

"But my dear, it is a rooster," the earl said weakly.

"A poor, tired, and worn-out rooster," Miss Mayton said.

Marvin chose that moment to crow rather loudly, which did nothing to support the idea that he was tired and worn out.

"I knew it! I knew some creature would be found!" Tattleton said. Their butler stared at Marvin as if he was a bear escaped from the circus.

"Now, I have to put my foot down, I really must," the earl said. "I cannot have a rooster in the house."

"Goodness no," Juliet assured her father. "Once our dear Marvin regains his strength, he will be quite happy in the garden."

"That's what they said about the goat!" Tattleton said, clutching his chest.

Juliet nodded. "We all remain terribly sorry about that, Tattleton. Our darling little goat was delighted with his one day in the garden. It was just…the garden was not delighted with him."

"Well, I—" the earl stuttered.

"Marvin will not tear out the flowers though," Miss Mayton said. "He'll only keep down the insects."

"Dear Papa, we could not allow Marvin to be killed, could we?" Juliet asked. "What sort of people would we be if we had allowed such a thing to go forward?"

"The type of people who eat chicken?" Tattleton muttered.

"He will be no trouble at all," Juliet said.

"As to that," the earl said, "I really cannot have the servants inconvenienced. I do not think the string of animals that have arrived over the seasons have been at all good for Tattleton's nerves."

"Finally," Tattleton said, throwing up his hands and talking to the air, "somebody mentions my nerves."

"I have full faith in you, Tattleton," Juliet said cheerfully. "You are made of admirably stern stuff. I imagine if you had not become a butler, you would have been a warrior of some sort. A general, even."

Tattleton, as much as he wished to denounce the rooster and stop it getting into the ladies' carriage, always had a very hard time arguing against the idea that he was warrior-like. He puffed out his chest.

"Now," Juliet said, "we really best be off if we are to see Darden for dinner."

As they loaded Marvin into their carriage, Juliet said to Miss Mayton, "They will both grow to love Marvin. I really am very confident about it."

THE FAMILY HAD arrived in Portland Place in very good time, if one were measuring by Bennington time.

It was at least before dinner and, as always, a note had been sent to Darden's club to deliver the good news that his family had arrived to the house.

Juliet and Miss Mayton left the unpacking to Lynette and Fleur, while they acquainted Marvin with the back garden.

The rooster took to it terrifically well. He marched to every corner, pecked at the ground, took a drink from the fountain, made a determined run on the grass, launching himself into the air before coming down with a thud and setting off in a new direction.

Tattleton even began to believe that his fears were all for naught. As he said to Miss Mayton, he did not care if there were a giraffe in the garden, as long as it stayed in the garden.

Though, things did take a turn at sunset. Marvin began crowing and flapping at the window and using his claws to scratch at the door.

Charlie finally let him in and he promptly relocated himself onto the piles of yarn atop Mrs. Huffson's sewing basket. He closed his feathers tight around himself and looked very pleased to be there.

Tattleton walked round the basket muttering, "I should never have let my guard down. Never! Hopes up and hopes dashed."

Juliet counseled that they could not blame Marvin for his fear of the dark. Any rooster would be, what with foxes wanting to creep up on them. The poor rooster could not know that there was not a fox lurking round every corner of London. Marvin only had the good sense to be frightened of predators.

"And yet, he does not have the good sense to be frightened of *me*," Tattleton said darkly.

Juliet had patted the dear butler's cheek and said, "Anybody not knowing you would be very persuaded that you were a frightening character. We love you too well to think so, though."

Tattleton let out a great sigh, as if he had been keeping in no end of insults to Marvin and now that Juliet had soothed him, they must be released.

Now, Juliet had thrown herself at her brother to welcome him back into the family fold and they'd gone into dinner.

"What is the news?" Darden asked, taking his usual seat. "I've already seen Viola and Baderston. I understand Cordelia and Harveston are set to arrive. I have not seen Rosalind, but I know she came in two days ago—the news that Conbatten is in Town always travels quickly. I am only missing news about Beatrice and Van Doren."

"They will be here in the next week or so," the earl said. "They'll bring Lily, as Van Doren cannot bear to leave her in the country. I'm very pleased with the idea—my dear granddaughter will be right across the street. I imagine I'll be walking over quite a lot, or she'll come here and we can examine the flowers in the garden."

"What's this?" Darden said in a joking tone. "No goat tearing up the garden this year? No parrots, no dogs, and no cats roaming the place? The house shall be positively silent."

The earl looked away. Tattleton set a plate of beef on the sideboard with a decided clatter.

"Well now…" Miss Mayton said quietly.

"We rescued a rooster," Juliet said. "His name is Marvin and I have every confidence that Lily will adore him."

Juliet proceeded on to tell her brother the sad story of Marvelous Marvin, his near brush with death at Basingstoke, his bedraggled state, and his heroic rescue.

"So you've brought a rooster to Town," Darden said, laughing.

"It seems so," the earl said with a sigh.

"You shall love him, Darden," Juliet said.

This was met with more clatters from the sideboard and Juliet had the distinct impression that Tattleton had not yet fallen in love with Marvin.

To take his mind off it, she said, "I suppose we go to Almack's on Wednesday?"

Darden nodded. "Indeed we do."

"Now, Darden," Juliet said, "I am a poetess. I believe I have mentioned that I must marry a poet?"

"More than once, Jules," Darden said, laughing.

"As to that," the earl put in, "it is my understanding that most poets are exceedingly poor. I will not have you living in a garret, Juliet."

"Papa, I cannot know what circumstances my poet may be in just now. But if he does live in a garret, I would live quite happily there. We would have our poetry between us, you see."

The earl did not at all look as if he saw.

"Mr. Wordsworth seemed to be doing very well for himself," Miss Mayton said.

"Ah, Wordsworth," the earl said, as if recalling a fond memory. "Very genial fellow."

"Though Darden," Juliet said, "do not recommend to me a Wordsworth."

"Wait, how do you know Wordsworth?" Darden asked.

"We met him at Basingstoke," the earl said. "He dined with us—I quite think he enjoyed himself."

Juliet nodded. "I spared his feelings out of kindness, as he does seem a very nice man. But really, I have begun to think he uses so many words because 'word' is in his surname. Perhaps he imagines he must get his words' worth. Very misguided, really."

"You did not say any of that though?" Darden said, his knuckles going white around his wine glass.

"Certainly not. It is not to be supposed that everybody in the world can capture a feeling in only four lines as I can. Far be it for me to throw the idea in Mr. Wordsworth's face."

"It is very true, Lord Darden," Miss Mayton said. "Juliet only ever writes four lines, and they are always so very poignant."

"Now Papa," Juliet said, "I am not even certain every poet lives in a garret, perhaps only the bad ones do. Except poor Mr. Wordsworth of course."

"He is popular though," Darden said. "His poems, I mean."

"But then, dear Phillipe did live in a garret before he hanged himself over unrequited love," Miss Mayton said, ignoring Wordsworth's popularity. "I thought his poems were rather good."

"I am certain they were, Aunt," Juliet said. "Had he lived, he would have ended very rich."

Miss Mayton nodded, acknowledging the truth of it.

The earl did not look convinced as to Phillipe's brilliant career that was suddenly and violently cut short. He said, "My dear, I rather expect you will have some of your sisters' experiences of thinking you are sure of what you want, only to decide you want something different."

Juliet was rather sure she would not. She'd watched Cordelia wish for a Corinthian and end with an intellectual. It had seemed the silliest thing in the world. Her sister was deliriously happy of course, and that could only be approved of, but Cordy had not really known her own mind.

Juliet knew her own mind very well.

"Darden, is there anyone in your club who is a poet?"

Darden shook his head. "None that would advertise it, anyway."

Juliet chewed on her lip. Cordelia had found that Corinthians were not falling out of the trees, but now it looked as if poets were also running a bit thin on the ground.

"Do you know anybody at all who writes poetry?" she asked.

"Only Mr. Roundbat, eldest son of some baron or other in the north. He keeps angling to get an invitation to the Young Bucks Club."

"A baron would at least be acceptable," the earl said.

"He certainly would not live in a garret," Miss Mayton said.

"Why do you not let him into your club, Darden?" Juliet asked, becoming intrigued to hear more of this Mr. Roundbat.

"Because it is a club for young bucks and Roundbat does not seem much of a buck. Or young, for that matter, though I believe him to be only twenty-three."

"But he is a poet?"

"So he says. He's always going on about the graceful moon or some such nonsense."

Juliet sat back. Graceful moon? Now that she thought of it, the moon *was* graceful. Goodness, she had never thought of that particular phrase. And as for him not seeming a buck, what care did she have for that? Quite naturally, any man spending his waking hours exploring the world of words and poetry would not have time to be powerfully built.

She cared nothing for any of that. It was a gentleman's mind she was interested in. It would be his ability to commune with the glories of the written word that mattered to her.

She was most interested in meeting this Mr. Roundbat.

"Do you suppose he will be at Almack's?" she asked.

Darden shrugged. "Probably. He's the type that might get passed over, but he's got Lady Jersey enthralled by how he describes her manner as 'a medieval queen, all benevolence to her loyal subjects.' She's taken to nodding her head condescendingly at the rest of us as if she's just woken up in Henry Tudor's court."

A medieval queen, all benevolence. How striking.

Juliet began to wonder how Mr. Roundbat would describe *her*.

Well, she would find out soon enough. She would go to Almack's and he would be there.

CHAPTER THREE

MRS. HUFFSON HURRIED into the servants' hall. She stared down at Marvin asleep, nestled in her sewing basket. "Oh dear," she said, "some of Miss Mayton's darning is in there. You know Fleur, she cannot get a stitch straight, so I took it from her."

"If there is anything in the entire world of less interest to me, Mrs. Huffson," Tattleton said, "than the state of Miss Mayton's darning, I do not know what it is."

"Well, I suppose it will not be ruined. Animals never soil their sleeping place."

Of course, Tattleton could see that was perfectly true. That rooster had got up several times, strutted around, and soiled elsewhere. Of course, that was between the creature making very determined pecks at his shoes, as if to drive him out of his own hall!

He poured out a brandy for the housekeeper and a second for himself.

"Now I know all these animals that keep turning up year after year do fray your nerves a bit, Mr. Tattleton," Mrs. Huffson said in a soothing voice.

"Keep *turning up*, you say? They never just turn up, Mrs. Huffson. They are actively sought out. It is my understanding that Lady Juliet and Miss Mayton interrupted a cockfight to deliver this latest specimen."

"Aye, so said Lynette."

"As always, the problems pile up the minute we set off for London," Tattleton said. "Did you know Lady Juliet remains determined to find herself a poet?"

"So I understand. But then, that does not sound so bad, does it?"

"Not so bad?"

Tattleton was of the opinion that the housekeeper grew more naïve by the year. How did she manage to convince herself that it was not so bad?

"I fear you have not played out the situation in your mind," Tattleton said. "None of them above stairs have either. All the earl is worried about is that his daughter does not end up living in a garret. That is the least of their problems."

"But you *have* played it out in your mind?"

"I have, Mrs. Huffson. I most certainly have."

Tattleton grew silent, once more playing out the situation in his mind.

"Come on then, I must know it," Mrs. Huffson said. "You cannot leave me in the dark, as it were."

Tattleton nodded slowly. "Picture this: our Lady Juliet somehow manages to dig up a poet. She is already thinking about one, Mr. Roundbat is his name. And then, imagine they hit it off, talking about poetry and such."

"That all sounds rather promising," Mrs. Huffson said.

"Oh yes, everything seems to go very well. She's got her heart set on the fellow, but then we come to the disastrous moment."

"The disastrous moment, Mr. Tattleton!"

"The disastrous moment. The moment when Lady Juliet recites one of her odes. Perhaps she performs *Ode to a Bovine*. Or *Ode to a Fence*. Or her latest creation, *Ode to Rocks on the Road*."

"Rocks on the road…" Mrs. Huffson said.

"That's right. Rocks. On a road."

"Oh dear."

"Oh dear is right! That fellow will run off like his hair is on fire. And why? Because all along, this family has convinced Lady Juliet that she is a poet of the first order. Just like Lady Viola's dreadful painting and Lady Rosalind's disconcerting playing of the pianoforte and Lady Cordelia's fraught version of Desdemona."

"They do very solidly support each other in their endeavors," Mrs. Huffson said sadly.

Tattleton shook his head so violently that some of his brandy sloshed from the glass and he felt a little dizzy. "No, good lady, that is not what they do. These sisters, and I will include Miss Mayton in this, are positively blinded by one another."

He leaned forward and said confidentially, "Why do you think the Duke of Conbatten has designed a special room in his house for 'family things?'"

"I thought it was a nice gesture?" Mrs. Huffson said.

"No, it is to hide those things from the rest of the world! It's all there—terrible paintings, awful odes, and even the pianoforte that Lady Rosalind uses as if she were beating dust out of a rug!"

Tattleton had been thinking these things for some time. He'd hinted at them before. However, he found it a special sort of relief to just say it as it really was.

"Well, there is no real harm in it," Mrs. Huffson said.

"No harm? Our Lady Juliet is soon to discover that she is no more a *poetess* than I am the King of England! Now, were she to set her cap on some gentleman who spent all his time riding out and gambling, he would likely not notice how wretched those odes are. But a real poet? He *will* notice. His sensibilities will be affronted, just as my own have so often been."

"Perhaps, though, even after he notices her odes are not very good, he will not mind it?" Mrs. Huffson said hopefully.

"A real poet not minding wretched poetry? I hardly think that is likely. And then, will he really not notice when she begins criticizing his work? Oh yes, she is that up in the clouds about it. She feels sorry for Mr. Wordsworth. Sorry! For Wordsworth!"

Mrs. Huffson patted his arm. "Perhaps she will find a gentleman whose poetry is equally bad. Perhaps this Mr. Roundbat is just as delusional as she is."

Tattleton paused and considered the notion. It was, at least, one single shred of hope bobbing in a sea of despair.

RUPERT WAS ON his way to Almack's. They all were.

Theodora was looking very good on her first time out of the gate. His mother and father were discussing which old friends they might meet with.

All Rupert could think of was his decision to marry.

Naturally, he would be cautious and take his time and keep his options wide open. He was determined to end as happy as the duke and duchess had done. For all that, though, he did find that just having come to the intent led him to all sorts of genial thoughts.

He imagined riding out with his beloved, and playing tennis, and taking her out sailing. They might take long walks and she would likely be very good at lawn bowling by candlelight. She might even wish to run barefoot across the park's grass with him.

And then of course, he looked very much forward to becoming a father. His own father was such a fine old fellow always ready for fun and he aspired to be just like him. Would a son or a daughter enjoy their family tradition of lawn bowling by candlelight? It was interesting to think of.

Rupert looked forward to being introduced to Lady Juliet, as several of his friends had married her sisters. Conbatten, Baderston, and now Harveston must have been on to something. They all did seem exceedingly pleased with their choices. The sisters he'd met were all very genial and Darden was one of the jolliest men he knew.

He'd seen Darden at the club and gotten confirmation that he would bring his youngest sister to Almack's.

Rupert had attempted to ask about Lady Juliet. Very casually, of course. Though he still could not work out what Darden meant by his answer.

He'd said, "By the by, I understand your youngest sister is out this year?"

Darden had nodded.

"Your other sisters are all very pleasant. I assume Lady Juliet is as well."

"Exceedingly so," Darden said.

"Excellent. What is she like, exactly?"

That was when Darden had laughed and said, "What are your feelings about wondrous orbs?"

They'd been interrupted before he could say anything further.

What *was* a wondrous orb? He'd meant to ask Theo about it, but he'd never got the chance.

They neared the entrance. As his mother and father chatted happily, Rupert noticed his sister had gone rather pale.

He should have known she would be feeling her nerves. They all should have known it. They'd become too used to composed and serene Lady Theodora to think of it.

Rupert patted her arm. "All I can tell you is, it is not nearly the life-altering event it seems to be this moment. Just be yourself and everyone will admire you."

Theo smiled gratefully. "Precisely what I needed to hear this minute. Gracious, I did not imagine I would be nervous."

"Nervous?" the duke said. "My Theo? I will not believe it."

"Goodness," the duchess said, "I should have remembered my first entry into this place. I thought I should faint and make a spectacle of myself."

"But you did no such thing. I took you to supper," the duke said, "and that was rather that."

"That *was* rather that," the duchess said, laughing.

"Anyway," Rupert said reassuringly, "you are a duke's daughter. Even if people do not like you, they will not let you know it. I expect there is no end of people who find me tedious, but do I have to think of it? No, I do not."

Theo laughed. "And so concludes another encouraging speech from my brother."

"Come now, chin up and remember you are a Doncaster," the duke said as the carriage doors opened. "We go in."

They stepped inside and Theo's card was procured. Rupert looked about him, and then his eyes stopped abruptly.

A veritable goddess stood next to Miss Mayton. And there was Darden and the earl.

My God, could that be Lady Juliet? The other sisters were all very pretty, but she…she was divine!

She was tall and slim, with the darkest of hair and dark eyes to match. Her lips turned up ever so slightly at the edges and there was something about her air that spoke of confidence and determination.

It suddenly occurred to Rupert that what he was seeing, every other gentleman was seeing too.

There was not a moment to lose. He would get himself on her card and gain Lady Jersey's nod to do it afterward.

He leaned over to his sister and said, "Come, Theo. There is Lady Cordelia's sister. You must be introduced."

"You mean, *you* must be introduced," Theo said with a smile.

"You, me, we must both be introduced."

⟥⟩⟩⟩⟨⟨⟨⟦

JULIET SUPPOSED SHE was not as nervous as some of her sisters had been when first walking into Almack's. She was hard-pressed to imagine how Beatrice must have felt, being the first one to venture into this den of patronesses without knowing what to expect.

At least Juliet, herself, had the benefit of hearing it described four different times over four different seasons. If any lady had been more prepared, she did not see how it could be so.

She knew she would be looked over by those lofty matrons, particularly Lady Jersey. It was likely to go off without a hitch, as Lady Jersey had a soft spot for the earl. All Juliet need do was curtsy low and smile—Lady Jersey would do all the talking.

Juliet gazed round the ballroom and could not help but notice that there were various gentlemen looking her way.

Her gaze stopped short at a man who had just come in.

He was marvelous! A powerfully built brick of a man with hair the color of late summer honey and dark blue eyes.

If that was Mr. Roundbat, she might faint on the spot. It would be too miraculous for a poet to be housed in such a personage. She had not thought it possible, but then…

He was looking at her. She was looking at him. Would the fates point him out so decidedly if he were *not* Mr. Roundbat?

He was coming over. He brought another lady—who was she? She had the very same hair color, so fingers and toes crossed it was a sister.

Juliet looked expectantly at Darden as the glorious man approached.

"Hamill," Darden said jovially.

Hamill. It was Lord Hamill. Goodness, of course it was. He was a Corinthian of the first order. He was the one Cordelia was meant to like, but she had not.

How positively tragic that he could not be Mr. Roundbat.

As they were introduced, it was confirmed that Juliet's idea that the lady might be a sister was correct. It was Lady Theodora, whom she recalled Cordelia liked very much.

"Lady Juliet," Lord Hamill said, "may I enter my name on your card?"

Juliet nodded. Of course he must be let on. He was not her poet, but he did look a wonderous specimen to dance with.

In any case, it had been drilled into her head the protocol of such things. Were a lady to refuse, she must sit out. When she'd been younger, she'd argued that idea with her governess very bitterly and claimed it was most unfair. Miss Weldy had only shrugged and pointed out the world would not be modifying its habits on account of what Lady Juliet thought about it.

That had also seemed unfair.

As she handed her card over, a prepossessing lady approached. Juliet thought she knew who it was. Despite her earlier confidence, she quaked just a little.

"Earl, Lord Darden, Miss Mayton," Lady Jersey said, sweeping into their presence. "This must be Lady Juliet, very pretty."

Lady Jersey eyed Lord Hamill scribbling his name and almost furtively handing Juliet back her card.

"Hamill? Do you go forward without a sanction?"

"I did rather," Lord Hamill said, "though I intended to seek you out promptly, of course. I pray you indulge me."

Lady Jersey frowned. Then she turned to Lady Theodora. "Finally, our Lady Theodora is with us. How often I have fondly reflected on meeting you at your father's house."

"I am honored to be here, Lady Jersey," Lady Theodora said.

That was very prettily done. Juliet wondered why she hadn't thought to say something similar.

"Nonsense, the honor is all ours. Now," Lady Jersey said, "though your naughty brother has thrown over the rules, just this once I will overlook it. You can be assured, Lady Juliet and Lady Theodora, that the rest of the gentlemen approaching you *have* been sanctioned by me."

Juliet was left to gather that Lord Hamill had put himself on her card without bothering to ask leave to do it. It was rather bold, and she supposed she ought to be flattered by it. Which she was, rather.

"I have given particular approval to a delightful young man— Mr. Roundbat," Lady Jersey said. "You will find he is gifted with the ability to form a unique turn of phrase. Though, he is rather a flatterer, I warn you. Goodness, who would imagine I am to be described as a medieval queen, all benevolence to my loyal subjects? Really, who?"

Lady Juliet dearly hoped somebody else would answer who.

"Those queens did rule with an iron fist," Miss Mayton said nodding. "That is my understanding of it anyway."

Juliet's father's eyes went just a little bit wider than they ought. He said, "I must think that's where Mr. Roundbat went wrong, Lady Jersey—the queens of yore may have required iron fists, but *you* only require your elegant presence."

Fortunately, Lady Jersey whipped out her fan and tapped the earl's coat playfully. "And here is another one who can turn a phrase. Now, Darden, I give you leave to enter your name on Lady Theodora's card."

Lady Jersey drifted off. Lord Hamill bowed and followed her, no doubt hoping to smooth ruffled feathers over his defiance of the benevolent queen of Almack's.

"Lady Theodora," Darden said, reaching for her card.

As he filled it out, Juliet said, "Lady Theodora, my sister Cordelia spoke so well of you when you met last summer."

"I did like her very well too," Lady Theodora said.

"And Lord Hamill, your brother, I recall he was very helpful to Cordelia."

"Was he?" Lady Theodora said with a smile. "I only remember him driving Lord Harveston to become a sailor in time for the regatta, which resulted in a very banged up head."

Of course, that was true, but Juliet did not give a toss for how banged up Harveston had been. She was attempting to lead the conversation in a particular direction.

"Yes," she said, "I understand Lord Hamill is very sporting. I wonder, though, if that is all. What I mean is, I do not suppose he writes poetry?"

Lady Theodora took her card back from Darden and said, "Rupert? He would not know a poem if it grabbed his hat and beat him with it."

"Perhaps he reads it sometimes, though?" Juliet said, a little surprised by the hopeful tone in her voice.

"If he does, he has kept it a very great secret," Lady Theodora said.

Juliet sighed. What a shame.

Seeming to sense her disappointment, Lady Theodora said, "Of course, that does not mean he could not start if he were inspired to it. He *can* read. I at least know that."

A short, rather thin, and bespectacled man approached their party. His clothes were acceptable, but they looked as if they had not been tailored with precision. The sleeves seemed just a tad too long, his neckcloth a quarter inch too loose, the buttons on his coat just a hair's breadth droopy, as if they had not been sewn on properly.

"Lord Darden," the man said, "as always it is an absolute honor to encounter you."

"Roundbat," Darden said, with rather less enthusiasm than one might have hoped.

So this was Mr. Roundbat. He was certainly no Lord Hamill. But then, he had something that Lord Hamill did not have. He had poetry in his soul. She must keep that in mind.

After they were introduced, Mr. Roundbat said, "Dear Lady Jersey has given me leave to approach the two brightest stars in the sky. It is as if the heavens have sent twin blazing comets to grace these hallowed halls."

Though Darden's brow wrinkled, Juliet ignored him. Mr. Roundbat's phrases were rather clever. In any case, she did not suppose any lady would be opposed to being named the brightest star or a blazing comet.

Lady Theodora only said, "Goodness."

Mr. Roundbat had taken Juliet's card. He said, "Alas, Lord Hamill has taken supper. I rather despair of it, as I have heard that Lady Juliet is a poetess and had hoped to hear more about it."

"*Despair* seems unnecessary," Darden muttered.

Juliet was beginning to wonder if her brother was in some way intimidated by Mr. Roundbat's facility with language.

"I am indeed a poetess, Mr. Roundbat," Juliet said, "but I bid you not to be cast down over a missed chance."

Mr. Roundbat nodded enthusiastically and wrote his name

down for the first. "At least I will have the honor of escorting the poetess for her first venture onto the famed ballroom floor that knows no equal."

He turned to Lady Theodora. "My lady, if I am not too late, I would take *your* supper."

Lady Theodora smiled weakly. Juliet got the impression that she was not looking for her own poet. Naturally, not everybody was. And, of course, if one were to discount Mr. Roundbat's soul of a poet, well there was not much else left.

But he did have a poet's soul. He did have that!

That was the most important thing.

OTHER GENTLEMEN HAD approached, but Mr. Roundbat did not move away. Not even under Darden's rather dark stares.

Lord Hamill had returned, collected his sister, and taken her round the room. Though, he had looked at Juliet so pointedly before leading Lady Theodora away.

There was something about him. Something stirring. For just a moment, she wished to touch his face.

For just a moment, she imagined him carrying her off somewhere.

She dismissed the feelings though. After all, she well understood her own proclivities. To admire a gentleman's person was all well and good, but it was not what she required. A person's physical appearance would diminish over time, while a fine mind would only expand.

Juliet Bennington required a life of words and ideas, of admiring vistas and finding just the right phrases to poignantly evoke the scene.

She might almost be willing to throw over requiring a poet, but Lord Hamill did not even *read* poetry. Such a union would be a doomed one.

Now, the first dance was set to begin, and Mr. Roundbat led her to the center of the floor. They took their places in the line.

CHAPTER FOUR

A S THE TOP dancers executed their steps, Mr. Roundbat said to Juliet, "I understand from Lady Jersey that your sisters and Miss Mayton all speak very highly of your poetry, Lady Juliet."

Juliet nodded. "Of course, it must be so. They have been with me always and have ridden the journey alongside me. One cannot be very good when one begins, after all. It takes years of training to reach certain heights."

Mr. Roundbat said, "Yes! Indeed, it does. So few people really understand that. My father is only interested in estate matters—farming and tenants and such. As if cows were to be the beginning and end of a man's existence! I have attempted to explain to him many times that I am not just staring off at the horizon—at those sacred moments, I am composing poetry."

"Ah yes, capturing the inspiring vista," Juliet said. "I often do so myself."

It really was quite wonderful to speak to another person about the interior life of a poet.

"He complains about it no end and claims there is no money in it, as if a poet is a mercenary!"

"The notion is absurd—true poetry can only be created from a pure place."

"Just so. And, should the public see fit, one's poetry might be published and people like it and then there is money, though the poet never looked for such a thing."

"That is very true," Juliet said. "I have met Mr. Wordsworth and that seems to be the case for him, even though his poems are rather…well they are…"

"Long? For myself, I find they do go on a bit."

"Yes! They are too long," Juliet said.

It was as if she and Mr. Roundbat were of the same mind. He instinctively understood that Mr. Wordsworth's poems were too long.

And really, if she squinted a bit or looked just over his head or at his coat buttons, his being the owner of a rather unprepossessing person was nothing at all.

"I favor the Japanese style of poetry myself," Mr. Roundbat said.

"Japanese?" Juliet asked. How interesting. She'd not heard any Japanese poetry.

"It is very compact, which I have tried to explain to my father is harder to write than something longer."

"That is always true," Juliet said. "I had thought to mention that very thing to Mr. Wordsworth, but did not wish to hurt his feelings."

"For example, here's one about dawn," Mr. Roundbat said. "Pink light slow seeps, the world awakes in glory, the orb has risen."

Now that was something. How often had she herself written about the orb returning at dawn? Their minds were as one, it seemed.

It was their turn to dance and while Mr. Roundbat did not make any terrible missteps, it was clear enough that his time had been spent more on poetry than dancing.

Which was precisely what she had wished for.

She'd said so many times.

RUPERT HAD SPENT most of the night glancing at Lady Juliet Bennington. Naturally, he did look elsewhere. It was far too early in his decision to engage himself to make any sort of choice. There was no telling when another lady might catch his eye. There was no telling which lady was most suited to him.

And yet, was there anybody in the room to compare to her?

There certainly was not, and he was sure he wasn't the only gentleman who'd come to that conclusion.

Particularly Mr. Roundbat. As far as he could see, that fellow had only engaged himself to Lady Juliet for the first, and Theo for the one before supper. He'd spent the rest of the time toadying up to Lady Jersey which, if her expression was anything to go by, he was rather good at.

Theo was not at all enthusiastic about the prospect of dining with Mr. Roundbat, though he could not help but notice that Lady Juliet had seemed very engaged in conversation with him throughout the first.

But certainly, that was nothing to concern himself with. There might be competition all round, but that squeaky little man could not be included in it.

If there was anything at all that gave him pause, it was Theo's description of all the flattery that was heaped upon both she and Lady Juliet by that gentleman.

Where does a fellow think he is going by telling a lady she is a blazing star in the sky?

He must put all that aside for the moment. It was time to lead Lady Juliet.

Rupert could feel the heat of her through her glove and her eyes sparkled—she was so vibrant and beautiful, so brimming with vitality.

"How do you find your first outing to Almack's?" he asked, as they waited their turn.

"It is very pleasant indeed," Lady Juliet said. "I had the advantage of having four sisters gone before me, so I knew what to expect."

Rupert nodded, though he did not have a response. It was his usual opening gambit and the usual response was one of a description of nerves, to which he might say, "Nobody would have perceived it," or some such thing.

"Is it true that you put your name down on my card before being given leave to do it?" Lady Juliet asked.

Rupert had hoped that situation had been glossed over and not especially noticed. But then, he might as well admit his intentions.

"I did," he said, "and it is not a thing I have done before."

"No?"

"No," he said. "But I knew that the gentlemen would be flocking round Lady Juliet, so I had to be decisive about it."

"I see," she said, looking rather thoughtful.

He could not tell if it had been the right thing or wrong thing to say.

"Mr. Roundbat seemed rather keen," he said. He did not know why on earth he'd said it. It was really the wrong thing to say. Gentlemen who went on fishing expeditions very often caught a not-looked-for fish and ended wishing they'd never cast a line.

"Mr. Roundbat and I share a love of poetry," Lady Juliet said.

"I see. You read a great deal of it?"

"I *would* read poetry every spare moment," Lady Juliet said, "but I am far too busy writing my own."

She did not only read poetry, she also wrote it too. It seemed to take up all her time. That could not lead him to believe that she was well suited to him. She would be more like Theo—in a library half her life.

Still, he could not stop looking at her.

"Your brother mentioned something about you admiring wondrous orbs," he said. "Was that from a poem?"

"Indeed, yes, one of my own."

"Interesting. Yes. What is a wondrous orb, exactly?"

She looked at him very quizzically. "The sun. The wondrous

orb is the sun."

"Of course, yes. The sun. I was thinking that was it, but did not like to assume."

He had been thinking no such thing, of course. Why call the sun a wondrous orb when one could just call it the sun?

Lady Juliet got a faraway look in her eye. "Wondrous orb, you did not forsake me, instead you come to gently wake me. Be of good cheer life-giving circle, that you are yellow and not tragically purple," she said.

Rupert did not have the first idea of what she just said, but as she'd mentioned the wondrous orb again and seemed to be very fond of the phrase, he said, "Gad, that is something."

Lady Juliet graciously nodded. "It is one of my earliest works, but I feel as if it still holds up."

"Of course it must," Rupert said. "Nobody would like to see the sun tragically purple."

"Just so."

Lady Juliet was positively mystifying. Stunning to look at, rather irresistible, but mystifying.

⧽⧽⧽⧼⧼⧼

JULIET WAS GLAD the day had passed and her extended family were set to arrive to dinner. She'd spent what felt like very long hours feeling what she called "hoppy." She'd pushed around her breakfast, could not sit anywhere for long, went for a walk with her aunt and then abruptly turned round as she was in no mood for walking, and attempted an ode that went nowhere—nothing and no place seemed to suit.

She was torn and had not ever thought she would be so. She should have thought she would be, she supposed. It only made logical sense that if one had very specific requirements, then other lesser preferences must fall by the wayside.

Juliet had spent all her life certain that she must have a poet.

On her very first outing, she had met with a poet. A remarkable poet, really. She'd not dared to imagine that she would encounter a gentleman as interesting as Mr. Roundbat.

He was so dedicated to poetry that he'd even learned about the Japanese style. It rather gratified her that she could not lord it over him with her knowledge and experience. He was every bit the poet she was. They were equals in that regard.

Further, to know that he'd had to defy his father to pursue his passion for words? There was something romantic about the idea. It was just the sort of thing a poet would do.

But then, there was Lord Hamill. What a specimen of a man he was. That beautiful dusky hair and dark blue eyes, his broad chest and strong jaw—his looks shouted "man, man, man."

His dancing had been superb and he had expertly led her while seeming as if it were not the slightest effort. He'd defied Lady Jersey to put himself on her card. Then he'd outright told her why he'd done it.

She supposed Lord Hamill could sweep her up with one arm.

She also supposed Mr. Roundbat would sink to the ground if he made such an attempt.

Now, Juliet hurried down the stairs, determined to put it all out of her mind. There was no point in dwelling on it—she'd only been out once and there would be many opportunities to begin to see the attractiveness of Mr. Roundbat's person. She was convinced he would begin to appear different to her as they got to know one another.

Or, perhaps Lord Hamill would take up poetry.

There was no way to know what would happen. She must only trust that the fates were at their work.

For just this minute, though, all her sisters and their husbands were to gather in the house and she would be the greatest fool in the world if she did not enjoy it.

Beatrice and Van Doren were already arrived Tin the drawing room. "Bea!" Juliet cried.

After sufficient embraces and exchanges of how wonderful

each of them looked, Juliet said, "I thought you were to bring little Lily for a visit. Papa shall be very disappointed."

"She is below stairs, saying hello to everybody there. Tattleton took her down—you know how fond of each other they are. In any case, she is not yet old enough to sit at the table with any patience, so Lynette will give her dinner and she will come up afterward."

The sound of a distant crowing drifted through the drawing room.

"Is that a rooster?" Van Doren asked.

"Good evening to you, Van Doren," Juliet said. "And yes, that is Marvin."

"Why have you brought a rooster to Town?" the viscount asked. He paused and then said, "Wait a minute. Is that rooster in the house?"

"It is nighttime. Where else would he be?" Juliet asked.

"He is below stairs, isn't he? Is my daughter being exposed to a farm animal in your servants' quarters?"

Juliet did not answer, because of course she was and of course Van Doren would find some outrage in it. In his mind, Beatrice and Lily must be protected from absolutely everything. It would not have surprised Juliet to see Lily going round with pillows tied round her in case she fell over.

Before she had to answer one way or the other, the earl came into the room. "Goodness, our Lily has grown even since last I saw her. Oh, I could not help it, I heard her little voice coming from below stairs and had to investigate. She said, 'Gwandbaba, lub me to pieces,' and then held her little arms out."

The earl wiped a tear. "It really gets you right in the heart."

"Is she there with a rooster, though?" Van Doren asked.

"Yes, she's met Marvin. He's in the servants' hall, as apparently there might be predators in the garden. But did you hear what I said? She asked me to lub her to pieces," the earl said.

Van Doren looked at Beatrice, who only patted him on the arm. She did that a lot, Juliet noticed, as if she were calming a horse who was thinking to bolt.

Miss Mayton hurried in. After kissing Beatrice on the cheek and saying hello to Van Doren, she said, "Our Lily has got the touch. I just popped downstairs and wouldn't you know, Marvin has settled himself on her lap."

"Now that really is too far," Van Doren said.

"She will be all right," Beatrice said.

"It was just the most adorable thing," Miss Mayton went on, seeming to not notice or care about Van Doren's simmering outrage. "She was trying to teach Marvin how to say 'murder.' You know, just as the parrot does when he wants almonds."

"I knew she should not have been exposed to that parrot!" Van Doren said in his usual growly voice. "If she starts imitating the other one, well, I draw the line there!"

Juliet suppressed a giggle. The other parrot, Jemima, had been collected on the way to Viola's family elopement to Gretna Green. She'd been found in a shop and had been owned by a couple who apparently did not care for one another. Whenever Chester shouted "murder," Jemima shouted back, "Shut it, old man!"

Benny led Conbatten and Rosalind in, with Viola and Baderston on their heels. Not a moment later, Cordelia and Harveston arrived, being seen in by Johnny, as Tattleton was still happily shirking his duties with Lily below stairs.

After greetings had been exchanged, Benny said loudly, "My lord, if you are ready to go through."

This prompted various looks, as nobody had ever heard such a thing from anyone other than Tattleton.

"Ah yes," the earl said, "I have told Tattleton he might stay with Lily, they simply adore each other. In any case, it will give Benny and Johnny an experience at running the dining room on their own."

Both Benny and Johnny nodded, suitably grave over the idea.

"But we still wait for Lord Darden, Benny," the earl said kindly.

Benny blanched, as he had apparently forgot all about Darden. That very person hurried in, having let himself through the door and thrown his greatcoat in the hall. "Sorry, I am late," he said.

The earl nodded to Benny that it was now safe to proceed. The footman threw his chest out and practically shouted, "My lord, if you are ready to go through!"

The party followed those two boys to the dining room and what followed next was a service nobody would soon forget. Without Tattleton at the helm, Benny and Johnny were often seen looking to one another as if to ask, "What next?"

They had seemed to come to the conclusion that if all else failed, they would at least make certain nobody's wine glass was ever empty.

Juliet supposed nobody minded the awkwardness of the service, as their wine glasses were never empty and they were too caught up in exchanging news.

Beatrice said, "Now, we have gone on and on about our households, but the real question of the evening is for Juliet. How did you fair at Almack's?"

"The evening was very pleasant," Juliet said. "I danced the first with Mr. Roundbat, he is a poet, you understand."

At the mention of Mr. Roundbat, there were various sighs and frowns round the table. Juliet could not understand it at all. Why did they all look so unhappy?

"My only hope is," the earl said, "poet or not, Juliet finds a gentleman of sufficient means."

"Nobody knows much about Roundbat's circumstances," Darden said.

"I think his father is a baron in the north somewhere?" Lord Baderston said.

"I do not think his circumstances or lack of them are what annoy people about Roundbat," Conbatten said.

"Annoy?" Juliet asked, her tone incredulous.

"He's rather tedious," the duke said.

"Tedious?" Juliet could not believe what she was hearing. Of course, Conbatten did not like everybody in the world, but she could not imagine how he'd come to such a conclusion.

"Tedious. Yes, that's probably the word for it," Lord Harveston said thoughtfully.

"Mr. Roundbat is a skilled poet," Juliet said. "He has even studied the Japanese style."

Lord Harveston snorted. "He tried to use that to get into my literary society. Wrote me something about the dawn seeping in somewhere."

"That's the thing with him," Darden said. "He tries to join everything everywhere. He's always angling for an invitation to the YBC."

"If you let him in, I will never consider joining," Conbatten said.

Darden dropped his fork. "You would consider it?"

"Do you suppose he's a climber of some sort?" Lord Baderston asked.

"A climber?" the earl said. "I would not like that."

"He is not a climber!" Juliet said, feeling a rush of outrage and a determination to defend poor Mr. Roundbat. "He is a poet of the first order. We spoke thoroughly on the subject and I am a better judge of such things than anybody here."

"Lady Jersey seems to like him," Miss Mayton put in helpfully.

"I will be interested in meeting him," Beatrice said. "To form my own opinion."

"As will I," Viola said.

"I too," Cordelia said.

Juliet was gratified to be supported by her sisters. She looked to Rosalind, who had not yet answered.

Rosalind said, "Goodness, he may well improve upon further acquaintance."

Before Juliet could question her meaning, Van Doren said, "I do not give a toss for this Roundbat fellow. What I want to know is if Lily is quite safe with that rooster roaming the house."

"Jules," Darden said, ignoring Van Doren, "what about Hamill? He was rather brazen, putting himself on your card before asking Lady Jersey. That did seem promising, I thought."

Now all the gentlemen were nodding in approval, but for Van Doren, who was still fretting about his daughter's proximity to a rooster.

It was so vexatious! Yes, of course, Hamill would be liked by all. What was there to dislike in such a fellow? He was a man's man, an excellent dancer, a Corinthian, a friendly sort, he would be a duke, and he was very lovely to look at.

But those qualities in no way detracted from Mr. Roundbat's accomplishments. It was as if none of them could see Mr. Roundbat's skills as a poet.

"Lord Hamill made himself very pleasant," she admitted. "Though, he does not even *read* poetry. He had to ask me what a wondrous orb was."

"A what?" Lord Harveston asked.

Cordelia leaned over toward him and said softly, "It's the sun."

"Lord Hamill seems a likely chap," the earl said. "He's to be a duke."

Why were they all so against Mr. Roundbat? It was as if she were the only one who could perceive his worth.

A stubbornness began to settle into Juliet's heart. They may not be able to see his true worth now, but they would. Over time.

They may not ever fully understand it, as none of them were poets. But she did. She was a poetess.

Mr. Roundbat was a poet, not some shallow Corinthian.

"Well now," the earl said jovially, "I believe we have worn out Benny and Johnny with this first foray into managing a table."

Juliet could see that was perfectly true—the two footmen were looking rather limp, leaning on the sideboard.

"I suggest we have our port in the drawing room," the earl said. "That way, Miss Mayton can read aloud our latest story and

Lily can visit with us. Gentlemen, you will not believe where this book is taking us."

"I thoroughly believe I will not believe it," the duke said drily.

And so, they did all retreat to the drawing room. Amidst Lily's occasional shout of "murder," various attempts to crow, and demands that somebody "lub her to pieces," Miss Mayton read from *The Ghastly Goings-on of Gallowing Glen*.

The gentle governess of the tale had her hands full, having thrown down the gauntlet to the angry ghost who was the duke's dead wife. The ghostly spirit had taken to following the gentle governess around and whispering insults in her ear, mostly about her hair. The ghost was quite put out that the governess kept whispering back, "The duke adores my hair."

Juliet felt sympathetic to the ghost—she was rather put out herself.

Somehow, Mr. Roundbat must be defended.

CHAPTER FIVE

"I UNDERSTAND BENNY and Johnny made out all right at table on their own," Mrs. Huffson said, sipping her brandy.

Tattleton nodded. "The earl congratulated them, though I think he was being kind. As far as I can tell from the empty wine bottles that came back down, their motto was 'when in doubt, pour more wine.'"

"No real disasters though," Mrs. Huffson said.

"No, not from them. They're good lads. Though, they told me all the lords view this Mr. Roundbat character very poorly. Lady Juliet did not like it one bit."

"Maybe that will turn her from him. I suppose that is what they were after."

"If it was, then they are fools, Mrs. Huffson. This is Lady Juliet we're talking about. Rather than turn her from him, they are turning this fellow into her persecuted Romeo!"

"You do not think—"

"Oh yes, everybody is against him? She will view that very positively. They had been better off to say nothing at all and allow Mr. Roundbat to do himself in by his own efforts."

"She does have a stubborn streak."

"Doesn't she just. Why, I still remember her at the age of seven in the kitchens with icing all over her face, boldfaced and lying to Cook about how it got there. No amount of evidence was sufficient—once she'd decided on her story, she would not be moved from it. Cook was to believe a thief stole in, took the fairy cakes, and then threw icing at her face to make his escape."

"Aye, she went three days with no dessert and never gave it up."

"Mr. Roundbat will be her latest fairy cake, mark my words."

Mrs. Huffson let out a gentle sigh. "Well, at least you were able to have a pleasant evening with Miss Lily."

Tattleton stared into his brandy. "She calls me Taddydon and she reached her little arms out and said, 'Lub me to pieces, Taddydon.'"

He wiped a tear from his eye. "She is the only thing good left in the world!"

Mrs. Huffson patted his arm. "I think you may be overtired, Mr. Tattleton."

⇒⟫⟫⟫⟪⟪⟪⇐

RUPERT HAD BEEN up and out of the house at dawn. He'd run through the park, ridden one of his horses, then taken out his phaeton, and rounded out the afternoon by boxing with Jackson in the ring. Even for him, it was rather a lot for one day, but it was done purposefully.

He was to attend Lady Hightower's musical evening and it would be well to be a bit worn out.

It was not that he was opposed to listening to music. It was only that depending on how many young ladies would play, he might be stuck in a chair for hours together.

Still, Theo would take her turn and he must be there. Even more still, he imagined Lady Juliet would be there too.

Over dry cake and sour lemonade, Rupert had attempted to get to know her at Almack's.

She was so lively! So pretty! And he really did like the way she had of saying things. She thought something, then she said it. She did not hesitate or appear unsure of her own opinions.

Unfortunately, while her style was straightforward, he'd understood little of the words accompanying it. She wished to speak on poetry, which was not a subject he was at all acquainted with, having always relegated it to a lot of blathering about nothing.

Lady Juliet had recited several poems, or odes, as she called them, written by her own hand. He'd floundered to understand their point.

There was one about a cow that was meant to live on, and then another about rocks on the road and whether or not the rocks may have seen the queen? Those two had followed the one about the sun rising, only to be relieved that it had not somehow turned purple.

He knew Queen Charlotte well enough to know that she would not be pleased to imagine the rocks on the road had eyes and were on the lookout for her.

The night before, he'd consulted with Theo, inquiring if it were usual to write poems about the rocks on the road and purple orbs.

Apparently, one could write a poem about anything at all and there was no particular point to be made. It was a matter of evoking feeling.

She'd sat him down in the library and gave him a book of collected poems so he could get the feel of it.

He'd read a page of something about yearning and dawn, got the feeling of being very tired, and then woken up two hours later.

Lady Juliet was inscrutable and mystifying and he could not stop thinking about her. She was with him as he ran through the park and rode his horse; she was alongside him in his carriage. He had even come close to taking a punch in the jaw when his mind had drifted in her direction while he boxed.

It was all very strange and wonderful.

Now, he led Theo into Lady Hightower's house and he scanned the room.

"There she is," Theo said.

"Yes, there she is indeed," Rupert said.

Lady Juliet stood by Miss Mayton and she looked smashing. Entirely smashing.

She wore a cream silk gown with very little adornment but for a thin gold necklace round her slim throat. The dress did not need adornment; it was cut with skill and the soft color set off her dark hair wonderfully.

She wore it with such elegance, as if she had not given a thought to her clothes and somehow ended leaving the house looking effortlessly smashing.

Just then, Rupert spotted Mr. Roundbat suddenly appear by Lady Juliet's side.

"Goodness," Theo said, "there is your rather irritating rival. If he forces me to endure one more poem of his, written in the Japanese style, I will throw myself out the nearest window."

"He is no rival to me, the notion is absurd," Rupert said. He guided Theo in Lady Juliet's direction.

"Lady Juliet, Miss Mayton. Roundbat," he said.

Lady Juliet had made a very pretty curtsy and smiled at both him and Theo. Rupert thought it a very good sign that she smiled at him, and that she and his sister appeared to like one another.

Mr. Roundbat said, "Lord Hamill, always the highest honor to encounter you."

Rupert nodded, though he really did not know why every encounter Mr. Roundbat had was meant to be an honor.

"You will play this evening, Lady Juliet?" Rupert asked.

"Yes, as have all my sisters before me," the lady said, "though we all despair of outshining my sister Rosalind. She does a travel through the world of music that none of us have ever been able to master."

Rupert had witnessed the now-duchess's travel through the world of music. It had been like a chaotic horserace with no destination—first going one way, then abruptly going another. It was positively jarring and he was rather relieved that Lady Juliet did not play in the same style.

"I am certain whatever you have chosen will be well-received," he said.

"Lady Juliet's choice has been most auspicious," Roundbat said. "It is the latest short melody from Hanfreund—*I Go Where You Go.*"

"I have not yet heard the piece, I look forward to it," Rupert said, unaccountably annoyed that Roundbat should have been privy to the information before he was.

Lady Juliet said, "Mr. Roundbat reminded me that the piece has also a part for a harp-lute and has graciously offered to accompany me."

Rupert was stunned. Was that little person, Roundbat, making some sort of move? It seemed impossible.

"How original," Theo said.

"That is what I thought too," Lady Juliet said.

"Do you play the harp-lute, Lord Hamill?" Miss Mayton asked.

"Certainly not," he said.

Of course he did not play the harp-lute. No man played such a thing.

No man except Roundbat, apparently. What was he doing, playing the harp-lute?

"It will be my deepest honor to serve as a humble backdrop to Lady Juliet's stylings on the pianoforte."

Humble indeed. That creature ought to be humble, but he did not seem as if he was!

Stylings? He was a puffed shirt. That's what he was.

Why was Lady Juliet looking so pleased with the whole thing? Really, she should be affronted that this person, this Roundbat, was inserting himself into her performance.

Theo would be irate if he had taken such a liberty.

"Hamill," a voice said behind him.

He turned to find Conbatten and Lady Juliet's sister, the duchess.

The duke said, "Juliet, Miss Mayton, how do you do?"

"Very well indeed, Your Grace," Miss Mayton said. "Do tell me if you find you must know how our gentle governess gets on with the dead duchess's rather irksome ghost."

Hamill looked back and forth, having no idea whose gentle governess and what irksome ghost.

"Our Miss Mayton always finds the most interesting books to read to us," the duchess clarified.

Hamill was rather relieved it was only a book.

"As the earl likes to say, we are on tenterhooks over it," Conbatten said with a small smile. "For now, though, we have come to support Lady Hightower in her noble efforts to ensure young ladies are heard, and Lady Juliet in her first performance in the wider world. The gentle governess and her tormentor must wait."

Lady Juliet smiled and said, "I am sorry you cannot look forward to anything as original as the playing Rosalind is capable of."

"There is nothing more original than my wife's particular style," the duke said.

Hamill was rather gratified that Conbatten had so far not deigned to see Roundbat was even standing there.

"Your Graces," Roundbat said, apparently not willing to be ignored, "it is always the highest honor to meet with you."

The duke said nothing. The duchess simply said, "Mr. Roundbat."

"I was just telling Lady Juliet of a poem I composed in the Japanese style to capture her debut at Almack's," Mr. Roundbat said. "In walks brilliance, the world awakens in awe, her star rises."

In walks brilliance? Who was he to write about Lady Juliet?

"Conbatten, Duchess," Rupert said, hoping to counter the man's poetry in the Japanese style, "Mr. Roundbat is going to accompany Lady Juliet. On the harp-lute."

Roundbat, seeming to see that it was rather bizarre after

glimpsing the duke's expression, muttered, "I play the harp-lute. My mother was very fond of the harp-lute."

"I see," Conbatten said.

Lady Hightower rang a bell from the front of the room. "My dear guests, we are ready to begin. Choose any chair you like, just do choose one this century. I say it every year, but once again, a reminder that the chairs are all identical and the location of your seat will not dictate your path in life going forward."

Hamill laughed a little. He could not help it. Every year, Lady Hightower pointed out the difficulty of getting a crowd seated into chairs.

Every year, she was ignored as people vied for seats at either the front or back and usually the ends of the rows. It was human nature, he supposed, as he did the very same thing.

He kissed his sister on the cheek. "Good luck," he said.

"Lady Juliet?" Mr. Roundbat said, holding out his arm.

Rupert watched in some amazement as that pompous fellow escorted her to the front of the room and then had the audacity to sit next to her.

"That is unfortunate," the duke said quietly to his wife.

Rupert was in full agreement. Roundbat and his harp-lute were entirely unfortunate.

JULIET WAS DOING her absolute best not to be cross. Mr. Roundbat had very gallantly offered to accompany her on the harp-lute. He'd shown very fine feelings when he'd explained that it had been his mother's favored instrument and he had learnt it when she had grown too weak to play it. As she was fading from some sort of consumptive disease, he had eased her hours by playing to her.

The whole notion showed very fine feelings indeed.

Alas, there were some who could not perceive it. Conbatten

had not even acknowledged Mr. Roundbat. Lord Hamill had taken the attitude that no man should play a harp-lute. Then Lady Hightower, in becoming apprised of the arrangement, had commented that it was very original.

Her tone had said it all! She thought it was silly.

Even so, Juliet had bravely carried on and marched to the pianoforte.

Mr. Roundbat had walked with her, and then explained that he would serve as a humble accompaniment to her musical stylings.

She could not help but notice the smirks from various people at being apprised of it.

Perhaps Mr. Roundbat was too humble and it allowed people to take advantage.

At least, the gentleman himself had not seemed to take in the various attitudes. He had played enthusiastically. At a particularly poignant moment in the piece, he had even risen and come to her side to play.

Naturally, a poet would understand the emotions of the music and act accordingly.

When they concluded, he set down his instrument and led the applause for her performance.

All in all, it was very well done, she thought.

Now, she was accepting congratulations for it, with Mr. Roundbat at her side. Everyone said very nice things, of course. But it was too late! She had seen their expressions.

Unlike the others, Lord Hamill had not been smirking at Mr. Roundbat though. He'd looked entirely aggravated throughout and Juliet began to wonder if he disliked Mr. Roundbat for more than the harp-lute.

She could not deny that Lord Hamill looked very well this evening, whether he was smiling or scowling. For that matter, Lord Hamill was the sort of gentleman who would always look exceedingly well.

For perhaps the hundredth time, Juliet so wished that she

could put Mr. Roundbat's soul of a poet into Lord Hamill's strapping physique.

Wishing was a waste of time though, and she knew it.

She must remember what she came to London for. She must remember what she'd decided was necessary to her happiness so long ago.

Juliet Bennington must marry a poet and that was that.

Even so, Lord Hamill was approaching them now and it was difficult to not notice how well he looked.

"Lady Juliet," he said, "that was a very fine performance. Very fine, indeed."

Juliet nodded her acknowledgment and tried not to be too flattered by it. All the ladies would be told their performance had been very fine.

"Very kind words, Lord Hamill. Very kind. It was my honor," Mr. Roundbat said, "to provide what little musical support I was able."

"I did not address you, Roundbat," Lord Hamill said curtly. "Lady Juliet, I do hope I will see you at Lady Rawley's theatrical evening."

She was rather taken aback by his manner to Mr. Roundbat. But then, unwillingly gratified that he inquired into her calendar.

"Of course I will attend. Miss Mayton is part of the troupe, and my sister Cordelia has been collaborating on the writing of the scene with Lady Rawley. It is to be *Hamlet* this year."

"I will be interested to see where it will go. Roundbat, I do not suppose we will see you there?"

"Uh…no, I have not had the pleasure of an invitation," Mr. Roundbat mumbled.

"I thought not," Lord Hamill said. "Until then, Lady Juliet."

Lord Hamill bowed and then set off across the room to collect his sister.

"Why does Lord Hamill seem to dislike you, Mr. Roundbat?" Juliet asked. Certainly, there must have been some argument between them.

"I am afraid a Corinthian such as Lord Hamill has no room for poetry or finer feelings in his heart. He takes an instant dislike to those who do."

Juliet nodded. She supposed that could be the case. Darden, Conbatten, Harveston, and Baderston disliked Mr. Roundbat too, and they also were not poets.

❯❯❯❯❯◀◀◀◀◀

RUPERT LEFT LADY Hightower's house very out of sorts. What did that Roundbat think he was up to? He struck Rupert as a scheming and sly sort of fellow.

There must be something sly about a man who wrote poetry in the Japanese style and played the harp-lute.

The only bright spot to the whole thing was Roundbat would not attend the theatrical evening. Roundbat may have wormed his way into Lady Jersey's good graces, but he did not cast a very wide net in society and had not yet had the chance to flatter Lady Rawley into liking him.

Rupert, himself, was not enthused about Lady Rawley's invitation and likely would have begged off if Lady Juliet were not going.

She was going, though. He would see her without the annoying buzzing of Roundbat irritating him.

His carriage had arrived to Lady Hightower's doors to take them home and he'd helped Theo inside it. He reminded himself that despite Mr. Roundbat's irritations, his sister had performed admirably.

As the carriage trotted through the dark streets, he said, "It was very well done, Theo. Mother and father would have been very proud to see it."

Theo laughed. "I am sure they would have enjoyed it very much, if they could bear to be seated for so long a time."

"True," he said. "Though, they will attend Lady Rawley's

theatrical on the morrow—Father calls it the most hilarious night of the season and well worth sitting down for."

"He has always delighted in describing it to me, and now I will attend myself. But the important question is, will Lady Juliet attend the theatrical?" Theo said mischievously.

"She will. And, thankfully, that Roundbat character will not."

"What was Mr. Roundbat about? Playing the harp-lute?" Theo asked. "I worked very hard not to laugh as all I could think of was what it might look like if *you* were playing the harp-lute."

"If anyone ever sees me playing the harp-lute," Rupert said, "I hope I am struck down by lightning shortly afterward. And that goes for spouting off poetry in the Japanese style too!"

"I do not like Mr. Roundbat," Theo said. "I cannot quite put my finger on it, but he seems false in some way. His flattery makes the back of my neck go cold."

"I do not like him either," Rupert said, "I think he is some sort of schemer, though I do not know what the scheme is. Perhaps he hopes to land a large dowry or perhaps he wishes to climb a few rungs higher on society's ladder."

"A schemer. Yes, that might be it. From what I could gather when I dined with him at Almack's, he is determined to make his mark as a poet, though his father is dead against it."

"As a father would be," Rupert said.

"He imagines a wife would wish to support his efforts."

Rupert sat up a little straighter. He had, so far, been unable to understand how somebody like Roundbat thought he was of a caliber to approach Lady Juliet. Now, he thought he saw the scheme. Somehow, he was hinting to Lady Juliet that a life of poetry was ahead. That was why she seemed to be tolerating him.

"That devil," he said. "He wishes to land Lady Juliet's dowry and he is using the angle that they are both poets. He is probably painting a very romantic and utterly ridiculous picture of marital felicity by way of spouting poetry all the day long."

Theo patted his arm. "I have full faith that you will not allow that to happen. I have never known you so intent on a lady, so I feel sure it must be a match."

Rupert did not answer, though he would not dispute it. Lady Juliet, for all her mysterious ideas about wondrous orbs and purple suns, was impossible to resist. He'd never been so drawn to a lady.

"And by the by," Theo said, "when you speak to Lady Juliet about poetry, perhaps do not describe it as 'spouting.'"

"Noted," Rupert said. "Though, perhaps my bigger problem is that I do not know how to speak about poetry at all. I did try to read the book you gave me, but I was asleep in minutes."

"Then maybe you should simply ask her about her own poetry. Listen to it, and then suitably compliment it. Be an audience for her."

"Yes, that is a very good notion. What sort of compliments might a poet appreciate?"

"How very moving the poem was. You felt the poignancy of it. It forces you to reflect. That's the sort of thing I would tell my governess at my lessons and she was satisfied with it," Theo said. "And remember that when any sort of orb is mentioned, whether it be blazing or purple or glowing or wondrous, it is always just the sun."

It was a very good idea, indeed. Lady Juliet—be prepared to be complimented.

CHAPTER SIX

J ULIET'S MORNING WAS a busy one, as Lady Rawley and her troupe had come to see Miss Mayton. Though they usually met at Lady Rawley's house, all in the troupe were intrigued to hear of Marvin and wished to view this new inhabitant of Lord Westmont's house.

Along with being introduced to the rooster, the last-minute adjustments to the theatrical would be worked out. Cordelia, being so familiar with Shakespeare through her hundreds of performances in the drawing room of Desdemona's death scene, had been helping Lady Rawley write a new interpretation of the last scene of Hamlet.

Juliet was glad it was busy. It took her mind off poor Mr. Roundbat's reception at Lady Hightower's musical evening.

"Now, Lady Juliet," Lady Rawley said, "perhaps you will stand in for our audience. We early on had a notion that it was impossible to untangle who wanted to kill whom in *Hamlet*, as it really is beside the point. The real point is Ophelia."

"Poor Ophelia," Cordelia said, "killed just as innocent as Desdemona was."

"I really wonder about Shakespeare's penchant for killing off women," Lady Agatha said.

"Yes, one does wonder," Mrs. Robinson said. "And to fall out of a tree and drown in a brook seems very odd. How deep could it have been?"

"No matter, *our* Ophelia does not die," Lady Rawley said. "She will rise triumphant!"

"Hear, hear!" Lady Agatha cried.

"We even have her triumphant final line, thanks to dear Cordelia. The only sticking point is how she will manage it. In the original version, we have Hamlet, Laertes, Claudius, and Gertrude all dying in the stupidest manners possible."

Cordelia added, "We'll bring Fortinbras in so he can be killed too and Ophelia crowned the Queen of Denmark. But how does Ophelia kill all four of them at the same time?"

As they pondered that, Tattleton softly knocked and brought in a letter on a tray. He handed it to Juliet and said, "The messenger insisted it be delivered immediately, my lady."

The butler frowned at it, then left.

Juliet opened it. Much to her surprise, it was an invitation to a dinner party that Mr. Roundbat was to host. It was in a few weeks' time and he prayed she and Miss Mayton would find room on their schedule to attend, and he would have a poetry reading after dinner if Lady Juliet would consent to read one of her own.

Of course they must go. It was precisely the sort of evening she planned to have when she was a married lady. Further, she would be interested in seeing Mr. Roundbat's house in Town. He'd not mentioned a thing about it. She supposed there would be all sorts of artistic things in it—framed poems, paintings of inspiring vistas, and who knew what else.

There was a postscript at the end of the invitation and Juliet was rather surprised by it. It said—

I hope I am not being too forward to mention it, Lady Juliet, but as we share the same love of poetry I thought I might be so bold as to note a particular habit of mine. I have always found walking to be conducive to thoughts and ideas soaring and I have recently found the pavements of Portland Place ideal for its lack of traffic. I like to walk in the afternoons and if you were at loose ends at such a time as three o'clock on any particular day, we might walk and ponder poetical ideas together with Miss

Mayton escorting you.

Ignatius Roundbat

It *would* be very interesting to walk and talk about poetry. And then there could be nothing untoward in it if Miss Mayton were to come along. She was sure her aunt would say so.

"I think I've got it!" Lady Agatha cried. "She might have a poisonous powder and blow it at them, killing them all in one fell swoop."

"Yes," Cordelia said, "that could work if she wears gloves and wears a heavy veil to protect herself from it."

"We could use flour from the kitchens," Lady Rawley said. "If it is ground very finely it should make a satisfying cloud."

"Do you suppose we might ask Lord Iverson to climb a ladder, hidden behind the curtains, and blow flour at the same time?" Mrs. Robinson asked. "It would seem as if the heavens themselves were assisting our dear Ophelia."

"Excellent notion," Lady Agatha said.

Marvin, who had settled himself by Lady Agatha's feet and had been happily taking bits of biscuit from her, crowed in approbation.

"He really is such a charming bird," Lady Rawley said. "I wonder if I ought to get one myself. It could become quite the fashion."

"My advice is," Juliet said, "rescue one from a cockfight—they really are so appreciative of it."

"Excellent notion," Lady Rawley said.

"What a productive afternoon, ladies," Lady Agatha said. "We've worked out the final detail for the evening and we've become acquainted with dear Marvin."

"Now, let us be off," Lady Rawley said. "We must locate a ladder, inform Lord Iverson of his extra duties, and get sufficient finely-ground flour from Cook."

Lady Rawley's acting troupe took their leave and took Miss Mayton with them. Juliet was left to her own devices for the next hours.

She wrote to Mr. Roundbat, accepting his invitation to dinner. In her note, she casually mentioned that she and Miss Mayton were in the habit of walking Portland Place on some afternoons so they might well encounter one another.

Juliet looked over the odes she kept in her commonplace and considered which she would read in Mr. Roundbat's drawing room. She worked very hard to happily anticipate a lifelong association with Mr. Roundbat and the delights of poetry.

But mostly, she was aggravated with herself that her mind kept drifting to the idea that she would see Lord Hamill this evening.

It seemed her mind and soul were deep and poetic, but her physical preferences were on the shallow side of things. She was highly disappointed in herself and determined to rectify the failing.

At three o'clock, she slipped over to the drawing room window and peered out. Just as he had said, Mr. Roundbat was strolling down the street, hands clasped behind his back and deep in thought. He was most certainly composing something in his mind. He might even be composing a poem about her.

She ought to be very flattered by it. She *would* be very flattered by it. Once she put her mind to it.

⇒⟩⟩⟩⟨⟨⟨⇐

THEO AND HIS parents were far more enthusiastic to see one of Lady Rawley's plays than Rupert himself was. He was only going for one thing—Lady Juliet.

As the carriage barreled toward Lady Rawley's house, his father said, "Duchess, do read the invitation once again, so we may fully prepare ourselves for the sights and sounds that will assault our eyes and ears this evening."

Rupert's mother nodded and pulled the invitation from her

reticule.

In this exciting new idea of Hamlet, renamed Hamlet in Justice, things proceed as expected, until the final question must be answered. Who will kill whom? Will it be as usual, with nearly everybody dead on the floor? Or will some righteous lady step in to decide their fates? (Heads are spinning as the innocent rise up!) All will become known in the most dramatic terms in a final revealing moment.

Cast:
Ophelia played by the incomparable Lady Margaret Rawley
Hamlet played by the indomitable Lady Agatha Montfried
Laertes played by the indubitable Mrs. Jemima Robinson
Fortinbras played by the indispensable Lady Cordelia Harveston
Claudius played by the ingenious Miss Eloise Mayton

Over the duke's roar of laughter, his duchess said, "I think we can be assured that Ophelia lives in this version."

"Now Papa," Theo said, "while we are there, you must be sure to be introduced to Lady Juliet Bennington. She is the first lady Rupert has ever paid any real attention to."

"Another Bennington, eh?" the duke said. "Well, we liked Lady Cordelia well enough when she stayed at the house. Aside from her and Harveston burning half the carpet on the stairs."

"They were both injured," Rupert reminded them. "It was an unfortunate accident."

"No matter," the duchess said. "Is this Lady Juliet as comely as Lady Cordelia?"

"More so," Rupert said. "She is marvelous."

"Goodness me," the duchess said, "if something were to come of it, we would be in some way related to Miss Mayton."

The duke and duchess looked at one another and erupted in laughter.

"Jolly good fun, that," the duke said.

"Rather," the duchess said.

Rupert supposed it was well that his mother and father were easygoing people who were prone to see the mirth of a situation. He was not so sure other sets of parents would see the hilarity of becoming connected to the bizarre Miss Mayton.

The duke and duchess, though, had found the lady endlessly entertaining when she'd accompanied Lady Cordelia to their house party.

"We'll see if something comes of it," Rupert said. "That is, if I can pry Mr. Roundbat out of the picture."

"Round-who?" the duke asked.

"Roundbat, Papa," Theo said. "He is a small and pasty fellow from the north who writes poems in the Japanese style."

After the duke and duchess recovered themselves from their laughter over the small, pasty fellow writing Japanese style poems, the duke said, "Look at you, Hamill—you're as solid as a house. Just pick up the blasted little blighter and move him out of the way."

That was precisely what he would like to do, and throw him over a fence while he was at it. It's what he *would* do if he were not certain Lady Juliet would frown at it.

JULIET HAD HER first experience of going somewhere in a carriage alone. Her aunt had been necessarily gone early to Lady Rawley's house for a last-minute rehearsal of the theatrical. Her dear Papa claimed he had a headache, though Juliet knew perfectly well he would sneak out for cards at White's after she'd gone. Darden had claimed an emergency at his club which she also imagined was invented.

Of course, she was in no danger whatsoever in traveling thus. Sandren was well-armed and at the reins, while two of their largest grooms rode the foot irons. It was just very odd to be in a silent carriage without the chatter of her sisters or her aunt.

The silence, needing to be filled with *something*, was very soon filled with her thoughts.

Her thoughts were so odd these days. It had always been her experience that she'd instantly decided on an opinion and then stuck with it. She was not a wavering sort of person. Her thoughts were always decisive and very well behaved.

Now, ideas came upon her like glowworms on a summer night—lighting up here and popping up over there and then disappearing only to turn up in another location.

She used all her might to stay concentrated on Mr. Roundbat's glowworm, even though Lord Hamill kept lighting up bright.

Finally, she gave up. She would see Lord Hamill this night and he would, she was certain, look glorious. Was her poetical soul to deny her pedestrian eyes their enjoyment? It hardly seemed fair. For that matter, there was not a thing wrong with simply admiring a person's looks. Admiration of physical beauty was no deep thing, after all. A person did have eyes for a reason.

Feeling very relieved that she'd resolved the conflict in her mind, she proceeded into Lady Rawley's house under Sandren's watchful eye.

Just as her sisters had described it to her in years past, Lady Rawley had set up her rather large drawing room with a wood-constructed stage at one end, and then groupings of chairs with small tables in front of them to set down food and drink.

Apparently, Lady Rawley was rather renowned for her sideboard. It had come to her notice some years ago that her audience could not partake in as much of her offerings as they would wish, were they to have to balance plates in hands. Hence, the tables had made an appearance, and everybody seemed very approving of the idea.

Miss Mayton waved from nearby the stage. She looked rather marvelous as Claudius in dove gray velvet, while Cordelia as Fortinbras wore a long blue silk cape with gold-braided trimmings. Lady Rawley, swimming in a diaphanous white gown, was busy directing two footmen.

Those two footmen were arranging the placement of the ladder behind a curtain, with Lord Iverson clucking round them as if they were not doing it right.

Lady Agnes and Mrs. Robinson, being old hands at appearing in the theatrical, were enjoying glasses of wine and nodding graciously as guests filed in.

"Lady Juliet."

Juliet turned, knowing the voice. It was Lord Hamill. He had such a deep voice, it almost rumbled through her.

"Lord Hamill, Lady Theodora," she said with a bob of a curtsy. They stood with an older couple who she guessed must be the Duke and Duchess.

"If I may present you to my mother and father, Lady Juliet," Lord Hamill said. "The Duke and Duchess of Castleton."

Juliet curtsied sufficiently low. Rosalind had explained to her once that a duke worth his salt liked to know he was at the top of the heap. The easiest way to accomplish the acknowledgment of heap-topper was a deep curtsy.

"Lady Juliet, well met," the duke said. "We very much enjoyed becoming acquainted with Lady Cordelia, well of course she is Lady Harveston now, when she stayed for a house party."

Juliet nodded. "She very much liked the visit, Your Grace. Though we were very sorry to hear about the burned-up carpet."

The duchess laughed. "As were we all, but it has all been replaced now."

"I much prefer the new carpet," Lady Theodora said, "so I really view it as ending in a happy accident."

"Yes, indeed," the duchess said. "That old carpet was getting very worn."

"That is very kind indeed!" Juliet said, grateful for their graciousness. "Cordelia will be most happy to know it, as I do believe she frets about that carpet sometimes."

"Put her mind at ease at once!" the duke said. "I should not be comfortable to imagine there is a young lady out there somewhere, fretting about my carpet."

"Well said, Duke," the duchess said.

"Lady Juliet writes poetry," Lord Hamill said. "I had the honor of hearing one of her odes that struck me in particular. It causes one to deeply reflect."

Juliet was taken aback. And wildly gratified. She had not imagined that Lord Hamill would have been reflecting on her poetry.

"I suppose poetry is all well and good," the duke said. "Though it does seem to drag on very long, I find."

Juliet nodded sagely. "You are thinking of Mr. Wordsworth, I'm afraid. For myself, if I cannot capture an idea in four lines, I know I have gone wrong somewhere."

"There now, that's a capital idea," the duke said. "One might sit through no end of poems if they are only four lines each."

"Tell us, Hamill," the duchess said, "what were the four lines that caused you to deeply reflect?"

"Oh, well…I am not so skilled at remembering the lines…exactly. It was just the idea that the sun is so reliable and we are so lucky it is not…purple. It was the feeling of the thing."

"It was one of my very early poems," Juliet said, "but it has always stayed with me."

"Well now, do not be shy," the duke said. "We must hear it."

Juliet nodded graciously. All her ideas of becoming a renowned poetess were slowly coming true. Here was a duke and duchess who wished to hear of one. For all she knew, Queen Charlotte would be next. She had not met the queen, but that lady might very well hear of her from a duke and duchess.

She cleared her throat. "Wondrous orb, you did not forsake me, instead you come to gently wake me. Be of good cheer life-giving circle, that you are yellow and not tragically purple."

The duke's face had gone positively red and he shook a little, clearly very affected by her words.

"So very charming, Lady Juliet," the duchess said. "I do hope we may hear many more of your compositions in future. Duke, do escort me to the sideboard."

The duke, so moved was he, could only nod and bow before escorting his wife away.

"Well, I, for one," Lady Theodora said, "could never have thought that up. I often wonder how artists create such things."

"I must believe poetesses are born," Lord Hamill said. "I doubt it can be something one simply decides one will excel in."

"I think you may be right, Lord Hamill," Juliet said. She had always thought so herself but had never heard anybody else express the idea! It had seemed somehow wrong for her to mention it herself.

Lord Iverson, who remained near the stage, said loudly to the now crowded room, "Gentle ladies, honored gentlemen, our actors will take the stage in five minutes."

"Ah look," Lady Theodora said, "Papa has saved us all seats. Rupert, do go and fetch us plates and glasses of wine. Lady Juliet, will you trust my brother to make a selection for you?"

"Indeed, yes," Juliet said, thinking it rather chivalric to be saved the trip to the sideboard.

Lady Theodora led her to the front row of chairs. The duchess and the duke sat five in, leaving three chairs on the end. Lady Theodora scooted ahead of Juliet saying quietly, "I must sit by my father, he may need an explanation or two regarding the play."

Juliet nodded and realized that would leave her sitting next to Lord Hamill. Her mind gently reminded her that she should be sorry for it. But she was not sorry for it.

What conversation had just transpired! Knowing that Lord Hamill did not at all involve himself in the creation of poetry, or even read it, it seemed especially moving that her poem should have struck him so deeply.

And then, the duke and duchess had been such an eager audience.

Goodness, it was something to think about.

CHAPTER SEVEN

RUPERT CORRALLED A footman to help him fill three plates from the sideboard. He hardly knew what he put on them, so taken up with his thoughts was he.

Theo had clearly been right—when in doubt, compliment. Though what a close call it had been after Lady Juliet recited the poem about a tragically purple orb. He knew well enough the look on his father's face—the duke had been holding back a roar of laughter, which was no easy feat for him.

The duchess was better able to control her mirth and had seen what was coming. She'd leapt to the rescue and led him away before he lost all control.

Fortunately, Lady Juliet's back was turned from the sideboard, so she did not see his father's shoulders shaking and his mother's patting him on the back with one hand while her other hand covered her mouth to stop herself from laughing.

The duchess really was a brick. He'd have to thank her later.

He led the footman to his seats and saw that Theo was just as much a brick as his mother. She'd positioned herself to leave him to sit by Lady Juliet.

The two ladies looked with some interest at the plates he had delivered. Which, now that he was really seeing them, were oddly composed.

There was a lamb tartlet, a stalk of asparagus, and a fairy cake.

At least he'd taken more care with the wine—it was a good Canary and would hopefully obliterate any memories of lamb with cake.

Lady Rawley's audience had speedily settled themselves into their places and Rupert thought Lady Hightower would be envious of the alacrity of the arrangements. Of course, one did dawdle when faced with a musical evening, while Lady Rawley's theatricals were all rather short and reliably startling. People were eager to see what lunacy she'd thought up this year.

"Ladies, Gentlemen," Lord Iverson said, "as always it is my honor to introduce this latest stroke of genius emanating from Lady Rawley's acting troupe. This year, I will even play some small part in it, which will be revealed in the fullness of time. I give you, *Hamlet in Justice.*"

As the audience clapped their applause, and none louder than the duke, Rupert examined the stage. Lord Iverson pulled the curtains back with gusto, revealing the actors standing round in a circle, but for Lady Rawley. That lady was to one side of the group, dramatically slumped on the floor. She was Ophelia, but he could not work out how nobody else seemed to notice she was there.

Lady Agatha, as Hamlet, faced down Mrs. Robinson as Laertes. "Before I fight thee to the death with my sword," Hamlet said, "I feel I hath to apologize about Polonius."

"You hath murdered my own father!" Mrs. Robinson said.

"And I hath apologized!" Hamlet said.

"Hath you get on with it," Miss Mayton said as Claudius. "Whoever hath landed two hits can have the wine in my hand."

"Oh give it over to me, Claudius," Queen Gertrude said, "we all know they'll hath be at it for hours."

Lady Rawley, having been collapsed on the floor all the while, majestically rose. The rest of the actors turned to her with suitable looks of horror.

"That's right!" Lady Rawley shouted. "I, Ophelia, hath no madness and am not dead!"

"Thou does seem a *little* mad," Queen Gertrude muttered.

"I hath madness? I? Ophelia? Mad?" Lady Rawley said, pacing the stage. "All of thee hath your poisoned swords and poisoned wine and think *I* hath madness?"

Queen Gertrude set down the wine she'd taken from Claudius, looking at him suspiciously.

"You," Lady Rawley said, pointing at Gertrude, "you hath married your son's enemy!"

Gertrude shrugged. "Everybody knows I'm weak."

"And you, Hamlet," Lady Rawley said, "can never make up your mind!"

"Well now, I suppose I hath, on the one hand…though on the other hand…one must consider…this thing or that thing…" Hamlet trailed off.

"Oh, thou all had your dastardly plans to be carried out this night, but you hath not taken one important point into consideration!" Lady Rawley said.

The rest of the actors looked at one another as if trying to work out the important point.

"The point is?" Laertes asked.

"The point is that I, Ophelia, would never be so stupid as to climb a willow tree, fall out of it, and drown in a brook! Everybody knows I hath a terror of heights *and* water! Now, I hath my revenge!"

Lady Rawley threw a veil down over her face, reached into pockets and threw something. Was it flour? Whatever it was, there was a lot of it and she'd pitched it high into the air.

A cloud of white powdery dust descended onto the actors as the audience gasped. The actors dramatically clutched at their throats as if poisoned. As they were sinking to the ground, more powder poured from the sky.

The cloud created was such that it encompassed the first rows of the audience and it was becoming difficult to see.

Rupert waved his hands in front of his face, along with everybody else who was just now in a cloud of powder.

At that instant, and very oddly, the curtain on the left-hand side of the stage began to move, as if some unseen hand clutched at the material.

Not a moment later, Lord Iverson and his ladder crashed down, fortunately missing the dramatically dying actors.

Lady Rawley, seeing her stagehand's mishap, paused for just a moment. Being a seasoned performer, she noted Lord Iverson was yet living and bravely carried on.

She crossed the stage to Fortinbras, usually known as Lady Harveston. Lady Rawley took the crown from her head, placing it on her own. "To thine own self be true and death to everybody who hoped I would drown myself in a brook! All hail the new Queen of Denmark! He who hath got the last laugh is a *she!*"

As the clouds of white powder slowly drifted down, a silence overtook the stage. Fortunately, somebody in the audience realized it was the end of the performance and led the applause.

Rupert surreptitiously glanced to his left. Lady Juliet was clapping wildly and looking admiringly at the actors as they both bowed and tended to Lord Iverson on the floor.

Theo had her lips pressed tightly together. The duke and duchess were using the applause as a cover for their laughter.

They were all coated in the white powder that he was now certain was flour. It had tinted Lady Juliet's hair from its very dark color to a greyish tone. It was as if he glimpsed the lady of future years. What she would be as an older matron.

She was still very marvelous to look at!

Their plates of food and glasses of wine did not look very good though—they too had been covered in flour.

"Lady Juliet," he said amidst the chatter of the audience, "may I escort you to the sideboard for a new glass of wine? That is quite ruined, I'm afraid."

She nodded and whipped a fan from her reticule. As she fanned herself, gentle clouds of flour rose and drifted off.

As they made their way to the sideboard, Hamill spotted Conbatten and his duchess. They must have come in when everyone was taking their seats and they had very sensibly seated themselves in the back of the room. Hamill could not imagine what the duke would do if he were covered in flour, but he was very glad he would not find it out.

Behind Conbatten's duchess, a man in a black suit stood by, hands clasped behind his back and seemingly unattached to any party.

"Hamill," Conbatten said. "I see you have been dusted in Lady Rawley's high ambitions this evening."

"Oh Jules," the duchess said, "you are covered head to toe."

Jules. That was her nickname amongst her sisters. He liked it very much.

"It was worth it though," Lady Juliet said. "We were right in the middle of the action."

"We hath been very much in the middle," Rupert said.

Conbatten pressed his lips together and Rupert was certain he did not dare laugh, as both his sister-in-law and Miss Mayton were part of the acting troupe.

"Who is that fellow behind you, Rosalind?" Lady Juliet said softly. "He keeps staring at you."

Rupert had been wondering the very same thing. He'd never before seen the fellow and he was wearing the wrong clothes for an evening out.

"That is the duchess's personal physician, Mr. Laurelton," Conbatten said. "He will be escorting us wherever we go for the foreseeable future."

Lady Juliet looked rather stricken until the duchess smiled and patted her midsection.

"Ros!" she cried. "Do Cordelia and our aunt know?"

"Not yet," the duchess said.

"We must tell them right away."

"Let's do," the duchess said.

Under Conbatten's affectionate gaze, the duchess and Lady Juliet hurried off, with Mr. Laurelton on their heels.

"I suppose one cannot be too careful with a child on the

way," Rupert said.

"Nor too careful of the duchess that carries the child," Conbatten said. "By the by, Lady Juliet sent a note to my duchess this afternoon. All the sisters send notes nearly daily between them— it is like a murmuration of starlings circling the house."

"They all do seem very close," Rupert said.

"Indeed. In this particular note, it was mentioned that this Roundbat person intends to walk Portland Place at three in the afternoon each day to reflect on his poetry. Naturally, Lady Juliet has been invited to join him at it."

"Does he really, that devil," Rupert said.

"Our thoughts are remarkably similar on the idea," Conbatten said.

"Perhaps I should walk Portland Place at three in the afternoon every day too," Rupert said.

"I do not see why not—you are always in motion doing *something* and that seems as good an activity as anything else."

Conbatten nodded to him and drifted off in search of his wife and the physician dogging her heels.

Yes. He would walk Portland Place every day. He would see how far Mr. Roundbat was able to get when faced with the Marquess of Hamill's walking. He was certain he could outwalk Roundbat from here to Bombay.

THE FOLLOWING DAY, Juliet and Miss Mayton had been asked to Lady Rawley's house for the afternoon to discuss the success of the performance of the night before and think about ideas for next season.

Juliet did wonder if Mr. Roundbat would be walking Portland Place at three o'clock but there was little to be done about it. Even if she had stayed home, she could hardly venture out without an escort. Her Papa was exceedingly liberal but would not favor her going out to meet a gentleman only accompanied by Lynette or Fleur.

It did not discompose her much, except that she was a little discomposed over how little discomposed she was to miss Mr. Roundbat's company.

Of course, it was all because Lord Hamill had managed to turn her head by explaining that he had been thinking of her poetry.

It might not be entirely true though. He might only have been flirting to amuse himself. She really must keep that in mind.

This evening they were to have a night in with her sisters. Juliet had assumed their various husbands would come too, but they all seemed to have need to be elsewhere.

Conbatten had been called to an errand for the queen, though Rosalind said she did not know the details of it. Lord Harveston was running his literary society meeting this night and while Cordelia did sometimes attend, she'd decided the subject of the evening was too dry to entertain her. Viola had given her blessing to Lord Baderston to go off with Darden on some urgent club matter.

Perhaps strangest of all, Van Doren had somewhere to go. He had somehow, despite his curmudgeonly ways, made a friend. A certain Lord Bertridge was said to be just as curmudgeonly, and they had hit it off talking about estate matters. It seemed they were to dine somewhere and thoroughly discuss the ins and outs of the rotation of crops and successful tenant relations. Beatrice was delighted for him.

The earl had briefly thought of going to White's for cards, but when he was apprised that all his daughters were coming and that Miss Mayton would read from her novel after dinner, he threw the idea straight out the window.

The only other fellow lurking about was Mr. Laurelton, Rosalind's physician. The gentleman kept himself to one end of the drawing room and read a book. He had been cordially invited to dine at table, but he demurred and insisted that he would be quite fine with a small tray and his book wherever they would like to put him.

They all supposed he must stay in the drawing room, as they could not imagine sending him below stairs.

"How like Conbatten to insist you be attended at all times," Beatrice said, glancing at the grim Mr. Laurelton. "Though, I am rather glad Van Doren did not hear of the idea when it was my time, I should have gone mad being followed about."

"Mr. Laurelton is no trouble at all," Rosalind said. "Conbatten consulted with an endless amount of accoucheurs; they were a regular parade through the house. He settled on Mr. Laurelton as having the very good sense to have a midwife by his side at the birth, to be of the opinion that most births naturally take their course with no interference, and to have some interesting ideas about preventing infection."

"Goodness," Beatrice said. "And here I was, just going along my merry way with the neighborhood midwife. I suppose Mr. Laurelton has given you all sorts of protocols to follow."

"The doctor has given me no particular restrictions, other than I ought to follow my own preferences and indeed I have noticed them," Rosalind said. "No more champagne in the bath just now, it is barley water or nothing."

"Oh yes," Beatrice said nodding. "For months, I was wild for salt and put it on nearly everything."

"Mr. Laurelton says the baby knows what it needs and will naturally drive me in the right direction. I have taken a sudden liking to vinegar."

Juliet was fascinated by the conversation. She did not know for certain with who or when, but sometime in the not-very-distant future she would find herself in the same situation.

"Though, I must ask you Beatrice," Rosalind said, "was it as frightening and horrible as I am imagining it will be? I did not like to ask until now, as I thought you might not wish to remember it."

"I will say no, it is not quite that bad, *if* your imagination is anything like mine," Beatrice said. "It was not a pleasant experience, I can assure you, but I kept waiting for the horrors I had conjured in my mind and they never came."

"I am much relieved," Rosalind said. "Conbatten would do it all for me if he could, but it will be my work alone. Now, where has that darling Lily got off to?"

"Tattleton has taken her below stairs to see Marvin and generally be fussed over," Beatrice said. "She has learned she can defeat nearly anybody by asking to be loved to pieces and I imagine Tattleton has been swiftly overcome."

"Now I think we must turn our attention to Juliet," Viola said. "What has happened these past days?"

Before Juliet could answer, and she was not certain how to answer, Cordelia said, "Lord Hamill was stuck by her side all evening at the theatrical last night."

The rest of her sisters turned to her. "That is true," Juliet said, "and he made a point of introducing me to his mother and father. They were very cordial."

"Oh, I do like them very well," Cordelia said.

"They say the carpet you and Harveston burned up has been replaced and they like it better, so it was all a happy accident."

"That sounds like Theo talking," Cordelia said laughing.

"It was, but also the duke said you are never to fret over it, as it would not make him comfortable to know it," Juliet said, gratified that she could once and for all put Cordelia's mind at rest on the subject.

"But do you like Lord Hamill?" Viola pressed.

"Lord Hamill is very genial. And he did remember one of my poems I told him of. He said it has made him reflect."

"That sounds very promising," Beatrice said.

"The duke and duchess demanded to hear it," Juliet said, reliving the glory of that particular moment. "They were very much struck by it—I recited the one about the orb not being purple."

"Oh yes," Cordelia said, "I always did like that one."

Just then, Miss Mayton hurried into the room. "Goodness, I am sorry to be coming in so late. You cannot imagine how Fleur can hold me up sometimes. How does one forget where one has put the hairpins? Nobody knows."

"We were just talking about Lord Hamill being keen to stay by Juliet last night, Aunt," Rosalind said.

"Yes, indeed, we all noted it," Miss Mayton said.

Juliet could see at once that all her sisters, and her aunt, were very approving of Lord Hamill. Yet, they had not asked her a thing about Mr. Roundbat.

"But you see," she said slowly, "I really feel that I owe it to my happiness to wed a poet. A real poet. I have always said so."

None of her sisters answered this idea, though they all looked rather frowny. Miss Mayton said, "One never knows…"

Never knows what?

Before she could ask the question and press for an answer, the earl arrived to the drawing room. "Ah, all my girls under my roof once more! What father could be so fortunate?"

With that genial statement, they proceeded to go into dinner. The service was once more absent of Tattleton and managed by Benny and Johnny, as their butler was below stairs being asked to lub Lily to pieces and finding himself entirely defeated.

After dinner, Juliet had hoped there would be another opportunity to discuss Mr. Roundbat, but the time was taken up by her aunt reading from her novel.

The gentle governess was waging war with the ghost of the dead duchess and had dodged no end of flying knives, slamming doors, and had taken to keeping sand buckets by her bed as her curtains and bedding kept bursting into flames.

Juliet wished the governess the best of luck with it, but she had her own matters to resolve. On the morrow, she and Miss Mayton would walk Portland Place at three o'clock. She would assess her feelings upon seeing Mr. Roundbat and discussing poetry.

She suspected that Lord Hamill's various attentions would

fade like mist in the morning once she found herself comparing notes on the high-flown words and sentiments of poetry emanating from a sympatico poetical mind.

CHAPTER EIGHT

ABOUT THE LAST thing Rupert had felt like doing this midnight was a foray into the Rats' Castle. He'd much rather be at home with a brandy, considering Lady Juliet.

Along with his physical pursuits, he'd begun to find that considering Lady Juliet was becoming a regular pastime.

Nevertheless, the call had gone out. Conbatten had sent a message. Fortunately, his mother and sister were long abed and his father had been an original Queen's Knight so was perfectly aware of why he'd been called out of the house at such a late hour.

The duke wished him well and would make his excuses at breakfast if he had not yet returned.

This particular case was an odd one indeed. It seemed that a dozen moneylenders had formed some sort of cabal. They'd all been operating independently, and they'd all faced their troubles of getting repaid. Especially if the debt was owed by a lord.

Each had their various strategies for pressing such a gentleman to pay up. In general, those gambits would begin with threatening an embarrassment of some sort. A father or a wife would be told. Dunners would begin to come to the house, alerting all the neighbors to the disgrace. Shopkeepers would be informed that their bills would never be paid, and they ought to stop extending credit. Even caricatures were produced and circulated—Lord Bellingham recently had one depicting himself trying to sell his neckcloth to a dealer of old clothes on a narrow thoroughfare of St. Giles.

The moneylenders only ever occasionally coordinated with each other before now. They would sometimes alert one another that they'd lent to a fellow who was in dun territory. A young lord finding himself unable to pay one lender would often attempt an approach to another. A rob-Peter-to-pay-Paul strategy. None of them wished to be Peter.

If the amounts of the debt were significant and spread across them, the lenders might gather together to share the cost of a writ. Even then, it was difficult, as they generally found their young man had slipped out of London to lay low elsewhere. If the debt had grown to such proportions that it could never be repaid, the gentleman would fly to the continent, never to be seen again.

It had all rather been like a game and Rupert knew plenty of fellows who would joke they were in it up to their eyes before laying a bet on a horse race. Rupert found it rather stupid to bet on luck and therefore only bet on himself if he had a horse in a race or was in the boxing ring.

Now though, a new and alarming strategy had emerged. It seemed these lenders were fed up with being cheated out of their money and had turned to more threatening solutions.

Just last week, Lord Manchinley's carriage had been forcibly stopped on a lonely road on the outskirts of London. It seemed he had been watched and then followed when he'd decided his debts in London were getting too hot for him.

The lenders had hired some suitably rough and burly fellows and the whole experience had ended with Lady Manchinley's jewels taken to pay the debt. The lady had been entirely traumatized by the experience, and then had swiftly made arrangements to stay at her father's house for the foreseeable future.

It was well planned, well executed, and violent. Sooner or later, some lord would get himself killed trying to fight back. The queen was outraged by the sheer audacity of it and said that putting hands on a lord crossed a serious line—respect for nobility of person must be maintained. Therefore, the scheme must be stopped.

"We are told that they meet in a rented room on Tuesdays at one o'clock in the morning," Rowndale said. "None of them live there—they have taken it exclusively for their meetings. There is a boy in the next apartment who regularly listens against his wall. He is left alone at night as his mother has…a certain occupation. Fortunately for us, he is willing to sell any and all information he comes upon."

"And you do not think he makes up half of it for coin?" Conbatten asked.

"I do not think so," Rowndale said. "He's been told if he tells one false story the bargain is at an end. He strikes me as uneducated but not stupid."

"Will we be crashing in and taking them all to the magistrate?" Rupert asked. "If so, I would prefer to be the one knocking the door down."

"Whenever there is a door to be knocked down, you are always the one to do it. We would not dream of taking that away from you," Conbatten said drily. "However, the boy thinks they keep books and records of debts in there. He's heard mention of them. I propose we listen in the boy's apartment and when the meeting concludes and they've all gone home, we break in and have a look at the books."

"I agree," Rowndale said. "I'd rather get them for everything they're up to than just Manchinley's recent adventure. I have taken the liberty of sending a message to the boy to expect us."

Rupert nodded. Though, he was the slightest bit disappointed that there would be no kicking down of a door.

They had gone deep into the Rats' Castle and Rupert's driver, Davis, stopped the coach. He, Conbatten, and Rowndale slipped out and made their way down the deserted alleyways. At least, they seemed deserted.

Rupert was well aware that there were those in the shadows

who would like to rob a person, but would not dare attempt to rob three well-armed persons.

Though, he supposed anybody watching must have wondered why they were not just well-armed, but also carried paper and writing instruments. It was not their usual armor, but if there were indeed books of debts to be found, they could not just abscond with them—they must copy down what they found.

It was no great matter to find the building, nor to get up to the third floor. The boy, a ragamuffin of eight or nine, let them in while laying his forefinger along the side of his nose.

If Rupert had expected the little ruffian to be alarmed at finding three lords in his ramshackle room, he was much mistaken. The boy, Petey was his name, seemed all enthusiasm as he led them to the corner of the room where he listened.

"It's just here," Petey said, "right here with my ear pressed against the wall, is where I get all my information."

Rupert looked round the room. It was as so many of the accommodations were in this neighborhood—bleak in the extreme. The landlord, whoever it was, could not be bothered to fix anything and a slow deterioration had set in. There were rags stuffed in holes in the wall and floor, to keep out the drafts. There was one small bedstead with a thin blanket, and another two blankets on the floor. A cup and a plate seemed to be the only kitchen accoutrements.

How every single person who was born into such conditions did not turn to crime he would never know.

Petey seemed rather cheerful, despite his circumstances. He'd been chattering to the duke for a quarter hour. As the hour grew near, Conbatten finally laid a forefinger against his lips.

It was quiet for some time, but as a distant clock tower sounded one o'clock, they heard footsteps on the stairs. Then the clink of a key in the lock next door and voices softened through the thin wall.

"We just wait for Freddie."

"I'm here, comin' in right behind."

"I propose we make this speedy. My wife is gettin' all kinds of ideas about these middle-of-the-night adventures."

"What ideas?"

"You know what ideas. She thinks there's another woman."

The other men guffawed. One of them said, "Nobody even knows how you got *one* woman."

"Can we attend to business?"

"Aye."

There was the soft sound of shuffling papers. "That one is all set—the letter went out to the baron and the messenger with the answer should come in on the night of the 15th. The fellows are all set for it."

"I'm not sure I like the idea of that one—involving other people."

"We have no choice. The fellow is cagey and does not seem to have a set schedule we can plan on, but for this one evening at his house where we know for sure where he'll be."

"Aye, and he's not like the others—everything in that house is rented. None of us is comfortable robbing a landlord to get repaid by a tenant."

"So we're left to count on his father to pay up."

"We've set it in motion, there's no turning round now."

"Who else?"

"What about that one? He owes us all too."

"Aye. I'm tired of that one's excuses. He's secured more money from somewhere else and don't bother to pay us a farthing."

"How we do it is the question. We don't got no information that he's ready to fly out of Town."

"No, but we know he lives alone, gambles late, walks out drunk, and goes home to his family's house. Should be easy enough to escort him there and do a little shopping—jewels, clothes, furniture, whatever will get us a price."

"I say Thursday."

"Done."

"All right, gentlemen, let's conclude this thing. *Somebody* needs to get back to a jealous wife."

Rupert did not move a muscle until he heard the key locking the door and footsteps fade on the stairs.

"It's like that every week," Petey said. "They's done it five or six times already and it's workin' out grand for 'em. One of 'em even said it would send a message to others what been slow to pay."

"Five or six times?" Conbatten said.

Of course, they only knew about Manchinley.

"I suppose a gentleman wouldn't want it getting round if they've been waylaid by their moneylender's hired men," Rowndale said.

"They did not give much away," Conbatten said. "They would accost a drunken gambler—that could be one of a hundred gentlemen."

"And they sent off some letter for the 15th," Petey said. "Why? To who? To where?"

Conbatten gazed down at the boy. "We are well aware of the questions to be answered."

"We'd best get in there and have a look at their books," Rupert said. "I'll have to break down the door after all."

"No you won't," Petey said. "I got a key. Nicked it off the landlady's ring while she was feelin' sorry for me and makin' me tea with biscuits. I turned on the waterworks as I was peckish and she's got a soft spot for my weepin.'"

"So you robbed her while she was kind enough to make you a cup of tea?" Conbatten asked.

"I ain't a monster!" Petey cried, seeming mortally offended. "I thought I might blackmail them fellows. Then I would'a split the profits with her all fair and square. She'd a thanked me for it."

"Delightful," Conbatten said. "Hand over the key."

The resourceful Petey took the lone chair in the room, climbed up on it, and pulled the key from a large crack in the wood beams in the ceiling.

They slipped out into the corridor and into the next apartment.

Conbatten had ordered Petey to stay in his own room, but apparently ordering Petey to do anything was just whistling in the wind. The boy threw himself into a padded leather chair and made himself comfortable.

"I wouldn't mind confiscatin' this chair if ya throw them gentlemen into the Old Bailey," Petey said.

Nobody answered this wish, and so the boy went on.

"I'd help ya read through all them books," the boy said, "if anybody'd ever bothered to teach me how it's done. I can make my mark though, so if you need somethin' signed, I'm available."

Rupert ignored his chatter. They split the books, and there seemed to be one for each moneylender involved.

Lists and lists of young and foolish gentlemen in over their heads.

The question was, who were the moneylenders targeting? Who would be next? They could not go after all of these debtors at once.

"I reckon we look out for those that are in deepest," Rowndale said.

"Them that's deep," Petey said. "That's how I'd do it."

"Well look at this," Conbatten said to Rupert. "Your Mr. Roundbat is on this list."

"I've got him here too," Rowndale said. "He's into somebody for three hundred pounds."

The blighter! Rupert scanned the pages of his own book. "He's here too, down for two hundred."

"Adding it all up," Conbatten said. "it seems Mr. Roundbat owes near a thousand pounds. Did he not arrive to Town with any funds at all?"

"What would one expect from a fellow come in from the hinterlands, composing poetry in the Japanese style?" Rupert said derisively.

He'd like to say far more than that. Lady Juliet did not know whom she dealt with. Rupert had guessed the sot must be after the lady's dowry, but now he saw that Roundbat had an absolute necessity to get his hands on it.

"Let's keep going," Conbatten said. "Mr. Roundbat won't be the only person with high figures—we need a complete list."

"Aye," Petey said, "That's 'xactly what I'd do, if anybody ever bothered to teach me how to read."

"It is very inconvenient that none of the lenders' names are on these books," Rowndale said. "Though I suppose that would have been too much to hope for."

"We'll probably have to set up a watch," Conbatten said.

Petey sidled up to the duke and fingered his coat. "I could find out for ya. If you three fine gentlemen could see your way clear to getting me a new suit a clothes."

"First, what do you plan on doing with a new suit of clothes?" Conbatten asked. "Second, how would you discover their identities?"

Petey hoisted himself up on the desk. "Nobody's gonna hire me dressed like this to do nothing better than crawl up a chimney. If I clean myself up, I might slide into an apprenticeship or I might make my way into a great house." He stared directly at Conbatten and said, "If anybody got a great house with a spare bed in it and was lookin' for a good worker."

"How would you discover their identities?" Rupert asked, thinking the boy had very conveniently left that part out.

"I follow 'em. One by one so it would take some weeks, mind. *You* can't follow 'em—ya'd stick out like peacocks hidin' amongst the pigeons. I can follow anybody, as nobody in the wide world pays any mind to a poor wretch like me."

A tear ran down Petey's cheek and he whispered, "A poor, pathetic wretch like me."

"Do not attempt your waterworks on us," Conbatten said. "We are not your sentimental landlady."

Petey shrugged. "All the same, ya know what I say is true."

Rupert glanced at Conbatten and Rowndale. They did know

what he said was true. It would be vital to know the identities of these men, as when the next attack struck, it would not be these men in attendance. They would have sent hired thugs and there must be solid evidence to connect them.

"Very well," Conbatten said. "If you are able to do as you say, you will receive one item of clothing per identification. All we need is the address. If you manage to follow them all, I will throw in new boots."

Petey nodded, all confidence. "Consider it done. Though, there is the matter of my expenses. A half-crown ought to cover it."

"What expenses, you little blighter?" Rowndale said.

Conbatten held his hand up. "There are no expenses so there is no point attempting to force the boy to invent them." He pulled a coin from his pocket.

"I can't do anything with that," Petey said. "I need it in pence, else I'll be nabbed as a thief."

"You *are* a thief, as far as I can tell," Conbatten said drily. "I'll send someone over with pence on the morrow."

"Now, as I'm the sort to think ahead," Petey said, "I'll need to know where you lay your head when you need to be told a thing."

Rowndale threw up his hands. "For the love of—"

"Never mind," Conbatten said to Rowndale. He gave the boy his address and said, "Do not dare come to the front doors. The servants' entrance if you please. I'll not have my duchess disturbed."

"She's a looker, eh?" Petey said.

Both Rupert and Rowndale stared at Conbatten, as the boy had just stumbled into very dangerous territory. Conbatten did not, in general, appreciate a joke. A joke about his wife was akin to saying, "Please do kill me instantly, if you would be so kind."

"You are getting very close to discovering that you have just flown out a window and are plummeting to your death," the duke said.

Petey held up his hands. "All right, all right. Just tell them servants of yours to let me in, else they'll slam the door shut in my face. Ya see, because I'm a poor wretch."

"We are at least agreed that you are a wretch," Conbatten said.

They spent the next hours making a very long list of gentlemen who owed significant amounts of money. Roundbat was just a drop in a very large bucket, but Rupert could not help thinking about him. He almost hoped the moneylenders would seek out the rotter and take their vengeance. And, if that vengeance were to expose him or lay Roundbat low for a few weeks, well, after all, borrowing money was a stupid thing to do.

Petey paced the room, rubbing his chin and looking thoughtful, as if he were supervising them all. He watched carefully whenever one of them wrote something down.

When they had done, Petey had somehow managed to convince Conbatten to leave the writing instruments in his care until they returned again.

After that was accomplished, the little devil had made a very great show of how sad it was that he was to look upon writing instruments for a whole week and not know how to write anything himself.

The duke had given him one sheet of paper he might keep as his own and had written the alphabet across the top. He was to only use the ink left behind for the single paper he'd been given.

Rupert did not know if Petey would actually attempt to teach himself to replicate the letters, but the boy had carried out the sheet of paper as if it were the crown jewels.

JULIET HAD THOROUGHLY discussed her plan with her aunt. At some minutes past three o'clock, when it was confirmed that Mr. Roundbat was indeed taking his constitutional up and down

Portland Place, she and Miss Mayton would casually stroll out themselves.

She did not wish to appear overeager. After all, she and Mr. Roundbat might share a meeting of the minds when it came to poetry, but it must still be *him* chasing, if any chasing was to be done. Which she was certain she would wish for once she had further discussions about poetry.

Tattleton entered the drawing room and said gravely, "There is a person I take to be this Mr. Roundbat aimlessly strolling round the avenue and attempting to give every appearance of thinking deep thoughts."

"Tattleton," Juliet said, "that was not very complimentary. Do not tell me that even you are against Mr. Roundbat."

"I am against nobody, my lady. I am only *for* the Bennington family."

With that cryptic comment, Tattleton made his exit.

Miss Mayton patted her hand. "You must recognize, my dear, that not everybody is so swept away by the idea of poetry as you are."

Juliet sighed. "What do you say, Aunt? You are not against Mr. Roundbat?"

"When have I ever been against anything you girls were for? Mr. Roundbat may not have the heart-stopping looks of my Philippe, or the passionate nature of my Gregorio, or the well-cut coat of my Hans, nor can he hope to have the riches of my Transylvanian duke. But then, I do not imagine he's likely to kill himself either, so that is distinctly in his favor."

Juliet knew her aunt was attempting to buoy her up, though she thought "not likely to kill himself" was not the sort of praise to start hearts fluttering.

"If you like him," Miss Mayton said, "that is good enough for me."

Juliet sighed. "We'd better go out, then. I suppose I must discover precisely how much I do like him."

CHAPTER NINE

JULIET AND MISS Mayton proceeded out of the house under the grim stare of the butler.

Mr. Roundbat, who despite being engrossed in deep poetical thoughts had certainly been keeping an eye out for them, hurried to their side.

"Lady Juliet, Miss Mayton, how propitious to encounter you," he said with a bow. "I have found this avenue so inspiring!"

"Have you composed another poem in the Japanese style, Mr. Roundbat?" Juliet said.

Mr. Roundbat blushed. "I suppose I have. But then, I am not certain I ought to recite it, as it may be stepping out of bounds."

"Bawdy, is it?" Miss Mayton asked. "I do not prefer such compositions myself, but mind you, when in Rome one does hear things."

"Bawdy?" Mr. Roundbat said, nearly choking on the words. "No, my dear lady! I have not written a bawdy thing in my life, nor would I dare to think bawdy thoughts!"

"Perhaps you will recite it and we may come to our own conclusions," Juliet said.

Mr. Roundbat nodded and they began to stroll down the street. He clasped his hands behind his back and said, "There, a wide window. The lady resides within. Hidden mysteries."

Juliet could not make much of it, other than she must assume she was the lady in question. And, of course, she was not entirely opposed to being named mysterious.

"I see," Miss Mayton said. "Because you've never been in the earl's house it seems mysterious. Well, it is very usual I suppose. Except for Marvin. Never was a creature so raised up from the gutter to take his proper place in the world."

"Who is Marvin?" Mr. Roundbat asked, his tone sounding full of dread.

Before Juliet could tell the tale of the rooster rescued from a cockfight, the sound of hoofbeats came fast upon them.

They all turned to the sound, as one never did hear of anybody barreling down Portland Place at such a speed.

Juliet's breath caught to see Lord Hamill rein in his horse. He was sitting very finely on a magnificent black stallion. She knew perfectly well from even glancing at the horse that it would not be an easy one to keep under control. It was a massive beast, its eyes wide and nostrils flared. It pawed the cobblestones to further emphasize the point.

And yet, there was Lord Hamill smiling and looking very relaxed as if it were no trouble at all to manage such a creature.

He leapt off the horse and handed the reins to a boy who had come up behind on a smaller horse. "Find Hercules some shade, George," he said to the groom.

Turning to Juliet, he bowed. "Lady Juliet, Miss Mayton," he said. "How pleasant to encounter you." With a sudden frown, he said, "Roundbat."

"My lord," Mr. Roundbat said, looking a little nonplussed to see him there.

"Lord Hamill," Juliet said, bobbing a curtsy. "Do you visit one of our neighbors?"

"I do not."

"I see. Perhaps you have taken a wrong turning?"

"I have not. Conbatten mentioned you might be found strolling your neighborhood at this time of day and I could not think of where else I would rather be."

Juliet certainly hoped she had not blushed when it had come

upon her that Lord Hamill had sought her out.

"The marquess is most kind," Mr. Roundbat muttered.

"Shall we walk?" Lord Hamill said, putting his arm out so she might rest her hand upon it.

Juliet did so and could not help noticing that Mr. Roundbat had not offered his arm.

But then, she must remember that Mr. Roundbat's thoughts had been entirely taken up by poetry in the Japanese style.

Lord Hamill had expertly moved them in front of Miss Mayton and Mr. Roundbat as they walked along the pavement.

Feeling she had to defend poor Mr. Roundbat in some way, she said, "Mr. Roundbat has just recited a poem he has composed while strolling this very street."

"Indeed," Lord Hamill said. "I must hear it, Roundbat."

There was a long silence behind them. Finally, Mr. Roundbat muttered, "Very well," and recited the poem.

Juliet detected a distinct snort emanating from Lord Hamill, which did put her hackles up. It was true that she'd not made much of the poem herself, but then not every poem was meant to please every person. Or be understood by every person.

"It captures a moment, you see," she said to Lord Hamill. "In the Japanese style."

Lord Hamill nodded. "Perhaps I might capture a moment myself. The lady is unparalleled and exists on a plane too high for most to reach. Some delude themselves to aspire to it."

"Oh no, Lord Hamill," Mr. Roundbat said. "You see, the Japanese style is very proscribed regarding syllables—it is five, then seven, then five again."

"No doubt, Roundbat," Lord Hamill said. "But as we do not live in Japan, I preferred to speak in the English style."

Juliet was in no doubt as to Lord Hamill's hint—he did not consider Mr. Roundbat to be sufficiently elevated to approach her.

She was both flattered and prickly over it.

"No, of course we do not live in Japan," Mr. Roundbat said,

"but I have always felt it is man's duty to take on a worldly view of things."

"Perhaps you ought to go there," Lord Hamill said, a small smile on his lips. "Really immerse yourself. What would be a continental tour compared to that?"

"Well naturally I have considered traveling thus to study under the great masters…" Mr. Roundbat said.

"Do not put it off, Roundbat," Lord Hamill said, clearly controlling his laughter. "Men are always saying they will do things and then not managing to get out of bed in the morning to do them. It is a laziness of character, if you ask me."

"Or perhaps it is just waiting for the right time," Mr. Roundbat said. "The fullness of time, as it were."

"I see," Lord Hamill said. "And what particular time have you put down as being the time to set off for Japan and study with the great masters?"

"That has yet to be determined!" Mr. Roundbat said, beginning to sound a bit hysterical. "A wife who was also interested in poetry might wish to accompany me."

Juliet's eyes did widen over that idea. She had not the slightest interest in traveling across half the world to Japan, nor had she the need to. She had developed her own style of poetry and the Japanese masters would have nothing to teach her. She had firmly settled on four lines, as opposed to their three, and she also preferred that they rhyme.

They had reached the end of the street and crossed over to make their way back.

"A lady traipsing round the world on ships, broken down hackneys, and cattle-drawn carts, only to sleep in flea-infested accommodations?" Lord Hamill asked. "Oh, unless you happen to be a friend of the emperor, in which case I imagine it would be very comfortable."

"As it happens, I have written to Ayahito to express my congratulations on Japanese culture!"

"Has he written you back?" Lord Hamill said with a loud

snort.

"Not as of yet, Lord Hamill," Mr. Roundbat said. "Though his response may very well be wending its way to me."

"I see. Well, I have not written a note of congratulations to the Japanese emperor myself," Lord Hamill said. "I hardly need his advice on how *my* wife is to be treated."

"I did not write him for any advice of that sort."

Lord Hamill continued as if Mr. Roundbat had said nothing at all. "She is to have a figure of allowance that could never be entirely spent, even if she used all her waking moments to spend it. She is to be a marchioness, and then in *my* family's fullness of time, a duchess. She is to direct what the household looks like and how it operates, with me her dutiful servant. Naturally, she is to pursue her interests to the fullest and with my unflagging support. Of course, I cannot know how that stacks up to traipsing round Japan."

"Well goodness!" Miss Mayton said. "This was a more lively conversation than I had been expecting. Here we are, back at our door. I will insist on taking Lady Juliet inside. Fresh air is all well and good, but too much of a good thing cannot suit."

Juliet was rather surprised at her aunt, but also relieved. Her thoughts were in a whirl and she did not mind coming to the end of the "lively conversation."

TATTLETON HAD BEGUN to view his life in Town as skating on a frozen pond. One moment he was gliding along, the brisk wind ruffling what hair he had left. The next, he had come to a hard crash and wondered if he had broken any bones.

Sometimes, the skating even ran in reverse. He'd begin the adventure splayed on the ice, only to be unexpectedly thrown to his feet and skate happily away.

Such was the situation this afternoon. He'd been lying face

down on the ice upon watching Lady Juliet stroll with that Roundbat person, only to come flying to his feet upon the appearance of Lord Hamill.

He could not, naturally, overhear what was said between the parties as they walked along, but he was not too proud to spy out the windows of the drawing room.

It must be presumed that Lady Juliet had by now recited one of her dreadful odes to Lord Hamill and he did not seem the least put off!

He was a strapping sort of fellow, a regular Corinthian. Tattleton guessed he wouldn't know the difference between good and bad poetry if it hit him over the head. He was precisely the sort of fellow who had been hoped for.

As well, it would make Lady Juliet a marchioness, and eventually a duchess.

That was very satisfying to think about. There would come a time when Horace J. Tattleton would manage a table with *two* dukes sitting at it. It would be the very pinnacle of a butler's career and he could peer down that glorious mountain at other butlers who'd only managed a viscount or a baron. Or even more hilariously—a mister.

If there had been anything that made Tattleton wobble on his skates in viewing the scene out of doors, it was that Mr. Roundbat did not seem put off by bad odes either. He was an actual poet and Tattleton had been certain that a poet would have fled upon hearing of orbs, bovines, rocks, and fences.

Lady Juliet and Miss Mayton had since come indoors, and he brought a tea tray into the drawing room.

"Goodness," Miss Mayton said, "Lord Hamill was exceedingly spirited today."

"He made it abundantly clear that he does not like Mr. Roundbat either," Lady Juliet said. "Darden, Van Doren, Harveston, Conbatten, Baderston—they are all so against poor Mr. Roundbat."

Tattleton had set down the tray and would have usually

exited the room, but instead he went to the other end with a dustpan and small broom. He set about pretending to clean the carpet.

Neither lady would say anything of it as they would both assume he was cleaning up after Marvin again. They knew very well it was outside of his duties. That it was, in fact, outside of *everybody's* duties. They would not like to call attention to the matter.

"Well," Miss Mayton said, "Lord Hamill and Mr. Roundbat are rather chalk and cheese."

"I must say," Lady Juliet said, "that I was rather startled by the idea of going off to Japan."

To Japan? Which of those fellows thought they would drag Lady Juliet to the Far East? Anything could happen on such a journey! They might never again set eyes on the earl's youngest daughter.

It must be Roundbat. He wrote poetry in the Japanese style and, in any case, no English Marquess suddenly upped sticks and set off for Japan. They'd be locked in a sanitorium for a long rest before they set foot on a ship.

"I did think, in this particular encounter," Miss Mayton said, "that Lord Hamill rather prevailed."

Looking out of the side of his eyes, Tattleton could see that Lady Juliet knew the truth of it, but she was not at all happy to know the truth of it.

"Lord Hamill is more glib and perhaps has more confidence than Mr. Roundbat, I will admit," Lady Juliet said. "But unfortunately, he is no poet."

"No, sadly, he is not," Miss Mayton said. "Though, I did think his description of how his marchioness would carry on was very appealing."

Lady Juliet was silent. Tattleton hoped that meant she could not argue the point.

"I also must think his words were rather a declaration before a declaration," Miss Mayton said.

"A declaration before a declaration?" Lady Juliet said.

"Indeed, he wishes you to know that he is quite set on you."

"And you do not think Mr. Roundbat did the same with his mention of a wife going to Japan?"

"Perhaps so," Miss Mayton said. "But in any case, nobody has absolutely declared themselves, so nothing need be decided just yet."

"No, not just yet," Lady Juliet said.

She then looked over at Tattleton and said, "Tattleton, I am afraid Marvin has caused you much trouble."

Tattleton stood up and covered the contents of the dustbin, which were no contents, with the hand broom.

"Not at all, Lady Juliet," he said. "Marvin is now a part of the family, and the family never causes me trouble."

He hoped this sentiment would remind Lady Juliet that she was yet safe in the family bosom and no rash decisions about going to Japan need be made.

It was, of course, a sentiment full of rubbish. The only way he preferred Marvin to be part of the household was to be the main ingredient in one of Cook's pots. As for the family never causing him trouble…the absurdity of the statement was at a fever pitch.

"You are very kind, Tattleton," Lady Juliet said. "Very kind indeed."

Tattleton nodded graciously and took his empty dustpan from the room.

⇛⇚

RUPERT HAD EXHAUSTED himself by going out early to run around the park, then taking his horse out, then boxing with Jackson. He'd no choice in the matter—physical activity was the only thing that would suit when his thoughts were plaguing him.

He came into the drawing room with a full plate in hand. The kitchens were well used to his habits and knew he could not possibly make it from one meal to the next—he must have plates in between times. They'd set him up with sliced ham, cold chicken and roasted beef, a stack of buttered bread slices and globs of mustard and relish.

Theo was in there attending to some sewing and smiled at the plate. "It is just going on ten in the morning and you are eating again. How your waistline does not expand to enormous proportions, I will never understand."

Rupert stabbed a piece of chicken and said, "Did you know, that Roundbat character has hinted he would take a wife to Japan? He meant Lady Juliet. To Japan!"

"Goodness me," Theo said, laughing, "I see we change the subject."

"It is just, the idea is so outrageous."

"It certainly sounds unusual," Theo said, frowning and pulling out a stitch. "I shouldn't like it myself."

"Nobody should like it!"

"What does Mr. Roundbat plan to do in the Far East?" Theo asked. "Is he involved in some sort of trading venture?"

"Oh, no," Rupert said, "that would be far too usual for the likes of Roundbat. No, he wants to study with the masters of Japanese poetry."

Theo bit her lip.

"He spouted off another of his poems to Lady Juliet, which was meant to be understood as about her. It was all rather stupid."

"Oh do tell me," Theo said. "I do love a good bad poem."

"I cannot remember the words exactly, something about the mysterious lady living in a house with a window."

Theo's laugh rang through the drawing room. "Close enough—that is very amusing."

"Here is another thing amusing—he claims he has written to the emperor of Japan to congratulate him on Japanese culture. I do think I got the better of him there, though. I inquired if that emperor had written him back, which of course he has not."

"Goodness no, can you imagine if our queen received a letter from some Japanese fellow nobody had ever heard of, congratulating her on English culture?"

"Nobody can imagine such a thing. Queen Charlotte would expect to be addressed by the emperor, as I am sure the Japanese emperor would expect to be addressed by our king and queen."

"Were she to receive some missive from Mr. Roundbat's counterpart in Japan, she would not even know what it said. I will hazard a guess that none of her retinue can read Japanese."

"That's right! Roundbat would have sent his letter in English and nobody could even read it!" Rupert paused. "I wish I'd thought of that yesterday afternoon."

"But Brother, if you really are set on Lady Juliet, what will you do about it? Papa told you to pick the fellow up and move him out of the way. How will you do it before Lady Juliet sets off for Japan?"

"I am not certain," Rupert said. "Were I to physically pick him up and throw him across the road, I feel Lady Juliet would not like that at all. She seems to admire his poetry. Though, that's the only thing the rotter has going for him!"

"Then perhaps you ought to compose your own poetry. After all, Mr. Roundbat's poetry is dreadful, and Lady Juliet's poetry is equally dreadful."

"Is it that bad? It's hard to tell."

"Quite," Theo said laughing.

"I suspect you are right about that. She recited a poem for our mother and father and I thought the duke would roar with laughter."

"Yes, Papa told me all about it. He was entirely diverted. I have every confidence in my brother being capable of writing his own dreadful poetry."

"But won't she know it's dreadful?"

"If she does not perceive that both her own and Mr. Roundbat's compositions are dreadful, then I cannot think your bits of nonsense would be singled out."

"You are a genius, Theo," Rupert said. "After I finish this plate of meat and can think again, I will write my own dreadful poem. Then I'll take it to Portland Place at three o'clock where he will be waiting to stroll with Lady Juliet and I'll beat him at his own game!"

"That's the spirit, Mr. Wordsworth," Theo said. "Now, do remember what Lady Juliet told our mother and father—if she cannot capture a feeling in four lines, she knows she has gone wrong somewhere."

"That's right," Rupert said. "I only need to come up with four lines. How did I not think of that before?"

"Probably because you did not think of it *now*," Theo said. "What is a sister for, after all?"

"You're a brick, Theo," Rupert said. Then he turned his attention to his plate. Only four lines and they need not even be good lines—how hard could it be?

⟫⟫⟫✦⟪⟪⟪

PETEY HAD NOT wasted any time dividing up the pence the duke's man had delivered. He had several good hiding places in the room and his ma could not find out he'd come into the small fortune of a half crown.

She'd want to spend it all before the sun set over the rooftops, but he had bigger ideas. He'd get a new suit of clothes and with some of the extra funds he'd buy himself something that had some swagger—perhaps a hat of some sort or a coat with a beaver collar. He might even try for a walking stick, which would make him stand out from the crowd and also be used to beat to death anybody trying to rob him.

With any luck, he'd worm his way into the duke's house and begin collecting real wages. Then his ma could retire from her current employment and be a lady of leisure.

He'd told the duke it would take weeks to track all of the men who met next door to their various addresses, but he'd since had a better idea.

There were five men. Therefore, he needed four other boys to work for him. He could get the whole job done in a single night.

It had not taken a moment to get hold of four that could be trusted. Boys desperate for money generally *could* be trusted to carry out a task without inquirin' too deeply into it. He'd given them the simple job of following a fellow home and memorizing the address. It was to earn them a thruppence each.

As was natural, he had to throw some threats into the bargain to be sure they all did the job properly. He hinted that he worked for a powerful criminal who would wring their necks if the addresses were wrong.

This was totally believable, as powerful criminals were always wringing people's necks.

Now, the work had been done and it had been easy as mashed potatoes. It turned out that a fellow who didn't rob for a living was not forever looking over his shoulder when he was followed around in the middle of the night. It was also fortunate that the boys he'd hired were swift on their feet—every last one of those moneylenders had their own carriage waiting for them on a wider street.

Since then, he'd memorized all the addresses and gone to Grosvenor Square.

He'd had a little bit of a time of it reaching the duke's house. It turned out the gentlemen peacocks of the neighborhood didn't like the looks of him. Of course, that would all change when he got his new suit of clothes *and* boots.

After finally getting there, he'd had to argue his way inside, pointing out that he knew they'd been told to let him in and swearing he brought no fleas with him.

Finally, he'd been let in and led to a room to await the duke. It was twice the size of his ma's rented room, but not nearly as grand as he would have expected.

A thin and smartly dressed fellow came through the door with paper and writing instruments.

"I'm to write down the addresses for His Grace," the man said. He had a foreign accent. Petey thought he might be French but could not fathom what the duke was doing with a Frenchman in his midst.

"You ain't the duke," Petey said.

"You astound me with your insightful observations," the man said.

"Well who are you, then?" Petey asked suspiciously. "I ain't handin' over valuable information what's worth a new suit of clothes *and* boots to just anybody."

"Henri is not just anybody," the man said. "Henri is the duke's personal valet and Henri is the most renowned valet in England. Men would sell their souls to know Henri's secrets, but he never tells!"

"What's Henri got to do with it?" Petey asked, not entirely sure why this fellow was talking about that fellow. "I want to know who *you* are."

"Idiot anglais! I am Henri!"

Petey snorted. "I got ya now—ya talk like you're the king of England. Well, my good man, I can do the same. Petey here is gonna need some proof that Petey's got what's comin' to 'im. Petey ain't born last week and Petey ain't no fool. Petey ain't gonna get done by Henri, 'cause Petey ain't no donkey."

Henri whipped a long tape from his coat pocket and said, "Who do you think will measure you for this suit of clothes you imagine you deserve, imbécile?"

"I ain't never got measured for clothes before," Petey said.

Henri looked him up and down. "This is évidemment. Now, recite to me the addresses the duke requires, or I will give up all life and throw myself into the Arno!"

Petey didn't know where the Arno was, but if it was anything like the Thames he'd not likely come out again. "All right, all right, no reason to go drowning over it."

As Henri sat down at the desk in the corner of the room and prepared to write, Petey said, "I gotta be straight here, I was 'specting somethin' more—this room ain't as grand as was my imaginings for a duke's drawing room. Live and learn."

"Mon dieu," Henri muttered. "This is the butler's closet."

Petey glanced around. Now that he was looking at it, that did make more sense. There were only three chairs in the whole place and he'd been led to believe that a duke was forever having crowds in his drawing room.

At least, that was what Mrs. Hopewell said. That lady had once taken in washing for a fellow who knew a baron and seemed to be up on all the muckety-muck's doings. The fellow liked to tell all and sundry what he'd seen, including the washerwoman.

Though, Petey could not ignore that he felt a little stung that he'd not been led into the drawing room. He supposed he would be when he had better clothes.

He recited the list of addresses to Henri, who wrote it all down. Then, Henri whipped around his measuring tape and took a measure of every inch of him.

Satisfied that he'd got everything required, the valet said, "Henri is finished."

"Say, my good man," Petey said, leaning confidentially against the desk, "you seem like ya got too much work on your hands. I bet you probably need an assistant, a right hand, as it were. You're in a bit of luck there. As it happens, I'm just now considerin' my prospects career-wise. Ya'd be lucky to have me, that's all I'll say about it."

Henri looked at him as if he'd just suggested the valet run himself through with a sword.

"I'd rather tie rocks to my shoes and leap off a bridge!" Henri cried.

"You need time to think it over. Sensible."

CHAPTER TEN

MISS MAYTON HAD left for Lady Rawley's house, as they were to have another planning meeting for next year's theatrical. It was Juliet's understanding that they would decide on the play, and then Lady Rawley would use the summer to come up with a concept on how to improve Shakespeare's ideas.

Fortunately, she was not to be left to her own devices as Beatrice and Lily had walked over from their house across the avenue. Or rather, Beatrice had walked and Lily had staggered. The darling girl was always in a hurry somewhere, though she bounded forward as if all the world was a pillow ready to break her fall.

Juliet was grateful for the company. She'd found that when she was alone her thoughts spun around too much, and it was very uncomfortable.

Tattleton had brought in the tea tray.

Lily said, "Murder?"

Juliet bit her lip. They'd never got the parrot to understand that murder did not mean almonds, and now they'd never get Lily to understand that murder did not mean the parrot.

"No darling," Beatrice said, "the parrot is at home in the countryside."

Lily's eyes welled, as only a young child's can when crossed on any little matter. Beatrice said her daughter encountered world-ending catastrophes at least three or four times a day, but fortunately these disasters never lasted very long.

Juliet was most sympathetic. The earl still talked very fondly of the time she had wept at the nursery window as the sun set, in deep grief that it could not stay daytime forever.

Lily looked as if she'd suddenly had a new idea. "Marvin?"

"Yes," Juliet said, "Marvin is here. He is downstairs and I am certain Mr. Tattleton would be willing to take you to see him."

Tattleton nodded as gravely at the request as if he'd been nominated to escort the queen to her throne.

Lily, whose world had just been crumbling less than a minute ago, was positively elated. "Taddydon!" she cried, launching herself at his legs. "Lub me to pieces!"

Tattleton, as was to be expected, was entirely undone over it. Now *his* eyes welled. He picked up Lily and said, "Do not fret about a thing, miss. We will see Marvin this instant."

And so disappeared Lily and the butler to the servants' hall.

Beatrice took her tea and smiled. "She is very attached to Tattleton. Sometimes, she looks mournfully out the nursey window and across the avenue and whispers, 'Taddydon.'"

"He'd like to know it, I'm sure," Juliet said. "Perhaps I'll tell him at a moment when he's particularly irritated with Marvin—it will cheer him up enormously."

"And what of you, Jules?" Beatrice asked. "Do you need cheering up? You seem somehow not entirely yourself."

Juliet nodded. "That is because I do not know my own mind. It is so strange! After all, it is *my* mind. If I do not know it, who does?"

"I suspect your confusion is not on every subject in the world. Is it about a gentleman?"

"It is about two of them, actually," Juliet said. "Now, Bea, you know of my idea that I must marry a poet."

"Certainly. And you have met one. Mr. Roundbat."

"Yes, the one nobody likes."

"But you like him?"

"I think so. I mean, I must. Mustn't I? He is a poet and there do not seem to be other eligible poets and I did say I must have a poet. It really should be a very simple thing!"

"And it is not turning out to be simple because…?"

"Well, I think I must blame Lord Hamill for complicating things. It is his looks, you see. Which I find very unfair. Why should someone be liked for their looks, rather than the poetry of their soul?"

"I will not say anything against either gentleman," Beatrice said. "Though I do think Lord Hamill has other good qualities aside from his looks. After all, he was the one who brought Cordelia and Harveston together when it seemed it should never be possible."

"Yes, indeed he did."

"And I always do find him so cheerful, as if anything in the world is possible."

"I expect you'd find him so, what with Van Doren looking in every corner for an oncoming disaster."

Beatrice erupted into laughter. "My darling husband is of a cautious nature, which I have come to admire. He is very careful of his family." Beatrice smiled to herself and said softly, "Though there are times when the bedchamber door is shut that he is less careful of me, which I also have come to admire."

Juliet knew very well what Beatrice was talking about, though it was near impossible to imagine Van Doren passionate behind closed doors. It practically gave her a headache.

She said, "I will also admit that Lord Hamill's mother and father are very genial people and Cordelia says they run a comfortable household. They do not stand on ceremony, which of course I do like."

"What of Mr. Roundbat's people?" Beatrice asked. "Do you know anything about them?"

Juliet shrugged. "All I know is the baron is dead set against Mr. Roundbat becoming a poet. Of course, there is a romance to the idea, but then I wonder if it is a very happy sort of household."

"I would wonder the same," Beatrice said. "A father and son at loggerheads on such a subject cannot be comfortable. I should not like to think of you tiptoeing round a tension-filled house."

"Although it mightn't come to that. Mr. Roundbat has had the idea of perhaps traveling to Japan to study poetry with the masters."

"Hmm. That would take him entirely out of the picture."

"Oh no, he was thinking of it after he is married."

"Jules! You cannot be considering going to Japan? It is so far away and you do not speak the language. You would be quite alone."

"I did initially recoil from the idea," Juliet admitted. "Not because I am afraid of the rigors of travel, but more because I do not think these masters he's interested in studying with would have anything to teach *me*. They will prefer three lines, while I am very set on four. They also do not work to make rhymes, which I find a bit lackadaisical."

"Wait. You *initially* recoiled? Do you think different now?"

"I have not ruled it out. Not entirely anyway. It occurred to me that sometimes great risks must be taken for the sake of art. What if traveling to study with the masters is the thing that catapults Mr. Roundbat into fame? Could I really say no to it? Could I be the person denying him his dream in life?"

Beatrice snorted. "I do not know if *you* can say no, but I would say no very loudly, clearly, and emphatically."

"Well it's all right for you—you are very happy with Van Doren."

"Goodness," Beatrice said, her eyes getting a faraway look. "I really am."

Juliet set down her teacup. "You see how my mind goes round and round. And then, I worry that I am being influenced by what other people think! Should I like Mr. Roundbat less because others do not like him? Should I like Lord Hamill more because all the world approves of him?"

"My advice is, make no decisions, Jules. You may not know

your own mind at this moment, goodness knows I did not for quite some time. However, I can promise you this—when your mind is ready, the truth of your feelings will fall on top of you like a crumbling wall of bricks. It will knock the breath out of you, and you will know."

Juliet nodded. She was actually very relieved to hear Beatrice's advice. She could simply decide to stop wrestling with her changing ideas and wait to be hit over the head with a wall of bricks.

"For now, it is quarter to three," Juliet said. "At three o'clock, Mr. Roundbat will be strolling the avenue. I did think I could not go out as our aunt is gone to Lady Rawley's, but if you were not opposed to a stroll…"

"I would be delighted," Beatrice said.

"And yesterday, Lord Hamill turned up to stroll too. I cannot say if he would come a second day, but he might."

"Now I am thoroughly delighted."

Benny knocked softly and came into the room to inquire if they needed anything.

Beatrice said, "Benny, do you think Mr. Tattleton would mind if we left Lily here for a time? We were thinking of going out for a walk and walking is not yet her strong suit. Perhaps you might ask him?"

Benny smiled. "There's no need to ask him any such thing, my lady. He's downstairs in a puddle over the little miss."

And so it was settled. Juliet would bring Beatrice along on her stroll down the avenue of Portland Place.

Who else would turn up to stroll and what would be said was currently a mystery, but she would be comforted to have her eldest sister by her side as she discovered it.

RUPERT HAD SPENT the remainder of the morning and into the

afternoon in the library, working on a four-line poem. He'd taken a break to eat a plate of Chelsea buns, then another break for a pot pie with roasted duck, and then another break for a large slice of berry pie and two mugs of ale.

It had been a lot of work, and he'd gone to Theo several times for advice, but he'd done it. His sister had pronounced his poem just as dreadful as anything Lady Juliet or Mr. Roundbat could think up.

Now, he was turning the corner into Portland Place with his groom behind, determined to arrive early so that Roundbat would have no time alone with Lady Juliet.

There was the scoundrel himself, just ahead, walking with his hands clasped behind his back as if he were Aristotle unraveling the mysteries of life. What a conniver.

Rupert reined in his horse just ahead of Roundbat. He leapt down and handed the reins to his groom. "Do you even have a horse, Roundbat? You seem to always be walking everywhere."

He fully anticipated that a fellow in for a thousand pounds to moneylenders would not have the funds to keep a horse, much less a carriage.

"Lord Hamill, good day to you," Roundbat said stiffly. "I have chosen to leave my stable of horses in the country. I do not believe the air in London suits them and there is so little need for them in Town."

"Where do you live, by the by?" Rupert asked. He was certain that wherever it was, it was rented.

"Yorkshire," Mr. Roundbat said curtly.

"I meant where do you live in Town."

"My father does not keep a house in London, and though I would prefer Mayfair there were very few rentals available. So, I am nearby St. Paul's, if you must know it."

As he had suspected. Roundbat had rented himself a house in Cheapside. Respectable enough, but easier on the pockets than some neighborhoods.

Of course, where Roundbat lived and his lack of horse and

carriage would mean nothing to Lady Juliet. Other ladies would turn up their noses at such circumstances, but Rupert was certain Lady Juliet would not.

There was not a thing he could do with the information.

Suddenly, Roundbat pushed past him and set off across the street. Rupert turned.

The devil. Lady Juliet and Lady Van Doren had just emerged from the earl's house.

Rupert set off in pursuit and easily passed by Roundbat, who clearly did not exercise in the park of a morning.

"Lady Juliet, Lady Van Doren," Rupert said with a bow.

Roundbat caught up with him and, sounding very out of breath, said, "Lady Juliet."

"Lord Hamill, Mr. Roundbat," Juliet said. "Mr. Roundbat, this is my sister, Lady Van Doren."

Roundbat bowed so low one might have thought he was picking up something from the pavement. "Lady Van Doren. An absolute honor to be introduced to one of Lady Juliet's relations."

"Mr. Roundbat," Lady Van Doren said. "Well, I understand we are all to stroll the avenue." The lady held out her hand and said, "Mr. Roundbat, do tell me of this poetry in the Japanese style you are keen on."

Roundbat had hesitated as if he did not know why Lady Van Doren was holding out her hand. Seeming to remember it, he put out his arm.

The fellow was such a rube!

Lady Van Doren, on the other hand, was an angel. She'd just very conveniently left him to escort Lady Juliet.

As Roundbat blathered on about the syllables required in Japanese poetry, Rupert led Lady Juliet.

"Lady Juliet," Rupert said, "I have found myself much inspired by your poetry, by your unique turns of phrase."

"Goodness, have you?" Lady Juliet said, her lovely face and dark eyes upturned to him. He'd very much like to kiss her, though he'd never travel so far out of bounds. At least, not yet.

"Indeed, I am most struck."

"Well, if you would like to hear another of them…"

"I definitely would."

"Hmm, I will tell you of one I composed regarding the glories of hay."

"Hay? Yes, that sounds terrific," Rupert said. He'd not the first idea that poems were written about hay, but he did not want to give away his lack of knowledge.

"Reaching for the sun and sprung from the ground, as we trot on by, we see it all around. A farmer joyfully feeds his horses and cows, while the ground that sprung the hay graciously bows."

"Yes, I see!" Rupert said. In truth, he did not see at all. The hay bows? Was it windy? He supposed there was all sorts of significance to it that he did not comprehend.

"It paints a picture of a moment in time," he said, hoping he'd got somewhere close to its meaning.

"Precisely," Lady Juliet said approvingly.

Encouraged that he was not entirely drowning in a subject he knew nothing about, he said, "Hearing your poetry has even inspired me to dare some on my own."

"Has it!" Lady Juliet said, seeming surprised and delighted.

"Indeed, yes."

"Now I know, Lord Hamill, that in such early days of exploring one's art, one might not wish to share one's work. I would only say that, as a poetess, I am particularly skilled at seeing where the initial talent might go, even if it is just now in its infancy."

Infancy indeed, Rupert thought. Theo had named his poem both dreadful and *infantile*. Though, his sister had not thought Lady Juliet would be put off by either of those qualities.

Roundbat had hurried forward, practically dragging Lady Van Doren with him. "Did I hear that Lord Hamill has written something?"

"You have heard correctly, Mr. Roundbat," Lady Juliet said.

Lady Van Doren wore a small smile. "How fortuitous," she

said.

"Now I have assured Lord Hamill that we all recognize it would be a first effort and could not, of course, be as seasoned as the work that I and Mr. Roundbat currently produce," Lady Juliet said.

"Nobody would dare imagine it," Rupert said, staring at Roundbat. He could see very well that the fellow was irritated to find another gentleman encroaching on what he took to be his particular specialty.

Annoyingly, the fellow also looked highly confident.

Roundbat said, "We must hear this feat of wordsmithing from Lord Hamill."

They had come to the end of the avenue and crossed over to make their way back. It was now or never, Rupert supposed. If Lady Juliet wished for poetry, then he would give her poetry, even though Theo had assured him it was dreadful.

He cleared his throat. "Youngest of five daughters at Portland Place, she writes poetry at a terrific pace. Each poem seems to be the best one yet, by the talented poetess, Lady Juliet."

Lady Juliet clapped her hands together. "Bravo, Lord Hamill. You've even made it rhyme, which can be quite tricky."

"I say, though," Roundbat said, "one cannot go simply naming the lady in the poem."

"Why not?" Rupert asked, enjoying the redness of Roundbat's face at the moment.

"It must only be hinted at. One simply does not come out and say it. It denotes a sort of…clumsiness and lack of finesse."

"Then call me clumsy and lacking finesse," Rupert said, highly amused.

"Lord Hamill's poem strikes me as heartfelt," Lady Van Doren said.

Rupert nodded to Lady Van Doren, as that lady was turning out to be quite the ally. "I said what I meant. But perhaps, Roundbat, you have some new creation, in the Japanese style, that you would wish to share? Even though it won't rhyme."

"It cannot rhyme, that is not in the Japanese style!" Roundbat said. "But as it happens, Lord Hamill, I will give you an example of hinting rather than saying. You might find it instructional."

Rupert stared blankly at Roundbat. If he ever was instructed by Roundbat on any matter at all, he would publicly announce it as proof that he'd gone as mad as a rabbit in springtime. He'd demand to be locked up until his sanity returned from whatever errand it had been on.

Roundbat got a faraway look and said quietly, "The lady emerged, cloaked lightly in an aura. The angels cry out."

"What?" Rupert said.

"Now, Lord Hamill," Lady Juliet said, "that really was very good. It was very evocative. For the Japanese style."

Rupert shrugged. "I will never understand the Japanese."

"That much is clear," Roundbat said curtly.

"Well, gentlemen," Lady Van Doren said, "I applaud you both. It is not often that one strolls while hearing original poetry. It was quite singular."

Rupert got the idea that Lady Van Doren thought both of the poems she'd heard were idiotic, but that she was very entertained by it all.

"Do you both attend Lord Dunston's rout this evening?" Lady Van Doren asked. "I understand he has invited the whole world."

Rupert nodded and was irritated to see Roundbat nodding too. It seemed Dunston certainly had invited the whole world.

He supposed Lady Jersey had put Roundbat on the list so she could hear more about how she was like a gracious medieval queen.

"And you, Lady Van Doren?" Rupert asked. "Do you attend?"

Lady Van Doren laughed and said, "Heavens, no. My lord refers to routs as the extra circle of hell that Dante forgot to mention."

"Van Doren is not very social," Lady Juliet clarified.

"Not with strangers, anyway," Lady Van Doren said.

"I find him a man of good sense," Rupert said. And that was the best thing he could say about Van Doren, as the fellow did come off prickly.

"I am free to go, and leave Van Doren behind to entertain himself, of course," Lady Van Doren said. "However, I do not find a rout compelling enough to give up my lord's company."

"I have not yet had the honor of being introduced to Lord Van Doren," Roundbat said.

"Do not rush into it, Mr. Roundbat," Lady Juliet said. "I shouldn't like to hear Van Doren's views of poetry in the Japanese style."

Lady Van Doren covered her mouth to stifle her laughter. "None of us would like to hear it, I suspect."

Rupert laughed too, as it was amusing to consider. As far as he could tell about Van Doren, one was safest sticking to talking about managing an estate and all the subjects contained in it. He'd rather like to see what Van Doren would make of Round-bat's lady cloaked in an aura coming out of her house only to make the angels cry.

"Here we are, back at home," Lady Van Doren said. "Now, I had better rescue my father's butler from the clutches of my young daughter. If I know Lily, she's wrapped Tattleton round her finger and finished it off with a bow."

Rupert bowed. "Lady Van Doren, a pleasure to see you again. Lady Juliet, I hope I can count on seeing you at Lord Dunston's rout."

He turned to collect his horse. Over his shoulder he said, "Roundbat, you'll likely need to go round the corner to find a hackney."

Rupert laughed all the way to his groom. Lady Juliet might not care that Roundbat would travel by hackney, but Roundbat himself would care very much to have it pointed out.

CHAPTER ELEVEN

Tattleton was well aware that Lady Juliet had once more walked the avenue accompanied by Lord Hamill and Mr. Roundbat. There was no possibility he would not be aware, as Benny and Johnny had kept a close eye on the proceedings.

Those two young fellows could not hear what was said, but they'd made very great leaps in imagining it. According to them, Lady Juliet had smiled more at Lord Hamill then she ever did at Mr. Roundbat.

Tattleton could only hope that was true, as Mr. Roundbat had some wild notions about taking a wife to Japan.

They also said Mr. Roundbat had a slinking and obsequious air about him, which Tattleton found himself agreeing with.

For all that, he could not spend too much time worrying over it. Miss Lily had spent hours with him this day and she always did buoy his spirits and give him the feeling that all must be right with the world.

What charm! What innocence!

Even that rogue of a rooster Marvin behaved himself in her company. The bird had sat respectfully at her feet while Tattleton taught her the proper word for biscuit so she would stop talking about murder.

Had anything ever sounded more adorable then when she tried to master it and shouted "Bitbit?" No, he was very certain that nothing more delightful had ever been spoken in the history of the world.

Now, the day was done and Mrs. Huffson hurried in and laid a bit of sewing on the table. That piece of work should have gone straight into her sewing basket, had there not been a rooster atop it like some god-forsaken sewing sentry.

"Well now, Mr. Tattleton, we'll have an easy night of it, what with them above stairs all going out. Lord Darden, Lady Juliet, and Miss Mayton go to a rout and the earl is off to cards. That must cheer you."

Tattleton nodded and turned his face away to brush away a tear. It would be an easy night indeed and he would spend all of it replaying the gentle scenes of this afternoon.

Miss Lily had demanded that he lub her to pieces and he *did* lub her to pieces!

JULIET COULD NOT have imagined that her thoughts would be even more mixed up than they had been. And yet, they were.

Lord Hamill had written a poem! Even more interesting, it had been four lines and rhymed, just as she preferred. Even more interesting than that, it had outright included her name, though Mr. Roundbat was very against the habit.

She was not unaware that it might only be a bit of flattery and the lord might never set pen to paper again. Still, she had been struck by it.

Juliet took comfort in the idea that she would take Beatrice's advice. She'd allow her thoughts to run all over the world and back, and simply wait for a wall of bricks to fall on her head.

Both Lord Hamill and Mr. Roundbat would be at the rout, and plenty of other people too. Darden would come with them, as Lord Dunston was one of his particular friends. Viola and Baderston and Cordelia and Harveston would come too.

They would only be missing Beatrice, as Van Doren would

rather have his teeth pulled out, and Rosalind, as Conbatten feared it would be too much of a crush and the personal physician who followed her every step would speedily lose sight of his wife.

Juliet had chosen to wear a deep violet silk dress as it was her favorite of Mrs. Randower's creations for her season. The lady had acted as all of the sisters' modiste and could be trusted implicitly. She'd told Juliet that her coloring would look well set off by vibrancy, and that deep plums, violets, clarets, and emeralds would suit. If they were to go for a lighter color, it must be cream or sage or dove gray. There were to be no pastels.

Juliet had been saving this one to impress. *Whom* she was out to impress, she could not decide, nor did she try to.

Sandren had brought the carriage round and she, Miss Mayton, and Darden had piled in.

"What's this I hear, Jules," Darden said, "about your strolls up and down the street with two gentlemen at your heels? My valet spotted them out a window and said he'd find out who they were from Benny or Johnny, as they were sure to know, but I said I'd go right to the source."

"Lord Hamill and Mr. Roundbat have come by two days in a row to discuss poetry," Juliet said.

"Hamill?" Darden said laughing. "Hamill is discussing poetry now?"

"And writing it," Juliet said.

"He never did," Darden said, roaring with laughter.

"He did," Juliet said. "Though, I have wondered if it were just a bit of flattery."

"A *bit* of flattery?" Darden said. "I'd say it was quite a lot of flattery."

Juliet had been afraid that was the case. She could not help but feel some disappointment over it.

"I have never known Hamill to do anything like it," Darden said. "He must be very keen."

"I have seen the signs of it, Lord Darden," Miss Mayton said. "I have been convinced he has made a declaration before a declaration."

"A pointed hint, you mean?" Darden said.

"Just so," Miss Mayton said nodding. "As has Mr. Roundbat. They are both very keen."

"Roundbat," Darden muttered.

"Darden, do not tell me again that you do not like Mr. Roundbat," Juliet said. "He is a poet and I know you cannot understand the importance of that, but it is important all the same."

"Do not get your back up, Jules," Darden said kindly. "No more teasing from me tonight."

Juliet nodded, and of course she would not get her back up with Darden for long. He really was the dearest of brothers.

"Now, I'd best tell you something of Dunston's rout," Darden said. It is to be the rout to end all routs. He's got all kinds of rooms set up—absolutely everything has been transformed and most of the furniture moved above stairs. An orchestra will be in the ballroom, but it will only play waltzes so we will see who dares it. Then the music room has been turned into the theatrics room—lots of costumes, musical instruments, and a stage if anybody feels moved to perform. There will be other rooms dressed in themes—I believe a pirate's den was mentioned."

"Goodness, I have not waltzed since I lived on the continent," Miss Mayton said.

"I have never waltzed," Juliet said. "Not in public, anyway."

It did indeed seem daring. She supposed that Cordelia and Viola might try it out, as they were married ladies.

"Well, I do not find anything so outrageous in a waltz," Darden said, "despite what panicky older matrons think about it. However, there is one thing specifically I wanted to mention. Dunston recently returned from Switzerland and there he visited a little village called Couvet that offered the most unique liquor. It's called absinthe."

"How interesting," Juliet said, "and now we will all have the chance to taste it?"

"No, absolutely not. That's why I'm telling you. It will be in the punch—do not go anywhere near it. I've already written to Cordy and Viola about it so they do not make the mistake."

"Why?" Juliet asked.

"It is very strong. Very strong indeed," Darden said. "We tried it out at the club and were…let us call it surprised."

"Ah, did somebody feel ill-effects from it the next morning?" Miss Mayton said.

Darden paused. "It was not so much ill-effects as it was we do not really know what happened. When I came to my senses at dawn, I was in the back alley of the club, talking to a stray dog. Another member had painted a floor and then walked all over it. Another had cooked up all the chops in the kitchen and then forgot to eat them. We ended up giving all the chops to the dog and as far as I can tell, the dog was the only creature who enjoyed their morning."

"Goodness," Miss Mayton said, "I am not so certain that Lord Dunston should serve this cordial."

"Nor am I," Darden admitted. "But he says everybody will be warned of its strength. He hopes that those who dare drink it will provide some hilarity to the evening, as no doubt they will."

Juliet had no intention of sampling that punch. She could not imagine the horrors of a lady awaking in the morning only to remember she had too much to drink and had somehow embarrassed herself.

Her Papa had always been very sensible about ensuring his daughters understood the pleasures and dangers of drink. At fifteen, they were permitted wine at table and sherry in the drawing room. This had allowed them all to have years of experience with their own constitutions, well before those constitutions were put to the test in Town.

There had only been a few mishaps with the strategy. There was the time Beatrice had announced that she really ought to be queen and Charlotte ought to step aside. She planned to be exceedingly liberal with her subjects.

Then the other time when Cordelia had wept over Desde-mona's fate in *Othello* and said she would ring Shakespeare's neck if she could find him.

And then the other time when Viola had made a speech about how much she loved ham, and then fell over when she rose from the table.

All lessons learned and not forgotten.

While Juliet rarely consumed her limit, she knew what it was. She could easily manage three glasses of wine as long as she'd eaten and they were spaced well apart. Or, two glasses of wine and a half glass of sherry afterwards. She had no experience whatsoever with absinthe and she thought it best to keep it that way.

"Ah, here we are. The line of carriages is long—shall we get out here and walk up?" Darden asked. "Miss Mayton, would it be too far for you?"

"Goodness, no," Miss Mayton said. "If I can climb to a Swiss meadow with Hans, I'm sure I can manage an English pave-ment."

Darden rapped on the roof and Sandren had them out of the carriage in a trice. It was time to discover what wonders Lord Dunston had prepared for the evening.

RUPERT READ THE large sign printed in bold black letters over Dunston's sideboard, which was just now lined with punch bowls. The punch itself was ghastly green, which would have been enough to put one off, even without the sign that hung above it all.

WARNING: This punch contains absinthe, a devilishly potent liquor from Switzerland. Drink if you dare and do not blame me if you have regrets on the morrow. Dunston.

It was just the sort of warning that might have Rupert hurrying to take up the challenge.

That was, if he had not already had experience taking up the challenge at the YBC one awful night.

They'd all been keen to try out this new cordial that Dunston had brought back from Switzerland. It had been odd tasting, almost medicinal—like licorice without enough sugar in it.

It was not a flavor any of them had liked. At least, not at first. Somehow, though, it had seemed to grow on them. Then Dunston said they ought to put sugar in it and they'd liked it even more.

One of the last things Rupert remembered before waking up on a club sofa the next morning, was that Bailey was going to cook chops. The man swore he knew how to expertly cook a chop and they were all in favor, finding themselves starving.

Bailey had in fact cooked the chops. He'd cooked all the chops to be had in the kitchens. However, nobody had been awake to eat them. Not even Bailey himself, apparently, as he was found sleeping on a kitchen counter.

Among the other discoveries that morning, the coffee room floor was covered in wet paint, and Darden was discovered outside in the alley, having a genial conversation with a dog.

Rupert's head had pounded as if his brain were fighting to get out of his skull for most of the day. That was enough absinthe for him, thank you.

"Ah," a voice said behind him, "this must be Switzerland's answer to Japanese Awamori."

He would recognize that weaselly voice anywhere.

Roundbat. Why was Roundbat talking to him and what was he on about?

Rupert declined to turn and acknowledge the man. Until he heard another voice answer Roundbat's stupid comment.

"I am told it is very strong. Is this Awamori you speak of strong as well?"

It was Lady Juliet.

Rupert spun round. "Lady Juliet," he said, bowing.

"Lord Hamill," Lady Juliet said. "Mr. Roundbat was just saying that Lord Dunston's punch must have some sort of similar cousin in Japan."

"Awamori," Roundbat said gravely. "It is carefully made with rice imported from Siam and treated with a special sort of black mold."

"It sounds rather awful," Lady Juliet said.

"Are you in the habit of drinking this Awamori, Roundbat?" Rupert asked, very certain he was not. "What is its flavor?"

Roundbat reddened just a little bit. "I have not had the delight of tasting Awamori myself, considering how far it would have to travel to our shores. I have, however, read extensively about it."

"I suggest you do the same with absinthe—only read extensively about it," Rupert said. "As Lady Juliet has pointed out, it is very strong and not for the weaker constitutions."

Of course, Lady Juliet had not said anything about anybody's constitutions. Rupert had only added that in for his own amusement.

"Lord Hamill," Roundbat said, bristling, "I am a Yorkshire man. Our constitutions can hold up against anything."

"Except absinthe, I'll wager," Rupert said.

"Have you tried it before, Lord Hamill?" Lady Juliet asked.

Rupert nodded. "I have and will not do so again."

"Ah!" Roundbat cried, as if he'd caught out his opponent on a point, "So you found it overcame you, Lord Hamill?"

"Rather," Rupert said.

"That is sad, really," Roundbat said, appearing all confidence. He picked up the ladle in the bowl and poured out a full glass of the punch.

"There is nothing sad about knowing one's own limits," Rupert said.

Roundbat drank down the glass in one gulp. "A Yorkshire man has no limits, my lord."

"We'll see," Rupert said laughing.

As if the comment had been some sort of throwing down of the gauntlet, Roundbat poured himself another glass.

"What ho!" Darden said, coming among them. "Roundbat, go easy with that stuff. Did you not read the sign?"

Roundbat bowed deeply, and only spilled a little of what was in his glass. "I did indeed have the honor of reading Lord Dunston's kind explanation of this offering, Lord Darden. However, as I have explained to Lord Hamill here, I am a Yorkshire man with no limits."

To prove the point, Roundbat downed another glass.

Darden was looking both wide-eyed and amused.

Rupert said, "We'll see what you think about a Yorkshire man's limits when you wake up in the morning."

In answer to this, Roundbat attempted to drink his third glass, but only got halfway before he choked on it.

Clearing his throat, Roundbat said, "Ignatius Roundbat has never woken with a head in his life. He will not begin the habit now!"

In the distance, over the chatter of the crowd, the orchestra had struck up in the ballroom.

Darden said, "Come, Jules. I will waltz you round the floor. It will be quite proper to dance with a relation."

Lady Juliet clasped her hands. "Will you, Darden? You are such a darling brother. And do not worry, I believe I know most of the steps. Now, Mr. Roundbat, I really do advise you drink no more of that punch."

Roundbat bowed. "At your service, my lady."

Darden took his sister away and Rupert could not blame him. Roundbat was acting the fool and as he was on his third glass of absinthe, things would only further deteriorate.

Though Roundbat was beginning to look a bit unsteady on his feet, Rupert had never felt steadier. He followed Darden and Lady Juliet through the crowd that headed toward the ballroom and left Roundbat in conference with his punchbowl.

JULIET HAD LEFT Mr. Roundbat and Lord Hamill at the punch-bowl. She thought it very right of Darden to lead her away, as it seemed Mr. Roundbat was intent on having a contest with Lord Hamill regarding who could drink the most absinthe.

It was a rather silly contest, as Lord Hamill refused to drink any at all.

Of course, she thought she understood what drove Mr. Roundbat. Lord Hamill was a Corinthian, a sportsman, a man whose arms were as large as some other people's legs. Other men *would* be driven to show that they were just as manly.

It was a thing Darden had once explained to her as being one of the great immutable facts of life—dare a man to prove he's a man and that man would throw himself into a fire and hold his fist up in victory, satisfied he'd proved his point as he went up in flames.

In any case, she was to waltz for the first time in her life. At least, the first time with a man in public. She and her sisters had of course tried it out with each other. Miss Mayton had been good enough to get them a pamphlet on the steps, their aunt certain that it would soon become as widely accepted in England as it ever was on the continent.

For all her dancing with her sisters, though, to behold a ball-room full of people waltzing was magnificent indeed.

"There is Harveston and Cordy!" she said.

"Now," Darden said, "as the dance has already started, we will need to slip into an open spot without banging into everybody. Just follow my lead."

Before she knew it, Darden had pulled her in and they became a four with another couple Juliet did not know.

The gentleman guided her through the turns and allemandes, and then she was returned to Darden and they set off, going round gloriously.

As the ballroom spun past her eyes, almost making her dizzy, she caught sight of Lord Hamill.

He led Lady Jersey, who was looking well pleased to be so escorted.

The music signaled they were to pair with another couple again, but this time it was Cordelia and Harveston.

Harveston led her through the steps and said, "I suppose you learned the waltz in the same manner as your sister?"

"Yes, we learned all together and it really is rather more glorious than it was in our drawing room!"

Harveston laughed and Juliet thought he really was becoming a rather jolly fellow under Cordelia's good influence. He'd been so serious all the time, but her sister had seemed to wrestle that out of him.

Now, she was back with Darden again and they spun round the floor.

The waltz nearly took one's breath away.

They passed close to Lord Hamill leading Lady Jersey, and that nearly took her breath away too. What a man he was.

She did not mind these oncoming feelings, now that she'd understood from Beatrice that she was to let any and all thoughts and feelings wash over her until she was hit with a wall of falling bricks.

Darden slowed and they paused into a quartet again. She found herself facing Lord Hamill.

What a lovely, lovely creature he was. It was as if God had rubbed his chin and thought, what would be the most perfect example of a man?

He held her fingertips and led her through the steps. "You are looking very well this evening, Lady Juliet. Very well indeed."

She smiled and did not mind the thrill gone through her at his words. Why not? She need only concern herself with the wall of bricks that would sooner or later fall on her head.

As she turned to Darden, she was suddenly whisked away by Lord Hamill. She saw Darden shake his head, though he did not seem angry. Her brother took up Lady Jersey and they set off.

Juliet was, for a moment, speechless. Both Lord Hamill's hands held up her arms and they were in such close proximity. Closer than she'd ever been to a man, short of hugging her father or brother.

She forced herself to speak, and to sound rational about it.

"This is rather daring, Lord Hamill," she said, as he spun her round. "I do not believe a single lady is meant to dance with a single gentleman unless…" Juliet trailed off, as she did not really care to say what the unless was.

"Unless the gentleman has declared himself," Lord Hamill said.

"Yes, unless that."

"Perhaps the gentleman will declare himself," he said pointedly.

"No! That is, I cannot speak for every lady, but for myself, I do not wish to hear any declarations. Just now. At this moment."

"I see," Lord Hamill said. "Will there be a future moment?"

Juliet felt rather panicked to be asked such a direct question. The room was spinning, the question was so intimate.

"I do not know!" she cried. "I must wait for the falling bricks!"

Lord Hamill had stared hard at her then, and even though she knew she was supposed to be looking at him as part of the dance, she turned her face away.

She could not bear to look straight at him, lest he see into her confused soul.

Thankfully, it was time to return to a four again and Darden was beside her.

CHAPTER TWELVE

"A LL RIGHT, HAMILL," Darden said, Juliet returned to him once more, "I will not hold it against you that you have stolen off with my sister for a round, but she is back with her brother now."

"I should say so, Lord Hamill," Lady Jersey said, "you have been exceedingly naughty."

"I blame it on the absinthe," Lord Hamill said.

Breaking apart, Lord Hamill and Lady Jersey spun away. Darden led her and said, "You are very red, Jules. Did Hamill…that is, did he say something?"

"I stopped him from saying…something," Juliet said. "It is too soon. There has been no pile of bricks falling on my head yet."

Darden looked at her quizzically. He did not ask her to elaborate though. He knew his sisters well, and he knew when they were not quite ready to explain themselves.

The rest of the dance went on with no further encounter with Lord Hamill. Darden kept a sharp eye out to see it was so, lest there be any talk about the lord stealing away Lady Juliet for a waltz.

At the conclusion, Darden asked if she wished to go again, but Juliet had enough of waltzing for one evening. It had been glorious, but also a little frightening.

Her plan to wait for the falling bricks on her head was all well and good, but she had not factored in the idea that a gentleman might not be quietly waiting for it to happen also.

Had she not stopped him, Lord Hamill might have declared himself and she really was not sure what she thought about it. The only thing she could be certain of is that she would have been pressed to give an answer and she had no answers yet.

She had at once wished to throw herself into his arms, and also to run in the other direction. The bricks, wherever they were, were not even teetering.

They found Miss Mayton at the edges of the ballroom and went off to explore what else Lord Dunston had prepared for the evening.

They would end in regret that they did.

Laughter rang out from the music room, and they strolled in to discover what was causing such mirth.

To her surprise, Juliet found Mr. Roundbat standing atop a stage of some sort while a crowd gathered round him, pointing and laughing. He'd wrapped a cloak around his waist to create what looked like a skirt.

"It is not a skirt! It is Hakama!" Mr. Roundbat shouted over the crowd's laughter. "The traditional dress of the greatest samurais of Japan!"

Juliet bit her lip. This, whatever this was, had happened because of three glasses of absinthe. After all, Darden had found himself in an alley in confidential conversation with stray dog, so it was no surprise that Mr. Roundbat now fashioned himself as a Japanese warrior.

"If someone will just bring me a sword," Mr. Roundbat shouted, "I will demonstrate the different Samurai stances! Like so, and like so and like so."

Mr. Roundbat was waving his arms around putting himself into different positions, almost looking as if he were an acrobat at the theater. He had several times teetered at the edge of the stage and looked menacingly at his audience as if he might leap at them.

"For the love of heaven," someone in the crowd shouted out,

"nobody bring this fellow a sword lest we all die tonight!"

This sent the crowd into peals of laughter.

Mr. Roundbat was not laughing though. He suddenly stood stock-still, his hand falling from his makeshift skirt. It slid to the floor in a fabric puddle.

"The fair Juliet!" Mr. Roundbat cried, pointing at her over the crowd's heads.

As heads turned, Darden grabbed Juliet's arm and spun her round, walking her out of the room, with Miss Mayton on their heels.

"We will not wish to stay for whatever is coming next," Darden said.

"I should think not," Miss Mayton said. "Mr. Roundbat appears rather intemperate at this moment."

"It is the absinthe, Aunt," Juliet said.

"I believe we will be safer returning home," Darden said. "I have a feeling that Roundbat would not have been the only person indulging in absinthe and while whatever shenanigans occur from here on out might be amusement for *me*, I do not think I wish my sister to be present for it."

"Part of me wishes to rail against the idea, Darden," Juliet said. "But the more sensible part of me thinks you may be right. That scene was almost frightening. We'd best go."

And so they did go, leaving Lord Dunston to manage the absinthe drinkers however he might.

RUPERT WAS CONFOUNDED by Lady Juliet.

He sat in his drawing room after a long run round the park, brewing and stewing over the lady's words. It was a quiet time of day, the rest of the family still abed.

He'd been rather daring in stealing Lady Juliet away for a turn at the waltz. Then still more daring in hinting at a declaration.

He would have gone forward with it too, had she not stopped him in his tracks.

The confounding thing was he did not know what she meant when she'd stopped him. Was it a permanent stop? Or was it a temporary stop? Did she say no, never? Or did she say no, not right this minute?

What were these falling bricks she talked about?

He heard the door open, and Theo came through it with a book in hand.

"Goodness, I had not expected anybody here," she said. "You are usually out and about already, and Mama and Papa will be breakfasting in their beds."

"I have been out, and now I am here brooding," Rupert said.

Theo sat down across from him. "Brooding? That is very unlike you. I must guess the cause to be Lady Juliet?"

"She is a confounded creature, Theo."

"Do not tell me that your poem did not go over," Theo said. "I will not believe for a moment that it was not every bit as equal to the tragic orbs she writes about."

"No, no, she was very approving of the poem. Apparently, I have a leg up over Roundbat because I made my poem rhyme."

Theo snorted. "So? If it is not your astounding rhymes, what is it?"

Rupert sighed. "Well you see, last night at Dunston's rout, and by the way, you were very right in skipping it, I came very close to…you know."

"To saying something directly?" Theo said, leaning forward in all interest.

"Yes. There was waltzing, and she danced with Darden and I took the opportunity to steal her away for one go round the floor. She said a gentleman ought not have done it unless he had already declared himself. I said maybe I would declare myself."

"So you did not? You just said you might?"

"I did not get further than that. She said she did not wish for anybody to declare at that moment. Then I asked if there might be a future moment."

Rupert paused, because this part was really the sticking point.

"And?" Theo asked.

"She said she had to wait until the falling bricks."

"The falling bricks?" Theo asked. "What are they? What does that mean?"

"I don't know! I was hoping you might know. Could it be some sort of lady's phrase that means something else?"

"I suppose, though I've never heard the expression."

"You see what I mean? She is a confounding creature."

"You will not give up, though?" Theo said. "It would be very unlike you to give up. Especially when you might be ceding the field to Mr. Roundbat."

"Roundbat! That fellow got himself entirely drunk, put on a skirt, and claimed it was a Japanese warrior's outfit. Then he searched the house for a sword, which thankfully he did not find. He was finally carried out by Dunston and a few club members, shouting, 'You fail to understand, it is hakama!'"

Theo's laughter rang through the room. "Oh dear, while I suppose it was good sense not to go to Lord Dunston's absinthe party, I am rather sorry I missed that."

"My only hope is, Lady Jersey did not miss it. That would end her favor of that smarmy rogue for good, I think. As far as I can tell, her favor is the only reason he seems to get invited everywhere."

"Let Mr. Roundbat be the author of his own demise," Theo counseled. "You have a lady's heart to win. And falling bricks to arrange, whatever that might mean."

As always, Theo had given him good counsel. What was he doing, sitting around morosely, brooding like a schoolboy?

He was Rupert Doncaster, Marquess of Hamill. He was not to be done in by falling bricks or any other thing falling from the sky. He must just charge forward and throw those bricks out of his way.

"Perhaps you will see her again in three days' time?" Theo

said. "Certainly she must attend Lady Bloomington's masque. I know Cordelia did last season—she told me all about it and how one must be careful of the constant trays of champagne coming round."

"Yes, I believe she will attend and yes, Lady Cordelia is right about the ever-flowing libations. If Roundbat somehow wrangled an invitation, perhaps he will drink too much champagne and start shouting about his Japanese hakama again."

"He'll probably wear one," Theo said, laughing. "You have got the costume I advised? You will not back down and go in a boring domino?"

"Henry the Fifth is ready to present himself."

"I really think it's the sort of thing Lady Juliet will admire—strong, passionate, and determined."

"It had better be, the breastplate had to be created from scratch—none that were available would fit."

"Too small, I suppose."

"Far too small. Roundbat would do very well in one, the measly creature. Anyway, I'll ride over to Portland Place this afternoon and see if anybody is strolling the avenue. With any luck, Lady Juliet will be out and Roundbat will be home in bed recovering from his over-consumption of absinthe. If I remember correctly, he will be having a very bad day."

There was a soft knock on the door and Graves came through with a letter on a silver salver.

"The Duke of Conbatten's man just brought this, my lord. He says it is to be delivered to your hands directly."

Theo smirked as he took the letter. She said, "I cannot imagine what you, the duke, and Lord Rowndale talk about all the time. You three write to each other so often one might think you were wooing one another."

"We are just particular friends with various business interests in common," Rupert said.

His sister smiled, took up her book, and went to the far side of the drawing room. Of course, Theo would not know why both

Conbatten and Rowndale wrote so often, as she did not know a thing about the Queen's Knights.

He supposed Conbatten had sent some sort of update on the moneylenders' scheme to violently shake repayments from their debtors. He tore open the letter.

Hamill—

The boy, Petey, has located all the addresses of the moneylenders faster than we had anticipated. Apparently, he hired some other boys to do his work, so he's clever regardless of what else he is. (And he's already been to my house demanding his new suit of clothes so we can add bold to his description too.)

Rowndale has set a watch on every house identified, but it gets us nowhere. They all have so many people coming and going that it is impossible to sort out who might be a hired thug, and who might be there for a loan.

Will send further news when we have it.

C

So, they were nowhere with that investigation.

Rupert shrugged to himself. Rowndale and Conbatten could carry on however they liked. If they had need of him, he would answer the call.

But in the meantime, he had a lady's heart to win.

And the confounding puzzle of falling bricks to untangle.

PETEY WAS WELL aware that he had not had any grand opportunities in life, but he also knew he was clever. He had been all along counting on his cleverness to turn something up.

Someday, an opportunity would be trotting on by, and he would grab it and use all the cleverness he could muster to hold on to it.

As he *was* by nature clever, it was not lost on him that the opportunity he had waited for had arrived.

How many people in his neighborhood had been inside the Duke of Conbatten's house? How many people did he know who were on speaking terms with that duke and his valet?

None. That's how many.

Since his first visit to the duke's house, he'd gone back twice. He still had not got past the butler's closet, but he was ever hopeful of working his way into the drawing room someday soon.

Henri, the duke's valet, seemed to be on the verge of madness every time he set eyes on him. Petey had now been told three times that he would be informed when his suit of clothes *and* new boots were ready. The measurements for the clothes had gone to the finest tailor in England, an Italian master, and could not be rushed.

Petey was not in a particular rush. For one, he'd have to explain to his ma where the clothes came from—she'd already asked him quite a few questions about the ink and paper that had suddenly appeared. For another, he could not wear any fine clothes in his current neighborhood—they'd be taken off him in a trice.

No, those new clothes were for his move-up in life. Those clothes were for the moment he would step up in the world.

Mostly, he went to the duke's house so that the staff could become accustomed to seeing him around.

He'd made great inroads with the maids by telling them they were beauties who ought to be on the stage.

The footmen liked him, as he told them bawdy jokes he'd heard spoken in the dank alleyways of his neighborhood.

The butler, Alden, seemed to find him amusing, mostly because of his effect on Henri.

He'd even begun to beguile the cook with compliments about whatever was wafting round in the kitchens. He'd actually clutched at his heart upon being given an almond biscuit with the duke's crest stamped on it. He claimed it was the finest almond biscuit that had ever been made. For all he knew, it was—he'd never had one before and it tasted pretty good.

But Henri, that rascally valet, was not so easy to get over.

On the bright side, the fellow looked near collapse from nervous exhaustion, so perhaps Petey becoming the duke's personal valet was not so out of reach as it might have at first looked.

He'd decided he needed something else to offer the duke, some other piece of information to tip the scales in his favor. Mulling it over and thinking it through had not produced anything.

But then, as luck would have it, something fell right into his lap.

It had been a Thursday night and he'd been carefully copying the letters of the alphabet the duke had written out for him. He'd already filled one side of the paper and now he was working on the other side. It was as quiet as it ever was—the distant shouts, shattering glass, odd thuds, and screams were so usual for his world that he did not even hear any of it.

There should not have been anybody meeting next door. It had been a surprise to hear voices from that room.

It was not the whole cabal of those moneylenders, as it always had been. Just two of them.

Like most conspiracies, this one looked to be falling apart as fast as it had been put together. It seemed these two fellows had some disagreement with the others regarding the list of gentlemen who were to be violently pressed for owed funds.

Petey could hear a cork pop and the clink of glasses. That was good. It was his understanding that the more a man drank, the more he said things he weren't never planning on saying. His ma said many a murderer had been caught out in a tavern, not being able to stop themselves blabbing about it after a certain amount of gin.

"Here's my opinion on the thing," one of them said. "It ain't only the amount that's to be the guide on who we go after. It's the attitude, the lies to get the loan, the audacity of the gent, and the rudeness we get treated with when we're so bold as to want repayment."

"Aye, Kramer, you're preachin' to a vicar on that point."

"Marty, my friend, there's some of these fellas that irritate me mightily, and somehow they aren't on the list."

"Aye," Marty said.

"Seems like maybe we make our own list."

"Seems like I might agree to the prospect. Just one thing, though, if we're gonna break with the others and go our own way."

"What's that?"

"Let's keep mum and go along until we got Roundbat tied up right and tight. I hate that fellow."

"Aye. I hate 'im too, the arrogant little creep. If ever there was proof life ain't fair—that bounder getting a leg up in in the world has got to be proof positive."

"I'd like to wring his neck after my last conversation with the rotter."

"Likewise. I 'spose he told you all about the rich lady what's gonna wed him and set him up for life and then we all get paid off?"

"Aye. I said to 'im, do I look like a babe born this mornin'? What rich lady is gonna have anything to do with *you*? Then he says it's 'cause he writes poetry in the Japanese style."

"If that's true, the people of Japan have something to answer for, encouragin' a bounder like Roundbat."

"I'll wager them poor Japanese people don't got the first idea of it. I'll wager they'd get one look at 'im and be mortally affronted."

"Aye. The Japanese know what's what, then."

Petey quietly stepped away from the wall.

Roundbat. When the duke and his friends had been here, they had talked about this Roundbat character being into the lenders for a thousand pounds.

It had been clear enough that none of the lords cared for this Mr. Roundbat. Now these two fellows next door downright hated the fellow and speculated that the whole country of Japan would hate him too if they ever set eyes on him.

Petey was not particularly sure where Japan was located, he guessed it was somewhere past France, but he could not imagine how hard a gentleman would have to work to have a whole nation despise him. Somehow this Roundbat fellow had managed it.

Now Petey knew the moneylenders were to go after Roundbat, and they would do it sometime soon, as those two fellows didn't seem inclined to wait for long before breaking with their group of associates.

It seemed exactly the kind of thing the duke oughta know about. It seemed exactly the sort of thing to give him a leg up.

He'd need a leg up—he was starting at the bottom rung of the ladder and he intended on getting very close to the top.

All he had to do was start haunting the houses of this Kramer and Marty. He already knew where they lived and he was very skilled at slipping around unnoticed under the cover of darkness. One cracked window or one loud talker might give him the details he needed to take to the duke.

Roundbat was targeted soon. All he needed to know was where and when.

CHAPTER THIRTEEN

THE DAY AFTER Lord Dunston's absinthe rout was to be a quiet one and Juliet was glad of it.

Lord Hamill had taken her so by surprise by hinting he might declare himself that she was grateful for the interlude before she would no doubt see him at Lady Bloomington's masque in three days' time.

For that matter, she would avoid Mr. Roundbat too if she could. She had no wish to revisit his performance at the rout and could not imagine what he would say about it. Or what he might say about other things.

What if he too were to hint that he might declare himself?

She was not ready for anybody to say anything! They must all wait for the bricks to fall down. She did not want to be rushed. She would not be rushed.

For all she knew, the bricks would fall on her head about another gentleman she'd not even met yet. She was pulled in two different directions, but what if there were a third to come along? It was impossible to know!

Juliet would make no decisions until she knew her own mind, and that mind was currently waiting on a pile of bricks.

Mr. Roundbat would be impossible to avoid, though. His dinner party was on the morrow, and she and Miss Mayton had accepted the invitation.

She'd peeked out the window at three o'clock to see if anybody might be walking the street, expecting her to come out for a stroll. Mr. Roundbat had not made an appearance and Juliet presumed he'd been laid very low by the absinthe.

Lord Hamill had arrived on his horse and lingered for a while, but seeing nobody was to join him, he cantered off.

He really did cut a figure on that horse. And off his horse. He cut a figure pretty much everywhere.

But the lord's looks were not to be thought of now. Rosalind and Conbatten and Beatrice and Van Doren had come to dinner. And Rosalind's physician too, ever watchful of the lady's expanding waistline.

Mr. Laurelton was just now having his dinner on a tray in the drawing room, even though the earl had urged him to come to the table. He respectfully told the earl that certain lines must not be crossed.

Apparently, the dining table was a line for Mr. Laurelton, though none of them were clear why. They'd often had their own neighborhood physician to the house for a large dinner or party.

"I find I am most gratified to see how well my daughters' husbands care for them," the earl said, smiling round at the table. "Down to a man, I think I have been very blessed in that department."

"Indeed, Papa. Now we only wait to see how Juliet makes out," Rosalind said.

Juliet, herself, had no wish to answer such a statement and was rather relieved that her aunt answered for her.

"Never fear on that front, my dear Rosalind," Miss Mayton said. "I am using my steady hand to guide our youngest girl through it."

Darden's eyes widened just a bit, as they did when he was surprised by something.

Conbatten snorted into his napkin. Dabbing his lips, he said, "One might even be shocked by your success so far, Miss Mayton."

Miss Mayton nodded graciously.

The earl said, "I'm very glad you mention that, Duke. I sometimes think our dear Miss Mayton does not get the credit she deserves. Five daughters and four of them already married so well—if that is not a certain skill, I do not know what is."

Juliet could see Van Doren gripping his fork, his knuckles turned white. He would surely like to launch himself into a lecture just now regarding some past incidents her aunt should not have allowed. Or helped. Or thought of.

Particularly, hiring people to stage a kidnapping, which it did not seem like Van Doren would ever get over.

However, Beatrice had done a remarkable job of reining in that scoldy part of Van Doren's prickly personality. Now, he mostly just seethed in silence.

"I realized two things many years ago," Miss Mayton said, looking gratified to be the center of attention. "One, I must depend upon my sharp instincts if I am to successfully guide five young ladies round the pitfalls of society. And two, the five young ladies I look upon as my own daughters were all born with amazingly good sense."

Van Doren's fork clattered to his plate. Tattleton fumbled with a tray at the sideboard.

Conbatten pressed his napkin to his lips. "Remarkable observations, Miss Mayton," the duke said.

"I, for one," the earl said, "had never imagined it would all fall into place with so little trouble to myself."

"But the job is not done yet, Papa," Rosalind said. "Our Juliet must still find her match."

"Juliet," Beatrice said, "how do you get on with Mr. Roundbat and Lord Hamill? Was there a stroll with those two gentlemen this afternoon?"

Juliet felt all eyes upon her. She was, at first, hesitant to answer. But then she recalled that this was her family asking and they were all on her side, probably even Van Doren. All on her side, even though she was not certain what side she was on.

She said, "I purposely did not go out this afternoon, as I really had no wish to see either of them. I know it was very contrary of me, but there it is. I did look out the window, though. Lord Hamill turned up on his horse, went up and down the avenue, and then left. I suspect Mr. Roundbat remained at home recovering from his unfortunate introduction to absinthe."

"You did not wish to see either of them? Are they both out, then?" Darden asked.

Fortunately, Beatrice took that moment to step into the breach. "It is not that they are both out, it is not being certain who is in."

"Make no decisions then, my dear," the earl said. "After all, there is no reason in the world why we should not come back for a second season. You have no younger sister waiting in the wings, eager to take your place."

"A judicious idea," Conbatten said. "One would not like to rush, and then discover one has chosen wrong."

Juliet of course knew precisely what the duke meant. He did not like Mr. Roundbat one bit. He found him tedious. The duke might be highly romantic with regard to his wife, but he did not have a poetical turn of mind.

"And then," Darden said, "one must consider if one is entirely comfortable with the idea of one's husband wearing a skirt, shouting about hakama, and looking for a sword."

"You know that was the absinthe, Darden," Juliet said darkly.

"Gracious," the earl said, "I always think I am living at the far edges of gossip and rarely know what's being said, but even I have heard of Mr. Roundbat's performance last evening. You do not suppose he is intemperate with drink?"

"No, Papa," Juliet said, once again feeling as if she must defend Mr. Roundbat. "He was only goaded into drinking too much to prove something to Lord Hamill."

"What was he setting out to prove, my dear?" the earl asked.

Juliet said, "Darden? Tell our father of the immutable rule about gentlemen."

"Ah yes," Darden said. "If a man feels he must prove he is

manly by jumping into a fire, he will happily do so with a fist raised in victory as he goes up in flames. Roundbat went up in the proverbial flames last night."

"Ha! Yes, indeed!" the earl said, laughing heartily. "Though, you ought to modify that stricture to *young* man. I can assure you I have not the energy to jump into a fire to prove anything to anybody."

"Ros," Beatrice said to her sister, "you see the problem here, do you not? The bricks have not yet fallen for Juliet."

Rosalind nodded. "Yes, I do see. My own bricks fell in an instant."

"And yet, mine took their time," Beatrice said, nodding.

"The bricks are never on anybody's schedule," Rosalind said.

Beatrice nodded sagely.

Though Rosalind and Beatrice understood the matter, it did not look as if any gentleman at table understood. They looked entirely perplexed.

"Juliet only needs time to know her own heart, wherever it will choose to go," Beatrice said. "I would suggest, Jules, that perhaps these daily strolls should come to an end for now. Give yourself some peace for the time being."

Juliet nodded in agreement. It had felt rather fraught this afternoon, not wishing to go out, but then worrying that she was letting somebody down by not doing so.

"I will tell them both when next I see them," Juliet said.

"No," Darden said, "as your brother, I will tell them both. I will write and simply say that Father views it as untoward."

"I imagine I would have, had I known about it," the earl said.

Nobody addressed that particular statement, as the earl was usually in the dark about things. They never really liked to trouble him on any matter.

"That way, Jules," Darden said, "nobody's feelings are stung over it. No gentleman in the world takes it personally when a father views something untoward. Fathers are always viewing a thing as untoward."

"If they know about them," the earl said.

Juliet felt as if a weight had been lifted off her shoulders. Daily strolls had seemed to become a pressure rather than a pleasure.

She nodded vigorously. "Yes, I believe you are right, Darden. Then, I will only have to consider seeing Mr. Roundbat at his dinner on the morrow, and Lord Hamill at Lady Bloomington's masque in three days' time."

"What dinner?" Both Conbatten's and Darden's heads had snapped up and they'd spoken at the same time.

"Oh yes," Miss Mayton said. "We accepted Mr. Roundbat's invitation quite a while ago. There is to be a poetry reading after the dinner and, naturally, our Juliet will be one of the featured artists ready to delight with her poetical stylings."

"I do not think it wise you go, Juliet," Van Doren said.

Of course, he would not. Van Doren barely thought it wise to get up in the morning.

"What if he decides he's a samurai warrior again?" Van Doren pressed on.

"I am sure there will be no absinthe," Juliet said.

"That at least I can confirm," Darden said reluctantly. "Dunston brought it into the country himself, there would be no place to purchase it."

"It is only a dinner," Juliet said. "In any case, it would be grossly unfair to cancel, there cannot be anything more awkward for a host than to be left with empty chairs and it is always difficult to scrounge up replacements at the last minute."

"Now, that is true, of course," the earl said. "And perhaps we make too much of Mr. Roundbat's unfortunate display of the other evening. A young man having too much to drink is hardly the news of the century. In any case, Miss Mayton shall be chaperoning, so we might all feel very safe on that point."

Despite the truth of her father's words, Juliet could see perfectly well that neither Van Doren nor Conbatten were very comforted by it. Not even Darden seemed convinced.

"Safe as a newborn bunny in its den," Miss Mayton said confidently.

"If bunnies are safe in their dens," Van Doren muttered, "somebody forgot to tell the foxes."

Beatrice laid her hand gently on her husband's arm. It was some sort of trick she did with him, like she was calming a wild horse.

"Your Grace," Miss Mayton said, addressing Conbatten and seeming to wish to change topics, "you have visited us at an auspicious moment. We are coming to the exciting conclusion of *The Ghastly Goings-on of Gallowing Glen.*"

Miss Mayton waved her hands as if the duke was on the verge of a question, which Juliet did not sense that he was.

"Have no fear," Miss Mayton said, "we will catch you up on what has happened since last you heard it."

"I am on tenterhooks, Miss Mayton," the duke said drily.

"As am I," the earl said.

THE DINNER HAD concluded, and the party repaired to the drawing room. The men would take their port in with them, so there would be no delay in hearing of the exciting conclusion of the ghastly goings-on in the glen.

It was well they did not linger over the table. Upon entering the drawing room, they discovered that Marvin had been exceedingly naughty.

He'd cornered Rosalind's poor physician, the rooster likely intent on securing whatever was on that gentleman's tray.

"Your Graces," Mr. Laurelton said, "every time I make the slightest movement, the creature claws at me. I have been trapped in here for an hour! Look! My pants are ripped!"

"You really should have called out, Mr. Laurelton," the earl said.

"Called out?" Mr. Laurelton asked. "Called out in an earl's drawing room?"

Juliet hurried forward and swept Marvin into her arms. The rooster was perfectly agreeable to find himself located thus, though he did keep eyeing Mr. Laurelton's tray.

"I apologize for Marvin, sir," Juliet said. "He has spent his whole poor life as a fighting rooster and occasionally does slip back into the habit. Only with men, though."

Mr. Laurelton did not look particularly soothed by the explanation. He stared at Marvin as if he were a man just thrown to the lions in ancient Greece.

"Perhaps a footman might relocate this latest avian acquisition elsewhere?" Conbatten said. "Mr. Laurelton, do see my valet on the morrow. We will right this wrong. Tattleton? Perhaps Mr. Laurelton could do with a large glass of port?"

The duke gave direction on how the situation should be righted, while Rosalind watched him admiringly. His orders were speedily carried out—Benny took Marvin in his arms, holding Marvin's feet away from him so he did not get clawed. Mr. Laurelton was resettled with a large glass of port.

As the rest of the party arranged themselves round Miss Mayton, she opened her book.

"Now, as we know," Miss Mayton said, "the duke is in love with his gentle governess. This governess is the seventh to come into the house, the first six disappearing mysteriously. She has discovered that all these governesses were driven out by the dead duchess's malevolent ghost. Ever since, our poor governess has been dodging flying knives, having doors slammed in her face, listening to terrible whispers in her ear, and has taken to keeping sand buckets by her bed as her curtains and bedding keep bursting into flames."

"She is brave," the earl said. "I do not know if I could stand up against it."

"She is certainly something," Van Doren muttered.

In answer to Van Doren, Miss Mayton shook out her black bombazine skirt, cleared her throat, and commenced the story.

The gentle governess, being not exactly as gentle as other governesses might be, had held up very well under the assaults of the duchess's ghost. She did find, though, that she was growing rather tired of it.

She was madly in love with the duke. He was madly in love with her. The ghost must be got rid of.

She rang bells at all hours of the day and night to drive the ghost away. She slept on a pillow filled with pigeon feathers, making it impossible that she die in her sleep no matter how many times her bed sheets burst into flames. She went to the vicar, who was at once dismissive of the idea of a ghost and too terrified to come near the house. She'd even prayed to all her dead ancestors, requesting they come and drag this harridan away. None of it worked.

But then, she'd had an idea. She'd done some research into the house, and all the dukes who'd died in its vicinity. There was a particularly handsome fellow who'd died in 1563 at the age of thirty. He had, according to his history, been a shameless philanderer and seducer in his life. Hopefully, the fellow was still lurking around somewhere and still as shameless as he ever was.

The fourth duke of Bedlington had been thrown from his horse in a nearby field and so she'd set off at midnight to see if she might find him and have a word.

He was there, under the moonlight, ghastly grey and forlornly sitting on a fence post.

"Your Grace," she said, addressing the ghost. "You would do well to follow me into the house, rather than sit out here for all eternity."

"That I cannot do," the ghost said morosely. "There is a new duke now, one of many that have come before him. It is no longer my house."

"Nonsense!" the not-that-gentle governess said. "The new duke will be perfectly sanguine to find you back, and the duchess, who is now in your very same ethereal state, is very pretty. Spirited too."

"Very pretty, you say?" the ghost said, beginning to look intrigued.

"Exceedingly pretty," the governess assured him. "Might it not be more pleasant to chase her round the house until the end

of time, instead of sitting out here doing nothing?"

"Rather!" the dead duke said, hopping to his ghostly feet.

And so it happened that the duchess's ghost found very little time to harass the stalwart governess. The ghost of 1563 was a womanizer to his core. Every time the duchess would attempt to throw a knife in the governess's direction or set her curtains ablaze, she was forced to run off to escape the clutches of him.

The still-alive duke was delighted, and he married his governess in all haste. They went on very happy with one another and hardly noticed the arguments and shouts that went on in the air around them.

The end.

"So the duchess's ghost was haunting the governess, and now she gets haunted herself by another ghost!" the earl exclaimed. "What a twist—I never did see that coming."

"Only the deranged would have seen that coming," Van Doren said.

"Your Grace," Miss Mayton said to the duke, "you seem particularly moved by the story."

"I am positively shaken by it, Miss Mayton," Conbatten said, a small smile playing round his lips.

Juliet sighed. If only her own matters of the heart could be concluded so easily.

CHAPTER FOURTEEN

RUPERT, BEING SO used to action as the single and obvious answer to every difficulty, had found he could not wait until Lady Bloomington's masque to drive his suit forward with Lady Juliet.

He'd gone to Portland Place in the afternoon. He did not find Roundbat there, which was excellent. But he did not find Lady Juliet there either, which was disappointing.

As he could not see Lady Juliet, perhaps he ought to see Roundbat. Perhaps he ought to tell that bounder to back away.

He could not communicate what he knew of Roundbat's debts. Nothing could ever be said that was related to Queen's Knights' business. But he could hint round it.

He'd gone to his house at eight o'clock that evening, thinking there was every chance the man was still nursing a head from the absinthe.

Roundbat was out, however.

A fellow answered the not very prepossessing door. Rupert took him to be the butler, though the man's cuffs were rather frayed for a man of that position.

Rupert claimed he had important business with Roundbat, and that Roundbat clearly had forgotten the appointment.

Any butler worth his salt would never have given away his master's location. This one did not seem so experienced, though.

In the most obsequious manner possible, Rupert had been

informed that Roundbat had gone off to Vauxhall Gardens with a friend of his from Yorkshire.

That was not ideal. Had Roundbat gone to some party or other, Rupert might have taken himself there and told the surprised host or hostess that he was certain he'd got an invitation. That person was likely to welcome him in, though no invitation had been sent. It was one of the many benefits of being a marquess who might need a wife—if the host did not have a daughter he was trying to marry off, he would know somebody who did.

Vauxhall was another matter. He'd have to search a crowd of thousands to locate his quarry.

However, he was at loose ends this night, and it was to be hoped that his years of spying for the Queen's Knights had given him some experience at tracking a fellow down.

Arriving there, and leaving his horse with his groom outside, he paid his shillings and went in.

Rupert weaved through the crowds of people, searching all the likely places.

Roundbat was not to be found in any of them. He was not eating and drinking, he was not listening to the orchestra, he was not standing by one of the endless sights and entertainments provided.

Finally, Rupert began to search the less likely places.

And he should have known—Roundbat and his friend were just ahead, escorting some flimsily dressed ladies down the dark walk.

Though the dark walk was not quite as dark as it once had been, it was still a gloomy trail and a popular place for assignations one might not wish to write home to one's family about.

"Roundbat!" he called.

Roundbat froze. The two ladies turned their heads.

As he had imagined, they were both heavily painted. Even in the dim light, Rupert could see that the one on Roundbat's arm must be nearly forty.

Roundbat himself slowly turned, as Rupert jogged to catch up with him.

"Lord Hamill," he said, looking rather pasty from his previous night's adventure with absinthe.

"A *lord?*" the lady on his arm said saucily. "And a looker, too. Where have you been hiding this specimen, Mr. Smith? Or should I say, Mr. Roundbat."

Mr. Smith. He'd gone so far as to use a false name. Rupert supposed his friend was Mr. Miller. A man like Roundbat, intent on climbing the *ton's* ladder, would not give out his real name nor address to a lady of such work.

"What's your pleasure, Lord Hamill?" her companion asked with a wink.

Rupert did not respond to the lady, as he did not have a wish to contract the pox on this day or any other day. He did not look down upon the lady's profession, as he knew it to be a necessity to keep body and soul together and in food, heat, and a place to lay one's head at night.

He did, however, look down on the gentlemen who bought their custom, thereby bringing disease and shame to themselves and their wives at home.

"Typical," he said to Roundbat, thinking that was all he need say upon discovering him in such a situation.

"Lord Hamill," Roundbat said, undeterred, "allow me to introduce you to my friend, Mr. Miller."

"What's your real name?" Rupert demanded of Roundbat's companion.

Mr. Miller bowed low, and then nearly lost his footing as he'd clearly had too much to drink. "Uh, Thanebury, my lord," he mumbled.

The lady on his arm assisted Mr. Thanebury in staying upright.

"To what do I owe this fortuitous encounter, Lord Hamill?" Mr. Roundbat asked.

"I came to find you and warn you off Lady Juliet," Rupert

said. "You are not worthy, and you know it."

"I know no such thing."

"I will see her at Lady Bloomington's masque, and if you persist, I will inform her of a few facts about you."

Roundbat bristled. "I do not know what facts you imagine you know about me," he said, "but perhaps I might invent a few facts about *you* to be communicated on the morrow."

"If you think I will not be there to waylay you at three o'clock, you are mistaken. You will not be strolling alone with Lady Juliet."

Roundbat snorted. "I will have no need to stroll, Lord Hamill. Lady Juliet is attending a dinner on the morrow. *My* dinner. We are to have a poetry reading afterward. You have perhaps noticed how Lady Juliet adores poetry."

"Do not be absurd. She would not set foot in your house."

"We'll see," Roundbat said, looking very satisfied with himself. "Now, ladies, shall we carry on with our own stroll? Lord Hamill appears out of sorts this evening and had probably best be served to go home."

One of the ladies tittered and said, "Lucky Lady Juliet." The other one winked at him. Roundbat turned them round and they walked off.

Rupert stood in the dim light of the dark walk, the trees overhead reaching toward each other to block out the moonlight.

That Roundbat had allowed one of those women to speak the name of Lady Juliet! It said volumes about the standards of the man.

He had a great wish to sprint after Roundbat and pound him into the pavement. He might even keep pounding until Roundbat was no longer living.

Though, he knew he could not do such a thing.

Was the man lying? It must be so. Lady Juliet would never attend a dinner at that fellow's rented house in Cheapside. Particularly not after his samurai performance at Dunston's rout.

Her chaperone, Miss Mayton, would never condone it.

Rupert paused. Miss Mayton. The lady in widow's weeds who'd never been married. The lady who told outrageous stories of various continental gentlemen dying of love for her in some horrible fashion.

Of all the chaperones in London, she was the single one who would, perhaps, fail to see the inappropriateness of it. The earl would not know anything of Roundbat. As far as Lady Juliet's father would be concerned, his daughter and chaperone were off to a very usual dinner, like so many other dinners before.

Miss Mayton had seen Roundbat in action, though. If she had a lick of sense, she'd steer her charge away from that house.

If she had a lick of sense.

Which Rupert was very afraid she did not.

What about Darden? Surely, Darden must see what Round-bat was.

Rupert was fairly certain that he had but did not take Round-bat seriously. He did not know all there was to know. In any case, Darden had a habit of not taking things seriously, it was one of the reasons the fellow was so popular.

Roundbat's pursuit of Lady Juliet must be stopped somehow. Though, it was the somehow that was the difficulty—Rupert could not use anything he'd discovered during his work as a Queen's Knight.

Regardless, she must be saved from that scoundrel. Even if not for Rupert's own cause, but for Lady Juliet, herself. Even if she were to turn *him* down, Rupert could not bear to imagine her tied to Roundbat forevermore.

She had no idea what he really was.

The problem would be, how to acquaint her with it? He could not mention the debts he knew of. He was not so sure he could mention having chased the man through Vauxhall to discover him with a lady of questionable lifestyle. He certainly could not utter the word *pox*.

Somehow, though, Roundbat must be unmasked for who he really was. He was a devil, and poetry in the Japanese style was only his cover. It was the veneer he wore to appear other than what he was.

Rupert had stormed out of the gardens and ridden home at a brisk pace, his groom struggling to keep up.

As if the whole evening had not been unsatisfactory enough, he found a note addressed to him, left on the table in the hall.

It was in Darden's handwriting, and he hardly knew what to make of it.

Hamill—

Do not take what I say next too much to heart. My father is finding himself rather against Juliet's going out strolling with two gentlemen every day, so that's off for now.

Rest assured, my letter to Roundbat on this matter will not be worded so pleasantly.

By the by, did you know Roundbat is hosting a dinner on the morrow and my sister is going? I suppose Lady Jersey will act the hostess for him and it will be safe enough, but I do not like it.

Rupert let the letter fall in his lap. So Darden did know about the dinner. He presumed Lady Jersey might preside over it and that might be right.

Perhaps his feelings were driving him to make more of this dinner than was actually there?

He picked up the sheet and finished reading it.

I cannot say what your intentions are, as you've not relayed them to me. But, old chap, if there are any intentions leaning in Juliet's direction, maybe nudge the horse forward a bit faster.

As for my sister, herself, she says she is waiting for bricks to fall. My sisters Beatrice and Rosalind seem to know what she means, but I remain in the dark about it.

All I say, Hamill, is if you can locate these bricks, kick them over and make them fall!

Darden

It was the bricks again. He'd got to find out about these bricks!

⟫⟫⟫⟪⟪⟪

TATTLETON, AS HE was becoming accustomed to, had experienced an evening full of highs and lows. No longer was his life to proceed in calm regularity. Now, he could not guess what was coming round the corner to lift him up or drag him down. Mostly, he could only hazard a guess that both those things were coming round the corner at the same time.

The duke had come to dinner. A decided high point.

His Grace had sipped the claret Tattleton had specially selected, and then caught his eye and nodded to him in approval.

A duke of the realm had sought out *his* eye. It was a moment he would remember all his life. It was a moment he might mention to other butlers of his acquaintance when he casually mentioned that His Grace, the Duke of Conbatten and his wife, the duchess that Horace J. Tattleton had known since she was a baby, had been to dinner.

What he would not be mentioning along with those facts, is the circumstance of a rangy rooster, who somehow had run of the house, holding the duchess's personal physician hostage, going on the attack, and having the temerity to rip that gentleman's trousers.

That rooster was just now roosting atop Mrs. Huffson's sewing basket, seemingly unaware of the affront it had offered to the earl's guests.

Mrs. Huffson sighed at the sight of it. "There is no convincing Marvin about that basket, he's quite taken it as his own."

"I'd like to convince that bird into a pot, but for the fact that the meat would be tough and stringy."

"And Lady Juliet heartbroken, I might add," Mrs. Huffson

said.

"And that," Tattleton said grudgingly.

"I understand Miss Mayton was to read the last installment of the latest book she favors. How did it all turn out with the ghost?"

Tattleton sighed. "Most conveniently for the invented duke and yet another governess," he said. "The ghost of another duke, who in life was a philanderer, was conscripted to take up the ghostly duchess's time by chasing her round the place."

"Goodness," Mrs. Huffson said. "That sounds verging on…unseemly."

"Entirely unseemly. Guess what else is unseemly? Miss Mayton is taking Lady Juliet to a dinner at this Roundbat character's house. The one who wants to take a wife to Japan."

"Well, there cannot be anything dangerous in it, Mr. Tattleton," Mrs. Huffson said soothingly. "She will be chaperoned and Mr. Roundbat can hardly whisk Lady Juliet off to Japan without the earl getting wind of it."

Mrs. Huffson was really very naïve. Miss Mayton had felt free to attempt to help Lady Viola on her way to an elopement to Scotland. Why would the housekeeper presume the deranged woman would rule out Japan? Miss Mayton might be counted on to set off for Timbuktu if the opportunity arose.

"The only good thing to say about Mr. Roundbat," he said, "was that his strolls along the avenue, pretending he is experiencing deep and remarkable thoughts, have come to an end. Lord Darden was to write him that they're off."

"Ah well, whatever is to happen with Lady Juliet, it is not as if we have any control over it."

No. They did not have any control over it. Though Tattleton could rest assured in the knowledge that if he *did* have control over the doings of this family, there would not have been nearly so many doings!

JULIET GAZED ROUND at her surroundings and wrestled with her opinions regarding Mr. Roundbat's circumstances. She and Miss Mayton had arrived to that gentleman's dinner and she was at once put off, but also condemning of herself for her snobbish ideas.

She was already acquainted with Mr. Roundbat's situation—his father was entirely against him. So, it really could not come as any surprise that the baron had not been generous in renting out a house for his son for the season.

The neighborhood was out of the way, the house itself was small, and the furnishings…well, they were very worn and she presumed they must be rented. There was a butler, though that person's cuffs were terribly frayed and he wore a panicked look about him, and then a footman whose pants were far too short.

She should be applauding these circumstances. After all, were they not the precise circumstances that a poet would find himself in? Had she not declared more than once that she would live in a garret, were she to find her poet?

Miss Mayton had just ripped a hole in the material of the sofa, only from sitting down. Her aunt had strategically fluffed out her black bombazine to cover it.

Were she to live in a garret, there would not even be a butler or footman. She would do everything round the place. That rip in the sofa covering would be her concern and she would be pondering a way to mend it.

She had assured herself that such things would be as nothing, compared to the joys of a poet's life.

And yet, here she was—faintly uncomfortable with where she found herself.

Juliet also could not say what she thought of the guests of the party. She had assumed it would be a large dinner, and that she would likely know people who attended. Was not Mr. Roundbat a particular favorite of Lady Jersey's?

There was no Lady Jersey in sight. The entire guest list was comprised of herself and her aunt, a particular friend named Mr.

Thanebury, and an elderly couple from Yorkshire named Robinson.

"Lady Juliet," Mr. Roundbat said, "our after-dinner reading will be glorious indeed. We will have only poets round the table this evening, excepting our dear Miss Mayton, who is such a terrific audience for our work."

"Oh I see!" Juliet said, thinking the guest list began to make more sense.

"Mr. Thanebury specializes in ballads and shall accompany himself on his guitar," Mr. Roundbat went on. "And our dear Robinsons—I have known them since I was a boy. They were the wonderful people who encouraged me and pointed out that I had a knack for poetry, you see."

"Goodness, that was very kind," Juliet said.

"And then," Mr. Robinson said, "little did we know the fellow would decide to go in for the Japanese style!"

"We are not so innovative, I'm afraid, Lady Juliet," Mrs. Robinson said.

"Innovative? Perhaps not!" Mr. Roundbat said. "But they are keen on rhyming, Lady Juliet."

This interesting exchange was interrupted by the butler, who fairly staggered into the room and said, "Uh, the dinner. It's on."

With that engaging invitation, they went into the dining room.

As they were seated round an exceedingly small table in an almost uncomfortably tight room, Juliet instantly perceived why they were such a small party. There would be no place to seat another person.

"Well this is cozy," Miss Mayton said.

The butler and the lone footman began to bring round platters. The footman was sweating profusely and Juliet began to wonder if he were also the cook.

It might well be so, considering what was on the platters. There was what once must have been a chicken, but it had been hacked into bits. A lumpy gravy was to accompany it, the butler gamely trying to pour it out without the lumps escaping the porcelain boat. Limp long beans and mashed parsnips rounded out the offerings.

Gracious. If she lived in a garret, *she* would have cooked the dinner. She did not know the first thing about it!

Mr. Roundbat, seeming to be aware that it was rather simple fare for a hosted dinner, said, "I am afraid now you see how a bachelor lives."

"Though we hope our dear Ignatius is not a bachelor for long," Mrs. Robinson said, giving Juliet a smiling and pointed stare.

Juliet put her attention on her bits of chicken. She did not at all like the direction the conversation was going.

"You cannot hope it as much as I do, Mrs. Robinson," Mr. Roundbat said.

"Hope costs a person nothing, after all," Miss Mayton said enigmatically.

Juliet did not know where to look while such a conversation unfolded. Her eyes drifted to the sideboard, where she found the poor footman, who was also likely the cook, mopping his brow with a napkin. She turned her attention to her plate, but there was nothing particularly pleasant to see there. She turned her head to the window to the right of Mr. Roundbat's shoulder, though it was dark outside, and she could not have hoped to see anything out of it.

At least, she should not have seen anything out that dark window. Except, she did see something.

A face had leaned close to the glass and then disappeared into the darkness.

CHAPTER FIFTEEN

"M R. ROUNDBAT," JULIET said, feeling as alarmed as if she'd seen a specter, "just this moment, there was a man peering in your window. Right behind you."

Mr. Roundbat fairly leapt from his chair. "Behind me?" he cried.

"Yes, not a moment ago."

All at the table had turned and now stared at the window. There was nothing there.

"Perhaps it was only your imagination, Lady Juliet?" Mr. Robinson said hopefully.

"Oh dear no," Miss Mayton said. "Juliet imagines poetry, not faces in windows."

"Hanson," Mr. Roundbat said to his beleaguered butler, "go out and see that nobody is there."

"Alone?" Hanson said, as if he'd just been directed to storm a castle on his own.

"Take Larry, I mean Lawrence, with you."

"Why me?" the footman cried.

"C'mon," the butler said, grabbing the footman by the collar.

Juliet was beginning to wish she had not mentioned the person at the window. She'd never seen such a staff.

Tattleton would go mad if he viewed such a thing unfolding. For that matter, Tattleton would have grabbed the staff he kept in the front hall for just such a circumstance and charged outside to mortally assault a person who had the effrontery to peer into their window. In truth, Juliet had always thought Tattleton had been eagerly awaiting that circumstance as an opportunity to show his mettle.

The two servants shuffled out of the room, while Mr. Roundbat attempted to put a good face on it.

"That's London for you," he said with a weak laugh. "All sorts out and about."

"I suspect you are right, Ignatius," Mrs. Robinson said. "I am sure we never had anybody peering in our windows in Yorkshire."

"Except for young Charlie Siddons," Mr. Robinson said. "After he fell off that barn roof, he was never quite right. He was always peering in round dinner time and asking what was on the table."

"Ah yes, poor boy."

Juliet heard the front door open and she hoped whoever had been lurking around had taken themself elsewhere.

There was a sudden shout of "Aha! We thought you'd be rubes enough to open the door for us."

It was a rough sounding voice and Juliet began to get the idea that something very bad was happening, though she could not think what it was.

Were they to be robbed? It was not out of the question—the neighborhood was respectable, but perhaps not as safe as Portland Place.

"You can't barge in here!" the butler cried. "Who are you?"

Juliet heard some scuffling and shouts as a reply. Whoever it was did not care to answer the butler.

Mr. Roundbat, rather than racing out to discover what was happening to his staff, merely sat wide-eyed.

Three men, very large and roughly dressed, filled the doorway to the dining room.

"I'll guess you're Roundbat," their leader said, pointing at the very gentleman. The man wore a cambric shirt that was stained and his pants were held up by a tied rope.

"What do you want?" Mr. Roundbat squeaked out.

"I reckon you already know," the man said. "A consortium of sorts, a consortium what you owe pounds to, sent us along for a visit."

A silence settled over the table and Juliet could only hear heavy breathing. She did not know if it was her own, or somebody else's, or everyone at table together.

As far as she could gather, Mr. Roundbat owed somebody money and that somebody had sent these men to get it.

Had he gambled and lost? Darden seemed to be very successful at the habit. At least, she thought so. However, if a person won, that meant another person had lost. She'd never considered all the gentlemen who had lost. How did they pay if they'd lost beyond their means?

"Mr. Roundbat," she said, trying to keep her voice steady, "I suggest you simply pay these men what is owed, and then we can go on with the dinner and forget there ever was an interruption."

The three men at the doorway guffawed, which was not precisely the reaction she had expected. Mr. Roundbat had turned a rather sickly white.

"He ain't got the money," the leader said. "If he had the money, he wouldn't a gone to the moneylenders in the first place."

"Moneylenders?" Juliet said, not quite believing that could be true.

"Oh dear," Miss Mayton said, "I understand they give very bad rates."

"Ignatius," Mrs. Robinson said, "do tell these ruffians they've got the wrong house."

"I so dearly wish I could, but they do not have the wrong house," Mr. Roundbat said resignedly. "It is only a series of misunderstandings with my father."

Juliet could not help but admit that she was shocked. And becoming rather terrified. Mr. Roundbat had gone to a moneylender! Likely more than one, as the man mentioned a consortium.

How on earth had a misunderstanding with his father led to moneylending?

She did not know too terribly much about the operation of borrowing money from unsavory sorts, outside of the bits and pieces she'd picked up from Darden. On occasion, he would mention some fellow who'd had to go hat in hand to his father, or worse, flee to the continent. Despite understanding little of it, she'd gathered from her brother that this sort of borrowing was a dangerous business.

Of course, she could see that for herself.

"Tell those heathens I'll get their money," Mr. Roundbat said. "I've written my father, he should send the funds any day."

The leader leaned against the doorframe. "That'll be two letters your da got then."

"What?"

"The consortium done wrote the baron too, letting 'im know that we got you under what we'd call a house capture, until he sends the funds. That letter went by a fella on a fast horse days ago. Accordin' to what I been told, the answer is to come in the next hours. See? That's why we're here, awaitin' your da's rescue of you to make certain the funds go into the right pockets. Which ain't *your* pocket."

The man looked about the table and said, "Though nobody said nothin' about you having friends here."

"Of course nobody would have mentioned it," Miss Mayton said. "Nobody could have imagined that you would crash in on innocent people. Now, I would suppose your employers would think you'd better let the rest of us be on our way."

All three men snorted. "So they can raise the alarm," one said.

"We ain't rubes," the other said.

Their leader said, "Nobody's going nowhere but that bigger room over there, this one's crowded and has got too many windows for the curious to peer through."

They were promptly hustled into the drawing room, the leader of the men being rather rough with Mr. Roundbat. Of course, they had been rather rough with the butler and footman too, as those two were currently tied to chairs and looking as if they'd encountered a ghost.

What sort of situation had Mr. Roundbat got them all into? What if the baron did not send the funds? What then?

Juliet had, for a moment, thought of attempting to escape. However, she did not see how she was to get past three large men to the only door out of the room. The windows were set high and not particularly large. And then, even if she could make a run for it, her aunt most certainly could not. One of the problems of yards of black bombazine was that it would not be ideal for running.

The men had placed themselves near the door. The rest of the party sat down, with Mr. Roundbat pacing back and forth like a nervous cat.

"Certainly, Mr. Roundbat, your father will be terribly alarmed and send whatever money is necessary forthwith," Juliet said hopefully.

"Lady Juliet, quite naturally he will," Mr. Roundbat said. "He does not understand my poetical temperament! He never has. However, I am his only son and heir."

"That is true," Mrs. Robinson said. "He is the only son."

"Your father is a codger, though," Mr. Thanebury said. "Hard to know how he took the communication. I expect he went right through the roof."

"He does have rather a short temper," Mr. Robinson said. "Particularly when it comes to you, Ignatius."

"Nonsense," Mr. Roundbat said. "Now, I know this situation is most untoward. But only think, Lady Juliet, in future I may use this fraught experience to inform my poetry in the Japanese style."

Juliet nodded, though she was not very interested in poetry in the Japanese style at that very moment. Or any poetry. She felt a sort of seething toward Mr. Roundbat.

"Now I wonder, Mr. Roundbat," Miss Mayton said, "how you ever got involved with such people."

"We're wondering the very same," Mr. Robinson said.

Mr. Roundbat stopped at the mantel of the small fireplace and leaned against it, as if he needed support to stay upright. "My father claimed that if I wished to go to London and, as he termed it, 'spout off poetry' then I could very well live in a garret like any idiot poet would," Mr. Roundbat said. "It was a ridiculous notion of course, those neighborhoods are not even safe!"

"This here neighborhood doesn't seem so safe at the moment," Mr. Thanebury said, glancing at the hulking figures at the door.

"My dear Ignatius," Mrs. Robinson said, "do you say, then, that the baron gave you nothing to fund your season? That you borrowed the money for the house and such?"

"I had no choice!" Mr. Roundbat said. "We had a terrible argument, as he just could not see that I am to be a leading poet! Quite naturally, I was forced to storm out the door, make my way here, and prove him wrong."

Juliet had, all along, been very against the baron. Now though, she began to see how a baron from Yorkshire might not be able to envision his son becoming a poet. Especially if it were to require a large outlay of funds.

Mr. Roundbat's eyes darted this way and that, as if searching for something. He said, "Someday, this will only be an amusing story. Just think, upon marriage, I would have the funds to bring my poetry…I mean, of course, my and my wife's poetry, to the world."

Juliet blanched. Certainly, he hinted that she was the future wife in question. Though, her poetry did seem to come as an afterthought.

Had he got himself deep into debt, and then her dowry was supposed to rescue him from it and support him while *he* wrote *his* poetry?

Where was the poetry in that? It was not even…gentlemanly.

Juliet began to look at Mr. Roundbat with new eyes. He might compose poetry in the Japanese style, but he did not seem to have the soul of a poet. A poetical soul would never have led her into such a situation. A poetical soul was all chivalric ideals. A gentleman with the soul of a poet would rather have suffered in a garret, starving and freezing, before going to a moneylender or angling for her dowry.

Mr. Roundbat paused his pacing and said softly, "The night falls softly, the air filled so gloomily, yet the sun will rise."

Juliet suppressed a sigh. She supposed that was meant to lift their spirits. What would lift her spirits far more is if one of these able-bodied men actually did something to get them out of this ghastly situation. Mr. Roundbat and Mr. Thanebury seemed to have no courage between them.

The leader at the door laughed heartily. "The sun will be risin' you said?" he said derisively. "The sun will only be risin' if your da comes through for you."

The man paused, looking critically at Juliet. "I 'spose that's the lady who's to bail you out with a heap of money when you wed?"

Mr. Roundbat went positively purple at the statement. "How dare you!"

The man shrugged. "That's the excuse you been using to my employers to put 'em off." He stared directly at Juliet and said, "If ya don't mind me sayin' it, Miss, I'd steer clear of that one. He's a rum sort."

Juliet was not so certain she did mind him saying it. She was beginning to think Mr. Roundbat was indeed a rum sort. Her suspicions seemed to be true—Mr. Roundbat's interest in her was not her poetry, but her pounds.

"Just a small note," Miss Mayton said to the man. "Juliet is not a miss, she is Lady Juliet, daughter of the Earl of Westmont."

The leader shook his head. "Roundbat, you shot a little higher than your worth, don't you think? Attemptin' to marry the daughter of a lord?" To Juliet, he said, "My lady, excuse the inconvenience, but it's not us that are the author of it. We're only a couple of poor henchmen, out to make a living. It's him that's brought you to such a pass."

Juliet found she had to agree.

Mr. Roundbat did not defend himself against the charge, nor would he have had the time to.

There was a sudden pounding on the front doors. The leader nodded to one of his associates and that man headed to the door.

"That'll be the baron's reply."

PETEY WAS NOTHING if not diligent. Once he'd determined to do something, he did it with gusto. He'd visited both Kramer's and Marty's respective abodes of an evening to discover more information on when they planned to put the squeeze on Roundbat. He planned to become a value to the duke, and he would do it somehow.

It had not taken him a minute to decide that Marty's was the one to haunt.

Kramer's house was locked up right and tight, but Marty's had a nice and dark garden in the back where one might creep about unseen. They also didn't have one of the items that Kramer did. That item that posed a thorn in the side for those who liked to lurk—a dog.

One of Marty's back windows looked into a small snug with two leather chairs and a whole sideboard of glasses and libations.

This room was used by just two people—Marty and his doltish son who looked near twenty. They would go in after their dinner and spend some hours drinking and smoking cigars. And talking.

Of course, it was mostly Marty talking and the junior listening.

Fortunately, Marty liked to talk a lot and most of the talk was about himself. Also fortunately, with all the smoking they did, the window was generally cracked open.

Petey had learned no end of things about the moneylending business. All that information relayed was meant to educate his doltish son on the family business, but Petey was pretty sure he got more out of it than Marty the Junior. The trick to it seemed to be all friendliness at the outset and then a cold iron fist when funds were due.

It had all been interesting, though not useful. But then tonight, finally, a piece of information he could bring to the duke.

"That Roundbat is just now gettin' the scare of his life," Marty said contentedly. He puffed on his cigar. "By God, I hate that fellow."

"What are they gonna do to 'im, Da?" Marty Junior asked, leaning forward.

"Roundbat has got a dinner on this particular evening. Ya know, where you invite those you know into your house to eat."

"We never done that," the son said.

"No, it's a stupid habit. If I wanna break bread with my fellow man, I'll go to a tavern."

"But what's he doin' feedin' his friends at this time a night? They must'a fell over starved by now."

"The fancy rich types eat late, as they don't get outta bed until late. Roundbat is tryin' to pass himself off as one of 'em. Convenient for us, as it told us right where he'd be tonight."

"What's a-happenin' to 'im?"

"Our men will have the whole party delayed, waitin' for the baron's response to our demands. Ya see, this little incursion accomplishes two things—we get our money back and we humiliate that little rotter. He'll be finished in the society he's tryin' to worm his way into and that'll be the last time Mr. Roundbat tries to cheat a moneylender."

Marty the Junior seemed very approving of these ideas. Petey was seized with the urgency of the situation.

Even now, Mr. Roundbat and his guests were held hostage by the moneylenders' men. If that information didn't get Petey a job in the duke's house, he didn't know what would.

He set off in a sprint. It was a long run to Grosvenor Square and he had to get there in time.

RUPERT PLAYED HIS cards with no particular skill. He'd been losing most of the night, as he could not keep his mind on it.

His fellow members at the YBC seemed delighted with his inattention.

Rupert's mind, deciding to go where it liked, kept drifting to Lady Juliet.

He had definitely decided that he would ask Lady Juliet for her hand when he saw her at Lady Bloomington's masque. Despite her claiming she did not wish to hear anything just yet, or ever, he still was not entirely certain which one it was. Despite the falling bricks he had no notion of. Despite all that, he must ask.

He'd just not determined how to ask.

What would he say?

In a normal circumstance, he might enumerate his strong feelings and then list the lady's good qualities. At least, that was how he understood the thing was done.

It was the usual way, but the usual way would not be sufficient for an unusual lady. It would not be enough for Lady Juliet, who lived in poetry. She would expect something more. She deserved something more.

As Baderston happily took his money, his friend said, "Come now, Hamill, this is like stealing a toy from a toddler. What is on your mind that you cannot keep track of your cards?"

Rupert glanced round to ensure nobody nearby was listening. The club had filled with various gentlemen at their leisure. Most were drinking and playing cards. None had their attention on him.

"I was just mulling over how to approach a lady. With a serious question."

"With *the* serious question?" Baderston asked.

"The very one."

"I suppose the approach depends upon the lady," Baderston said. "At least, that's what I've learned from it. I did not expect to find myself standing on a green, facing three challengers, after all."

Rupert nodded. He had, of course, heard the whispers about that particular morning. Baderston had engaged to meet three other gentlemen on a green, all in defense of Lady Juliet's sister, Lady Viola.

Conbatten had somehow put a stop to the whole thing. Or Lady Viola had, he was not sure which. Whatever had happened, none of the three duels had taken place and the couple's respective families had escorted them on a family elopement to Scotland.

Baderston leaned over the table. "Is this about Lady Juliet?" he asked.

Rupert had given away nearly every hand this evening, but he was not certain he wished to give away *that* hand.

He only shrugged.

"Well if it is, she's a poetess. The whole Bennington family considers her better than Wordsworth, if you can believe it. I reckon the successful suitor best come up with a crackin' good poem about her."

Rupert had been afraid of something like that.

"I also think a fellow might want to get to it, lest some other fellow thinks of doing the same."

"Roundbat," Rupert said, practically spitting out the name.

"Exactly."

Rupert stared into his wine. Roundbat had to be defeated. Mr. I-Write-Poetry-in-the-Japanese-Style had to be ground into the dust.

And then, he had a sudden idea.

Roundbat might write in the Japanese style, but Lady Juliet had made clear several times that she preferred rhymes. What if he were to concoct some Japanese style poetry that *also* rhymed? He would beat Roundbat soundly if he could do that. It would be English poetry and Japanese poetry combined!

Just as his spirits began to rise at the prospect, Rupert noticed an odd hush had settled over the room. The talking and laughing had ceased.

All he heard were whispers.

Then, a loud voice he recognized all too well.

"For the love of heaven," Conbatten said, "stop staring as if you've seen a ghost. Where is Hamill?"

CHAPTER SIXTEEN

R UPERT STOOD UP, very much wondering what Conbatten was doing at the club, while at the same time amused by the club members' awe in seeing him there.

The gentlemen of the Young Bucks Club had spent a full three years now debating how to ask Conbatten to join—still stuck on the idea that he might refuse. Or worse, he might accept and nobody would know what to do with him.

To most of them, the duke was a frighteningly well-dressed enigma.

Rupert stood up and various members looked at him as if it were just discovered that he was the King of England.

The duke hurried toward him, pulled him into a corner, and said, "The moneylenders have enacted one of their attacks this night. At Roundbat's house."

A sudden cold ice encircled Rupert's chest. Lady Juliet was there. She was there for a dinner.

"She is there," he said.

"Yes, she is, and so is the dotty Miss Mayton. I hope you've brought your carriage. We must go in all haste."

Rupert nodded. He had indeed brought his carriage, as he nearly always did if he were planning a long night at the club. One did not like to risk getting on a horse if one discovered themselves worse for wear in the early morning hours. His own horse had pointed out several times that he did not like it, by way of depositing its rider on the street.

They strode out of the club. Rupert raised his hand and Davis, always at the ready, slapped his reins and trotted up at a brisk pace.

To Rupert's surprise, the young fellow Petey emerged from the shadows. He instantly perceived that was where the information about the attack had come from.

"He rode on the back of my horse, determined to come on the adventure," the duke said drily.

Petey nodded. "I gotta mind to work in the duke's house, so I gotta mind to stick close to 'im."

"My delight is indescribable," Conbatten said.

As they piled into the carriage, Rupert gave his coachman Roundbat's address.

He put aside the notion of Petey becoming employed by the duke. Lady Juliet was in very grave danger and must be extricated from it at once.

⤗⤗⤗⧽⧼⫷⫷⫷

THE POUNDING ON the door had signaled that the messenger had come. At least, that was what Juliet gathered from it.

She prayed the baron's response would bring a quick end to this ghastly night. Those men would be paid and be on their way.

Once that happened, she and Miss Mayton would be on their way too. Juliet had no intention whatsoever of going back into that dining room to finish that wretched dinner.

She had seen what Mr. Roundbat was, and it had been eye-opening. What a fool she'd been!

Juliet realized that her determination to find herself a poet had positively blinded her to what was in front of her.

How could she be so stupid? So many of those in her life had expressed their disapproval of Mr. Roundbat, but it had fallen on deaf ears.

She had supposed they did not understand. She had presumed that only she understood, as she was a poetess. She knew better than all these other people.

As it turned out, they all *had* understood, while she had understood nothing.

Mr. Roundbat was an adventurer, coming to London to find the lady who would finance him. No poetry in the Japanese style could get round that awful idea.

One of the men carried in a packet. He handed it over to his leader and said, "Feels about the right weight."

The man in charge tore open the packet.

A one-pound note fluttered to the floor.

The man pulled out the rest of the contents. There did not seem to be any more money. Just a letter and a stack of blank sheets.

"What's this!" the man shouted.

Roundbat had squeezed himself into a corner of the room. "Now I am sure that letter will explain where to get the rest of the funds!" he cried. "I am certain of it!"

The man unfolded the letter and read, huffing and puffing as he did so.

"Well it don't, you boldfaced liar," the man said. "What your pa says is this:

"Tell the blighter to put down his Godawful scribblings and work off the debt, else he can take himself off to Japan and see if he gets a better reception there. I won't pay more than one pound to extricate him from this latest tomfoolery. Hesterly"

"I told you he'd go right through the roof," Mr. Thanebury said, as if he were happy to be found right and not at all cognizant of the dangers of him being found right.

"That cannot be all he said!" Mr. Roundbat shouted. "Was he drunk? Was my poor mother absent? Whatever his feelings about my poetical ambitions, he would not leave me deserted in such a manner. Go back to Yorkshire! Go back and try him again!"

Juliet could hardly breathe. The men would not get paid.

What would happen next? What would happen to her and Miss Mayton? The men looked so angry.

She would pay them herself if she could, but she did not have a thousand pounds. Who would have such an amount? As for herself, she only had eleven pounds of pocket money saved up, and that was in her bedchamber, stuffed in a drawer.

When would her father and Darden realize that she and Miss Mayton were missing? It was possible they would not know until early morning. Tattleton would wait up for them, but Juliet knew he usually fell asleep in a chair in the hall if the hour grew late, only to awaken to the sound of the carriage.

Nobody might know for hours that they were in terrible trouble.

Juliet paused. The carriage. Sandren. Sooner or later, Sandren would realize that they'd been in the house too long. Sooner or later, he'd take note of all these people coming and going who did not look quite up to snuff.

She and her sisters were always attempting to hide a plan from Sandren, but now Juliet wished with all her heart that he would discover them in this one.

The man in charge pointed at one of the other men. "Go to the bosses and enlighten them on the idea that we only got one pound for all our trouble and find out what they want to do about it."

The man hurried from the room and Juliet heard the front doors close behind him.

Mr. Roundbat was quietly sobbing in his corner and Juliet found she did not pity him at all. It served him right—who ever heard of financing an entire season through moneylenders? How had he got the idea he could dodge these people and fail to repay them?

Of course, she had begun to understand Mr. Roundbat's plan. He had intended to wed and be in receipt of a dowry.

She felt as if her life had teetered on a razor's edge and she'd not even known it. She'd come so close to being ruined by her own ridiculous ideas. This situation was dire, but it had made her see that at least.

If she had married Mr. Roundbat, she would have condemned herself for her whole life. It would not have taken long to discover her mistake, and then she would have been at her leisure to repent it, somewhere in the wilds of Yorkshire.

The window on the far side of the room suddenly shattered and she jumped at the shock of it. A flaming ball of some sort was thrown through the opening and rolled across the floor.

As the men stared at it and Mr. Roundbat jumped up and down on it to put out the fire, a large figure appeared in the doorway.

He grabbed both men's heads and brought them together hard. Then he released them and they crumpled to the floor.

The man stepped forward. "Lady Juliet, are you unhurt?"

Lord Hamill. It was Lord Hamill.

He stood, looming large in the doorframe. Looking as glorious as he always did. Being glorious. Acting glorious.

Her heart took off in a race, as if it had just been informed it had somewhere to go and it must get there in all haste.

Glorious Lord Hamill had somehow come to rescue her. It was if she might be anywhere in the world and he would know she was in trouble and he would come.

And just like that, a whole world of proverbial bricks fell on her head.

It was rather dizzying, really. It was a sudden understanding of where her feelings had been all along. It had just been her stubborn nature clinging to the idea of a poet that had played tricks on her. It had been her obstinance in never going back on what she said. She'd *said* she must have a poet, and then proceeded to tie herself to the idea forever.

Who cared for poetry when Lord Hamill was standing there, being his glorious self?

The feeling was almost too much to take in. Especially when he stood only feet away from the cowering Mr. Roundbat.

How could she have possibly viewed those two gentlemen side by side and not realized that one of them was far superior? How could she have had so many conversations with both of them and have failed to see it?

Conbatten came in after Lord Hamill. He checked that the flaming missile he'd launched as a distraction was put out, and then set about tying up the two men who lay on the floor.

"Juliet?" the duke asked.

Juliet did not answer, she could not answer. Too many feelings were coming at her at once, as if they were being launched by an army of trebuchets.

Marvelous, wonderful feelings. It was as if she were floating right off the sofa.

"We are quite all right, Your Grace," Miss Mayton said.

"Yes, everyone is quite all right," Mr. Roundbat said. "Really, it was just an unfortunate misunderstanding. Though, there is the one fellow coming back at some point, so you might have a lookout for him. But other than that, just an awkward misunderstanding. I do thank you, Your Grace, for your timely intervention into this matter, truly an honor. We were interrupted as we were having dinner, I suppose we might go back in? Lady Juliet?"

"Sit down, Roundbat," Lord Hamill said in a wonderfully growly voice. "Lady Juliet is not going into dinner, she is going home where she will be safe."

Mr. Roundbat looked as if he might answer this idea, until Lord Hamill took a step toward him and he very sensibly sat down.

"Well I suppose we should take our leave," Mr. Robinson said. "We are to set off for Yorkshire in the morning and we plan an early start. Ignatius, we will visit the baron and inform him of the condition in which we last left you."

"And that you will certainly not be traveling to Japan," Mrs. Robinson added for good measure.

Mr. Thanebury had leapt to his feet with alacrity. "I'll walk you out, Mrs. Robinson. Say, Roundbat, I'll just take myself off to an inn. You can send my things on by the morrow. No rush, of course."

Mr. Roundbat's friends had abandoned him in all haste.

"Lady Juliet," Lord Hamill said. "You look exceedingly pale."

"Do I?" she whispered, staring at him.

"We had best get Juliet and Miss Mayton into their carriage. It is sitting at the end of the street," Conbatten said.

Lord Hamill nodded. Juliet thought the idea was full of good sense, but she would really rather stay and stare at this marvelous man.

"Oh, we're all right here, I think," she said.

"You certainly are not," the duke said. "We've got two ruffians to deal with and another on the way back. Then there is that other unsavory fellow." Conbatten looked meaningfully at Mr. Roundbat.

Roundbat's teeth chattered.

Juliet rose, but felt unsteady on her feet. She could not tell if it was caused by the shock of the evening, or the fact that she'd not had much of a dinner, or the sight of Lord Hamill.

He rushed forward and held her up.

"Yes, goodness," Miss Mayton said, "we'd really better go. Mr. Roundbat, well, what can one say? This has all been…most unusual."

Lord Hamill supported Juliet to the carriage and helped her inside. His arm was as solid as the bricks that had recently fallen on her head by way of finally knowing her own mind.

He said to Sandren, "Stop for no one and see that the ladies are into the house safely."

Sandren, ever careful of the family, sniffed and said, "I know my business, my lord."

"Yes, of course you do," Lord Hamill said. "It is just…well let us say there are some dangers on the roads tonight."

Then Lord Hamill said, "I see, excellent."

Through her hazy thoughts, Juliet thought Sandren must

have shown Lord Hamill one of his two pistols. He was very fond of his pistols.

The carriage set off and Juliet peered out the window to see Lord Hamill turn and go back into the house.

What a fine figure of a man he was.

"My dear," Miss Mayton said, "Lord Hamill told no tales, you do seem rather pale."

"I am perfectly all right, Aunt. Very perfectly all right."

"I am relieved to hear it. Now, you know I always am on your side in any matter?"

"Oh yes. You are always so good about that."

"Yes, but it seems to me, that is…I cannot approve of Mr. Roundbat just now. It is not just the moneylending business, though that was rather unsavory. It was really his actions that took me aback. Or rather, his lack of actions."

Miss Mayton paused. Then she said, "What I mean to say is, I simply cannot imagine that if it had been my Hans, or Gregorio, or Phillipe, or my Transylvanian duke, that they would not have leapt into bold action."

"Like Lord Hamill did?" Juliet asked.

"Just so."

"Lord Hamill is marvelous," Juliet said dreamily.

What a wonder. Her mind and heart had come together and they were as clear as glass—Lord Hamill was marvelous.

He had been all along.

Mr. Roundbat could not know it, but he had just done her the favor of a lifetime.

RUPERT HAD EVERY intention of stamping out the annoying Mr. Roundbat and it seemed luck sat on his shoulder—Roundbat had seemed to stamp out himself.

He attributed the fellow's outsize confidence in his charms

and his blasted poetry for the audacity to have ever invited Lady Juliet to his house to begin with. Rupert would not have, had it been his own.

It was the worst sort of rented house—a barely respectable neighborhood, a cramped house, and the furniture very much the worse for wear. And then, he'd seen what was on the dining table. His own servants would march out en masse were they to be presented with such feeble fare for their dinner.

Roundbat's butler and footman were rented too, and not at all trained for their duties. The poor footman had told him that he'd only been informed about cooking dinner after he was hired.

That poor lad seemed a game young fellow, so Rupert gave him direction to see his butler on the morrow. If he wished to be a footman, he at least ought to be trained properly, wear a livery that fit, and work in a respectable house.

Of course, there had been every chance that Lady Juliet would not have paid attention to any of the shabbiness of Roundbat's household. Perhaps she hadn't. If Roundbat's evening had gone as he'd planned, the outcome could have been far different. She might have been bowled over by some ridiculous poem in the Japanese style and ignored the relative squalor surrounding her.

However, the evening had not gone as Roundbat planned. In fact, that bounder had been fully revealed.

According to the beleaguered butler, one of the moneylenders' thugs had informed Lady Juliet that Roundbat had claimed he would pay what he owed using a dowry that was to come his way some time soon. He also advised Lady Juliet to steer clear of him and named Roundbat a "rum sort."

Rupert supposed that would have been the real nail in the coffin—there would not be much poetry in the Japanese style about a fellow chasing a dowry.

In any case, even if Rupert had not been informed of any of those facts, he had been in full view of Lady Juliet's various expressions. He was sure, quite sure, that Roundbat was entirely finished in her estimation.

The field had been cleared and all he need do was joust his way forward by way of the right words. Words were everything to Lady Juliet and so he must find the right ones.

Other ladies might be impressed with his athletic prowess, but Lady Juliet would not give a toss for it.

The moneylender's men of the night before had been dealt with, secreted away and hidden so their employers would not know what happened to them. They were more than happy to comply, once they understood it was either the magistrate, or an extended trip to Brighton with accommodation and food included. The leader of them had even commented that he'd always wanted to dip his toes in the sea.

On Tuesday night, those moneylenders would convene once more in the Rats' Castle, and the Queen's Knights would be waiting for them.

Until then, he had a poem to write and a masque to go to.

The poem was turning out harder than he'd expected. He'd composed one and presented it as they'd strolled Portland Place, but it seemed that *only* one poem had ever resided within the mind of the Marquess of Hamill.

It was just a poem—what was wrong with his uncooperative mind?

Perhaps rhyming *and* the Japanese style together was too high a hill to climb.

First, he'd roped in Theo to help, but the two of them had not got far. His mother had come upon them and joined in, though mostly with laughing. Finally, his father had turned up, looking for them, and thought it jolly good fun.

The four of them had been making lists of words that rhymed all afternoon.

The duke had not had a lot to offer in the way of words, but he proposed any number of ideas on how to deliver the thing once they had it.

He'd pointed out that his son was not particularly a poet and was rather ham-handed with turns of phrase, so perhaps Rupert ought to hire some sort of herald to read the poem with more panache.

It was not a bad idea, if they ever came up with a poem to read. Further, assuming he did come out of this conference with a poem, it was not likely to be very good. As it would need all the help it could get, hiring a professional actor might be the very thing.

"Wait!" the duchess said. "Best rhymes with zest—certainly we can make something of that."

Lady Juliet was the best and had a lot of zest? It was a place to start, he supposed.

Whatever final form the poem was to take, it appeared it would be a family affair. It would also likely be dreadful.

He only hoped Theo was right and Lady Juliet really would not know the difference.

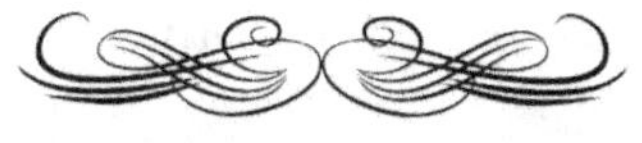

CHAPTER SEVENTEEN

TATTLETON WAS NOT entirely certain what had gone on the evening before. Miss Mayton and Lady Juliet had arrived home very late, which alone would not have set him wondering.

But then, they'd gone straight to the kitchens and ate everything they could find—slices of cold ham, chicken legs, slices of bread with butter, biscuits, and large glasses of ale.

It was possibly a good sign, but he could not be entirely certain.

"Mrs. Huffson," he said, "what would be your opinion of people arriving home from a dinner, positively starving?"

"I suppose I would wonder what had been served, Mr. Tattleton," the housekeeper said. "Was it inedible, or was there not enough? Neither being a thing that would occur in this house, in any case."

"Certainly not," Tattleton said, the very idea of such calamities occurring sending a shiver down his back.

"Are you aware of just such a dinner?" the housekeeper asked.

"I am. When Lady Juliet and Miss Mayton returned from that Mr. Roundbat's dinner, they came to the kitchens and ate *another* dinner. This was no light fare before retiring, Mrs. Huffson. They were two starving people."

"I hardly know what to make of that, Mr. Tattleton."

"Nor I, but I have some hopes. I pray Mr. Roundbat's dinner

was the most dreadful offering since Henry the VIII frightened his guests with blackbirds flying out of pies!"

"Oh, I never did like that idea," Mrs. Huffson said.

"Agreed. A bird ought to be sitting in a tree or properly dressed on a platter."

At that statement, Tattleton's eyes drifted to Marvin, roosting asleep atop Mrs. Huffson's sewing basket.

"And then there is Marvin, who does neither," Mrs. Huffson said with a laugh.

"Yes. Then there is Marvin," Tattleton said grimly.

He could not do anything about that rooster. For that matter, he could not do anything about Mr. Roundbat.

He could have hopes, though. Nobody could rip the hope from his breast and if that were all he had, he would hold on tight!

⇥⟫⟫⟨⟨⟨⇤

JULIET HAD BOUNCED out of bed the next morning, feeling freed from the confusion of her own stupid mind.

What had she been thinking in considering Mr. Roundbat?

She was afraid she knew. It had occurred to her that she had practically forced herself to admire Mr. Roundbat. She'd attempted to squeeze him into a preconceived box of a notion—a poet with no care for anything but words and high-flown sentiments, ranged against an uncaring world. Or in this particular case, *his* father and *her* sisters' husbands.

Juliet had ignored that she did not find Mr. Roundbat attractive. For heaven's sake, there was even a moment when she'd squinted at him, hoping a blur would render him more favorable to view.

She had pretended to herself that she admired his poetry, even though she knew perfectly well that she was in favor of rhyming.

She'd fooled herself that she would not mind living in a garret and that no amount of hardship would put her off her poet.

And why? Because she'd said she would.

Her old governess used to tell her she was stubborn as the day is long. Her governess had been right, of course. Once she decided upon a thing, especially if she'd announced it to other people, she clung to it like a life ring in stormy seas. No amount of common sense would convince her to let go and get in the lifeboat with other sensible people.

Despite her claims, it turned out that her feelings about creature comforts were a deal more pedestrian. She had flattered herself that she needed none of it, and then felt distinctly uncomfortable when faced with Mr. Roundbat's reduced circumstances.

Her feelings about physical attraction were just as ordinary. She could not make herself admire a person she did not in fact admire, regardless of how many poems were piled on.

She had, before the season began, considered herself extraordinary in some way. Unusual. Different. Superior. Decisive.

Now she supposed she was as any other lady and, strangely, it was a great relief to know it. Juliet Bennington was not nearly as complicated and mysterious as Juliet Bennington had once imagined.

She had gone down to the drawing room upon being apprised that Viola and Cordelia had come and they had settled into having a comfortable tea.

"I am not certain," Juliet said, "but I may be forced to stop writing poetry."

"Goodness," Viola said, "who would attempt to stop you?"

"Me. I would stop me," she said.

Her sisters' wrinkled brows hinted that she might want to elaborate on this new idea.

After a long sigh, she said, "You see, all along I have claimed I only need words to sustain me, but it turns out I was congratulating myself for something that is not at all true. And then, it occurred to me, that while I am lounging around in the luxury I claim means nothing to me and writing my poems, so many people are struggling just to eat. My efforts have been put in the wrong direction and I've discovered myself unconscionably shallow."

"So you will stop writing poetry and help the poor instead?" Cordelia asked. "Harveston has a lot of ideas on how the standards of living might be raised."

"I think I must do something," Juliet said. "Considering what I have learned about myself last night."

Juliet had told her sisters of the state of Mr. Roundbat's house and how put off she'd been, despite claiming she would live in a garret with her poet. She'd told them that she was firmly and finally done with all thoughts of Mr. Roundbat.

However, she had not told them *all* that occurred the evening before that had put her off. That he had been exposed as a fortune hunter and that they'd been held captive by moneylenders. Conbatten had warned her against it and Miss Mayton thought it was just as well forgotten.

She could not help but be relieved of the duty to explain it all. It was one thing to recognize that she ought not cling to an opinion that she no longer held just to be stubborn about it. It was another to admit how foolish she'd really been.

"I do not see why you might not do both things," Viola pointed out. "Help people *and* write poetry."

Just then, Tattleton brought a letter in on a silver salver. "This just arrived, Lady Juliet. I did not recognize the livery and there is no return on the outside of the paper. Furthermore, I happened to notice that the messenger's pants were short. Livery that was *short*, my lady. I've never seen the like of it."

Juliet took it, at once hopeful it was from Lord Hamill, and knowing full well it was not. Tattleton would have recognized the marquess's livery and, in any case, it was very doubtful that any of Lord Hamill's footmen would be wandering round with pants that were too short. She *had* seen one footman recently, though, who had been dressed in such a manner.

She tore it open while Tattleton pretended to straighten some things on the mantel, delaying his departure from the room.

My dear Lady Juliet—

Allow me to take this moment to apologize profusely for the grave misunderstanding that occurred at my house last evening. My father, ever the jester, sent that ludicrous letter and the one-pound note as a joke. The real letter arrived after your departure and all has been resolved regarding my financial arrangements.

I hope to see you at Lady Bloomington's masque. I am just now intent on arranging what might be my greatest poem yet and will deliver it to you at the masque in the most original style possible.

All my deepest regards,
Ignatius Roundbat

Juliet paused a moment to think through how she would explain Mr. Roundbat's letter, not a word of which she believed. It was ludicrous to imagine that a second messenger had arrived with the funds and the first with the one-pound note had just been a joke.

It was an effrontery that Mr. Roundbat wished to sweep it all away as if nothing had occurred. As if she were not now cognizant of his real plans.

Well, if he would attempt to read to her some poetry at the masque, he would end sorry for trying it.

Nevertheless, to refuse to show the letter to her sisters would hint that there was something scandalous about it.

She passed the letter to Cordelia, and she and Viola read it, heads together.

"What does he mean?" Viola asked. "What jest? What financial arrangements?"

"Well, as you know," Juliet said smoothly, "the baron is against Mr. Roundbat becoming a leading poet. As some sort of joke, the baron sent a messenger banging on the door with a strange letter and a one-pound note. Mr. Roundbat took it all in stride, as apparently the baron is an odd sort of fellow."

"Then just as well you are done with Mr. Roundbat," Cordelia said. "I would not like to think of you living in the same house with a strange baron. You would find it so off-putting—you are too used to your own family being so very sensible and regular."

"That is true, Jules," Viola said. "I do not think eccentricity would suit you, as you have not grown up with it."

"Now what about Lord Hamill?" Cordelia asked. "How do you view him at this moment?"

Juliet was quiet for a moment. Then she said, "Beatrice and Ros have both assured me that when the time was right to know my own heart it would come crashing down upon me like a wall of bricks."

"And has it?" Viola asked.

"Yes, yes it has."

Tattleton took that moment to drop a small statuette. It shattered on the tile surrounding the fireplace and splintered into dozens of shards.

It was just the sort of thing that would put him out of sorts for days.

Strangely, he did not look very cast down about it.

⟫⟫⟩⟨⟨⟨

As the carriage rolled forward, heading to Lady Bloomington's masque, Rupert said to Theo, "Well, we've done it."

"Indeed. Though it is fortunate nobody in the family must make a living at wordsmithing."

"Is it that bad?" Rupert asked, fairly certain he already knew the answer.

"Rather. But take heart, brother," Theo said kindly, "I really do not think Lady Juliet will judge it so. It will be the sentiment of it she'll be thinking about, not the skill."

He clinked and clanked as he shifted on his seat, Henry V's chainmail making the noise.

"In any case," Theo said, "you are quite the dashing knight this evening. That must play in your favor too. And then you said you are convinced Mr. Roundbat is out of the picture."

"Oh he's out," Rupert said. "He will not dare show his face tonight."

"That is a shame," Theo said laughing. "I was hoping to see him as a Samurai warrior."

"I am hoping to never set eyes on that weasel again."

"And your poem-reading herald? Did you fix it as Father suggested?"

"I did. I hired a young and handsome fellow from Drury Lane. He was only too happy to dress in a costume and read a poem for five pounds. I will point out Lady Juliet, who I already know from Darden is going as Elizabeth Melville."

"Who?"

"Who do you think?"

"Ah, *that* Elizabeth Melville. A fellow poetess."

"Just so. All I know is that this particular poetess was a Scot, and so Lady Juliet will wear some sort of tartan skirt. I do not know if she wears a mask of some sort."

"And here we are," Theo said, as the carriage slowed to a stop at Lady Bloomington's door. She kissed him on the cheek. "Good luck, brother. I have every confidence in your success."

Rupert hoped Theo's confidence was not misplaced. This was the night that would direct the course of his life. All he must do is find his herald, have the poem read to Lady Juliet to set the stage, and then use his own heartfelt words.

His own words wouldn't rhyme, but hopefully they would be good enough.

JULIET HAD EVERY hope that something would be said this night. Something would be said by Lord Hamill, and she knew precisely what she would say back.

As she had told him she did not wish to hear anything just yet, because the bricks had not fallen, she might well have to hint that they *had* fallen. She was prepared to do it.

As for Mr. Roundbat, despite his ridiculous letter, he would be well served to steer clear of her. She would have no time for him and was not in the slightest interested in the poem he was composing, nor in the original fashion he planned on delivering it.

Juliet did not require poetry this night, only the good and straightforward words of Lord Hamill.

She and her aunt had come on their own. The earl never did like a masque, as he always liked to say that if he would bother to talk to somebody, he'd much prefer to know ahead of time who it was he was talking to. All sorts of people wandering round with masks on their faces or cloaked in hoods or dressed as strange creatures made him feel as if he were about to be robbed.

Darden had gone off to his club first, and then would arrive with his friends from the YBC.

Her dress was marvelous. As she had not the first idea of what Elizabeth Melville might have worn, only remembering the lady's name as the first poetess to have her poems printed, she had used her imagination.

There was a high starched collar round the back of her neck, a tight-fitting bodice, and a billowing skirt in tartan.

Between her billowing skirt and her aunt's plentiful black bombazine and ghostly veil, it was well they were on their own—they had quite filled up the carriage with their clothing.

Now, they had gone inside and paid their respects to Lady Bloomington.

As Juliet had been warned, they were not two feet in the door before a footman arrived with a tray of champagne.

"Now do be careful, my dear," Miss Mayton said through her eerie black veil, "even I have fallen victim to Lady Bloomington's largesse. It can really tiptoe up on you and before you know it, you've somehow fallen on the floor."

Of course, she would be very careful. Though, one glass might go some way to settling her nerves. They felt at a fever pitch just this moment.

What was to happen? What was to be said? She wanted to rush time along to discover it.

As they entered the crowded ballroom, Juliet marveled at the costumes. Black dominos dotted a landscape of bakers, bespectacled clerks, jinns, bishops, ladies-in-waiting, dairy maids, cow herds, and she knew not what else. Lady Jersey had even styled herself a medieval queen, no doubt still under the spell of Mr. Roundbat's unctuous flattery.

Juliet searched the crowd for Lord Hamill. Regardless of what he wore, he would not be hard to spot. He was a mountain of a man. A glorious mountain of a man.

Ever since she'd come to understand her own mind, she'd been practically consumed by thinking about touching him and being in his arms. Her thoughts had even, on occasion, ventured into positively scandalous territories. Once she'd freed herself to think of the physical, it had come at her like opening the door to a gale wind.

She did not see him anywhere yet, but she knew he would come.

As she searched, she noted among the revelers a young gentleman dressed as a herald who seemed to be trying to catch her eye.

Yes, she was sure of it. He headed directly for her.

But who was he? She could not recall meeting the gentleman.

"Lady Juliet," he said, bowing.

Oh dear, they *had* met somewhere. Why could she not remember a thing about him?

"Have we been introduced to you, young man?" Miss Mayton asked.

"No, my lady," he said. "I am a herald sent to deliver a poem to a lady greatly admired."

He unfurled a rolled parchment. Juliet pressed her lips together. Mr. Roundbat really was a bold sort. And he also seemed to take her as unconscionably stupid.

The boy cleared his throat and said, "Well above the rest, she must now be secured lest, my life lose its zest."

So that was Mr. Roundbat's poem he'd been working on and this was the original style with which it was to be delivered.

She supposed that he'd taken in that she preferred rhymes and so had applied it to his Japanese style in an attempt to make some inroads.

How had he the gall to imagine that she would not remember what she had discovered about him? All she was to Mr. Roundbat was a purse full of money, and yet she was to be swept off her feet and made to forget all that had happened by rhyming in the Japanese style?

"Goodness," Miss Mayton said, "that was…something."

"Aunt, you know of course where this has come from."

"I'm afraid I do," Miss Mayton said. "He is a very persistent sort of creature."

Juliet turned to the young gentleman. "You may tell the originator of this poem that I know what he is. I have not the slightest interest in hearing from him again. I am quite set on a gentleman far superior."

"Are you?" Miss Mayton asked. "Entirely settled on whom I think?"

"Yes, Aunt. Indeed I am."

The young gentleman looked fairly struck down by her words and Juliet began to feel sorry for the poor chap. After all, he had only been sent to read the poem and could not know of any unsavory business that had transpired ahead of it.

"Now it is not your fault that you've got yourself involved

with such a person," she said to the herald. "My advice is, conclude your business, be on your way, and do not look back."

The herald nodded and hurried off, his complexion rather ashen.

Miss Mayton nodded approvingly. "You certainly gave Mr. Roundbat's messenger the what-for."

"I had to do it, Aunt," Juliet said. "His audacity knows no bounds. He is desperate to get his hands on a dowry and the only lady foolish enough to have been impressed by him is me."

Now, dear, we were all taken in by Mr. Roundbat," Miss Mayton said consolingly.

"Were we?" Juliet said. "As far as I can tell, it was only me that was taken in."

"Oh look, there is Lord Hamill," Miss Mayton said, kindly redirecting her attention away from her stupidity and toward her happiness.

Hamill!

Juliet turned. There he was and looking as glorious as ever. More glorious, really. He was costumed as a knight of old. Could there be any disguise more romantic? The silver chainmail of his hauberk rippled in the candlelight.

"What do you suppose he is doing?" Miss Mayton asked. "Goodness, he looks as dark as thunder and he's heading for the door."

Juliet watched him storm out. What was he doing? Where was he going when she was right here waiting for him?

CHAPTER EIGHTEEN

THE YOUNG ACTOR from Drury Lane, a certain John Crowder, leaned against a balustrade outside on the balcony for support.

He was glad he'd thought to bring his friend Luther along with him on this job, but that was all he was glad about.

"The lord looked pretty steamed," Luther said. "Did you fail to carry off the whole thing the way he told you to?"

"If words were a violence, this play I've landed myself in is a veritable *Titus Andronicus!*" John said. "It was all supposed to be so easy. I approach, read the poem, the lady is flattered, blushes and fans herself, and then the lord steps in. One, two, three, done."

"And it weren't one, two, three, done?"

"No!" John said, still hardly able to catch his breath. "Though we did get to the *done* part in terrifying speed. Just not the done destination the lord had in mind."

John shivered, as if a cold hand had run fingers down his spine. First, he'd had to approach a titled lady, then he had to recite poetry, then he had to inform an actual lord of the dismal results.

It had all seemed such a lark when he'd took the job!

"Spill it," Luther said.

"I read the poem, which was awful by the by—if Shakespeare yet lived he would have beat that lord round the head from here to Sunday. But who cares, I read it. The lady what's supposed to be bowled over glares at me, and I'm thinkin' she's against the poem, it's that bad. But no, she says she knows what he is and don't want to hear further from 'im, and that she's set on a superior fellow. And then *I* have to go and tell the lord that very thing. He's a marquess! I thought he might swipe my head from my shoulders, he was that irate."

"I reckon he's a rake or some such and she's kenned to it," Luther said. He rubbed his chin, looking thoughtful. "Still, he's a marquess, I'm pretty surprised she'd turn down a marquess even if he were a murderer. Me ma says that ladies of that style bet their life on marrying a duke or a marquess."

John suddenly felt his cheeks grow cold, as if a January breeze had come upon him. "Uh-oh," he said.

"What?" Luther asked him. "You look like you're dead and buried. Don't tell me you forgot to get the money upfront."

"I got the money, all right. It's just, I might'a forgot to say who the poem was from. I might'a left out the part that it was from the marquess."

"You never did."

John was silent, because he was in fact sure that he did.

Attempting to soothe himself about the oversight, he said, "It don't matter. She must'a knowed it was the marquess. How many other gents are gonna be sending a herald to read very wretched poetry?"

"You don't know, there might be fellas fallin' outta farmers' carts attemptin' it. We don't know what these titled people get up to. Ya gotta go catch 'im and tell him you forgot that part!" Luther said. "Or if you can't catch him, tell her."

John shook his head. "No. No I don't. I'm gonna slip out of here and back to the theater and hope I never see them two again in my life. Next time a lord turns up with five pounds, wantin' wretched poetry read to a lady, I'm runnin' the other direction as I'm informin' 'im I'd rather hang myself."

RUPERT HAD STORMED out of Lady Bloomington's masque and had not even waited for his carriage. A groom could come and tell Davis to bring it home.

He was too full of pent-up energy or feelings or…rage, even. Not rage at Lady Juliet, but rage at himself for being so stupid. He could not sit in a carriage. He had to walk and walk fast.

What had happened? Lady Juliet had told his herald that she knew what he was. What did that mean? It sounded like it meant she'd discovered he was a terrible person.

All he could think of was that she'd somehow figured out that he could not have possibly written that poem on his own.

Was it that offensive that he'd had help?

Or perhaps she'd perceived how bad the poem was and found it offensive, despite Theo being certain that she wouldn't notice its poor quality. Maybe it was so bad she thought he'd not put any effort into it.

And then, who was this superior gentleman she'd mentioned? It was not Roundbat, he was certain of that. Had somebody else been hanging about her and he'd failed to notice?

How could he have been so wrong?

She did not wish to hear from him further? At all?

How could she have arrived at such violent feelings against him when he'd thought just the opposite?

Had he been so obtuse to think that he would be successful when in reality she abhorred the sight of him?

None of it added up. Or did it add up and he was too dense to understand *how* it added up?

No. It did not add up. It just did not.

He might not be an intellectual, but he was not *that* much of a dolt.

Rupert stopped in his tracks and turned round.

She claimed she did not wish to hear more from him, but he

could not follow that wish until he had an explanation!

There was something unknown at work here and he would discover what it was.

JULIET WAS NOT entirely certain what to think upon watching Lord Hamill leave the masque. She was attempting to be hopeful about it. Perhaps he was called away on a family matter. Perhaps his horse suddenly needed attention—gentlemen did always have a great concern for their horses.

In the meantime, while she was hoping for his return, she had not allowed any other gentleman to put himself down for the last set of the evening by claiming it was already spoken for.

As it was Lady Bloomington's masque, there would be no sit-down supper. The trays of entremets would come by all evening, and charming sideboards would be set up after the dancing so that guests might linger at cleverly grouped tables and chairs at their leisure.

The musicians had been tuning and the ball was nearing its start and still no sign of Lord Hamill.

Very suddenly, a gentleman leaped in front of her and struck a pose. He was dressed as a warrior of some sort, with a breast-plate of interconnected pieces of leather and a metal helmet obscuring his face.

He threw the faceplate of the helmet up.

Mr. Roundbat.

"The dawn will rise up, whisking all troubles away, in time we will wed," he said dramatically.

The absolute boldness and effrontery of this man. How dare he approach her a second time after his herald had been told very directly that she had no wish to hear from him further?

Miss Mayton sighed quietly by her side.

"Mr. Roundbat," Juliet said, "I fail to understand how you

have somehow interpreted my message other than how it was intended."

"What message, Lady Juliet?" Mr. Roundbat said, removing his helmet.

"The message to the herald? Or perhaps he was too afraid to repeat it to you?"

"What herald?"

"Really, Mr. Roundbat, I find these games tiresome. Very tiresome."

"Lady Juliet, far be it for me to play games! I came this evening with very serious intentions. *Very* serious, if you understand me."

"You have no reason to have any sort of intentions in regard to me. Do you think I do not understand what you are and what you've sought to achieve? You were after my dowry, so that you might use it to launch yourself as a leading poet."

"Launch *ourselves*, Lady Juliet. You must believe me, I wished to launch both of us. We can be the leading couple of poetry."

The leading couple of poetry. There was a time that idea would have had great effect, but no more.

"You are a scoundrel, Mr. Roundbat, and you really should have listened when the herald told you I did not wish to hear anything further."

"What herald!" Mr. Roundbat cried.

Really, it was too much. She glared at him and said, "'Well above the rest, she must now be secured lest, my life lose its zest?' That does not sound familiar? You deny having sent that to me not a half-hour ago?"

Mr. Roundbat had taken a step back, as if the poem had assaulted him in some way. "You do not propose that I wrote such drivel?" he asked. "It is a lame attempt at the Japanese style and it *rhymes*. Rhymes? In the Japanese style? That is entirely absurd."

Now Juliet took a step back. He was right, it did rhyme, and she'd never heard Mr. Roundbat recite anything at all that rhymed.

Juliet looked to her aunt.

"Oh dear," Miss Mayton said. "If the herald was not from Mr. Roundbat…"

"It could not have been from Lord Hamill?" Juliet said in a near whisper. "It could not have been."

"That would be unfortunate," Miss Mayton said, "considering what was relayed to the herald."

The idea was too terrible to consider. The things she'd said! Certainly it could not have been…

As much as she attempted to convince herself, the pertinent question kept presenting itself. If the herald were not sent by Lord Hamill, then by who?

It had not been Mr. Roundbat and she did not know any other gentleman who would do it.

And then, another piece to the puzzle fell into place.

"It *was* Lord Hamill," Juliet cried. "He came as a knight and sent a herald! How could I have been so blind?"

"Now, Lady Juliet," Mr. Roundbat said, "if there has been some contretemps with that gentleman, it must be for the best, I think. He has not the mind or the depth of feelings to measure up to a poetess."

Juliet shoved his leather breastplate. "Get out of my way, Samurai. I have a superior man to find!"

As she raced toward the doors, she heard Miss Mayton say, "Well now, Mr. Roundbat, what can one say? Lord Hamill *is* rather superior."

She was out the doors in a trice, only slowing down as she passed Lady Bloomington and claiming she would take a minute of air.

Lady Bloomington would not be approving of it—what lady walked outside alone? However, the hostess did not immediately send anybody after her, so she seemed not to be *too* alarmed by it. Hopefully the lady assumed Juliet had forgotten her reticule in her carriage or was on some other little errand.

It was no little errand, though.

Juliet stopped where she was, looking up and down the line of carriages. Where had he gone? Was he at home already? Would she have to run all the way to Hanover Square?

Really, that was not so very far. She might get there in a quarter hour on foot, assuming she was not accosted on the way. A lady on her own at night would present an alluring target to those who looked for such.

There was no time to fetch the carriage though, even if Sandren could ever be convinced to drive her to a gentleman's house when she was meant to be at the masque.

She must just run faster than any thief or ne'er-do-well could catch her.

But what if he'd gone to his club? What if he just now walked into the YBC? That was another quarter hour in the opposite direction.

Juliet realized it was absolutely foolish to run off, but it could not exceed the foolishness of scolding Lord Hamill's herald and saying all those terrible things. In any case, she was feeling rather desperate and could not bear to simply go back indoors.

Her aunt had followed her out. From the doors, she called, "Juliet? Are you quite all right?"

"No!" she cried. "I've got to find Lord Hamill!"

"I believe he's just there, my dear," Miss Mayton said. "See? Just at the end of the street."

Juliet whipped around.

Yes, it was him. She would recognize that fine figure anywhere. He was striding in her direction at a very fast pace.

As he approached, he shouted, "Now see here, Lady Juliet, I think I am at least owed an explanation."

Juliet set off in a run, and he looked very surprised to see it. She had no care for ladylike behavior. She would get to him.

She launched herself at him, and it was probably well that he was a large and strong man, else they'd have ended in a heap on the pavement.

He held her against him and his arms were like two immovable branches on a seasoned oak, solid and strong.

"Have you changed your mind, then?" he asked, sounding a little confused as to why his herald had been told off and she'd now leapt upon him.

"I never changed my mind."

"Then I cannot account for your current location in my arms," Lord Hamill said, "but I do not much care."

He bent his head down and kissed her softly. Juliet returned the kiss with enthusiasm. Rather more enthusiasm than she imagined he'd been expecting. At least, it was more enthusiastic than she had been expecting herself.

She wrapped her arms around his neck and pressed against him. He was so solid! She felt like a willow against a brick wall and it was wonderful.

He kissed her neck and pulled pins from her hair. Were they on the street? Were they somewhere else? It did not seem to matter much.

"I thought the herald was from Roundbat," she whispered.

Lord Hamill laughed in her ear. "Roundbat? Roundbat could not write poetry in the Japanese style and make it rhyme."

"I should have known nobody but you could do it."

"Well, it was my whole family actually."

"Really?" Juliet asked. It was a very nice idea.

"They are very fond of you."

"And I am very fond of *you*."

"Fond? I see, so I am to have deeper feelings than you do? I am hopelessly in love with you. I save fondness for my friends."

Juliet giggled. "I am in rather desperately in love with you too, only I had to wait until you said it first."

"Is that the protocol?" Lord Hamill said, kissing up and down her neck.

"I do not know, really," Juliet said. "I have been a goose from start to finish, so do not depend too much upon what I may know about anything."

"Well, you're my goose, and that's quite enough for me."

"Whisper me the poem you wrote for me," Juliet said softly. "I wish to hear it from you."

"Did you think it was good?" Lord Hamill said, a note of surprise in his voice.

"It doesn't matter."

Lord Hamill said, "Well above the rest, she must now be secured lest my life lose its zest."

"She is secured. I will write a poem about it."

In the distance, Juliet heard Lady Bloomington's raised voice. "Miss Mayton? Do you look upon this scene and fail to intervene?"

"I imagine they'll get married," Miss Mayton said.

"I should hope so!"

"We will marry, will we not?" Lord Hamill said. "You will not change your mind and go running off?"

"Of course we must marry," Juliet said. "It has never been about changing my mind, only knowing my mind. My heart knew, but my mind took its time to catch up."

"And now you do know it? As I have known my own feelings since the beginning?"

"Now I know it, Hamill. I know it entirely."

He kissed her lightly on the lips and he held her—both strong and gentle—as Lady Bloomington fretted at the doors.

"Perhaps we ought to go in," Juliet said, as Lord Hamill nuzzled her neck. She had no wish to go in, but Lady Bloomington was beginning to sound rather distressed.

"Or perhaps," Lord Hamill said, "we set off to find your father so I might gain his approval. I do not see any reason to delay."

"That is a rather inspired idea," Juliet said. "He is at White's playing cards."

Juliet was fully cognizant that most gentlemen would sensibly wait until morning to seek out a father. It was beginning to occur to her that she'd somehow put Corinthians and poets into two different categories, as if they could not overlap in proclivities.

That had been wrong. Here was Lord Hamill, man of action, using his actions in the most romantic way possible.

"I'll call my carriage," Lord Hamill said. "Miss Mayton will come along; I will not damage your reputation by taking you alone."

Juliet sighed. He would not damage her reputation. More romantic action.

He picked her up in his arms and strode toward the doors.

Another romantic action.

Goodness, it was looking as if a man of action was full of romantic actions.

Lady Bloomington cried, "Now this is really too much!"

"It is all right, Lady Bloomington," Lord Hamill called. "We are to set off to gain the earl's approval of this union, if my carriage might be brought round and Miss Mayton consents to accompany us."

And so, Miss Mayton accepted the invitation with alacrity, Lord Hamill's carriage was speedily fetched, and Lady Bloomington was left praying that the Earl of Westmont would indeed approve of what had just transpired on her pavement.

RUPERT, HAVING BEEN nearly bowled over by Lady Juliet, and having been apprised that his herald had been told off because the lady thought the boy had been sent by Roundbat, had wasted no time securing her.

It had occurred to him that he ought to waste no time securing the earl's approval too. That earl was just now at White's playing cards. Rupert had not been there in ages, preferring to spend his time at Darden's YBC, but he was a member as was his father.

It would be untoward to interrupt a card game, but it must be done. Rupert would not take the chance that another Roundbat spouting off poetry would turn up.

The next one might be a bit more strapping than the original, not involved with moneylenders, and writing poetry that rhymed. Lady Juliet was just now in love with Rupert Doncaster, Marquess of Hamill, and he intended to keep it that way.

Davis, ever the unperturbable, had not blinked at the sudden summons, nor the fact that Lady Juliet and Miss Mayton were got in the coach, nor that they were to head to White's. He merely nodded and set off.

They were so nearby St. James that they would arrive in a matter of minutes, and Rupert speedily began to get the idea that was a good thing. Lady Juliet peered round the heavily reinforced carriage that did not house the sort of soft padding and comforts one might have expected in a lord's coach.

She said, "This is very unusual, Hamill. There seem to be compartments everywhere and the seats are not very well padded. Well, I suppose I'd never considered how a real Corinthian might travel."

Rupert nodded, hoping she was not thinking of opening any of the many compartments round the inside of the carriage. They were filled to the brim with weapons and he did not know when, if ever, he would apprise her of his activities for the Queen's Knights.

Her sister, Rosalind, knew all about it because of Conbatten's role and the duchess was highly approving, but Rupert could not think every lady would be.

"This is too masculine for your tastes, I know," Rupert said. "I will have a glorious carriage made for your use and it will be so well padded you will not even know you are out of your own drawing room. Velvet covers and fur throws, and braziers for your feet."

Miss Mayton nodded and Rupert got the idea she found favor in the idea. Lady Juliet, thankfully, did not reach for any of the compartments, but rather snuggled in the crook of his arm.

They arrived to White's shortly thereafter. Rupert could not bring the ladies indoors with him, as it was a gentlemen's club, but he did not like the idea of leaving them alone to explore the inside of his carriage either.

He opened the window and said, "Davis, please go in and alert the steward that the Earl of Westmont is wanted out of doors."

CHAPTER NINETEEN

Davis had hopped down from Rupert's carriage, ever unperturbable, and strode to White's doors.

"Excellent notion, Lord Hamill," Miss Mayton said. "The privacy of a carriage must suit at such a moment."

Rupert nodded, and gently untangled Lady Juliet from her current location in the crook of his arm. "Your father, perhaps, would prefer to see us not sitting so close."

Lady Juliet nodded and slid to the other side of the seat, though she did not look happy about it, which made Rupert very happy indeed.

It was not many more minutes before the earl hurried out, accompanied by Davis. The groom swung the door open, and the earl scrambled inside next to Miss Mayton.

"Juliet, Miss Mayton, are you quite all right? I was only told you were here and could not imagine the cause. Has something happened? Is it a house fire? Lord Hamill?"

"Something very momentous has occurred, Papa," Lady Juliet said. "Lord Hamill has asked for my hand, and I have accepted, and all there is to do now is for you to approve it."

"Gracious," the earl said.

"Now," Lady Juliet said, "I know I blathered on about wishing for a poet, but I must be brutally honest—Mr. Roundbat is entirely finished in my mind. I would not entertain that person for a minute longer, not even if you wished it."

It seemed to Rupert that the earl had not wished it for a moment, such was the relief on his features.

"I cannot claim to be too downcast about that," the earl said.

"I have been such a goose, Papa," Lady Juliet said. "All along, I have really loved Lord Hamill. I just would not face it, as I had not imagined I would fall in love with a Corinthian. You see? Because I am a poetess, I stupidly imagined I could only be happy with a poet."

"Yes, yes, you did say quite a lot about that," the earl said softly.

"I have been in love with Lady Juliet from the start," Rupert said. "And I find I have been lucky that things have broken my way."

"I imagine we've all been lucky," the earl whispered.

"Do say you approve, Papa," Lady Juliet said.

"Lady Juliet will be a marchioness," Rupert said, thinking he'd better lay out his case, "and then a duchess someday. Nothing shall be denied her. Nothing."

"My dear," the earl said to his daughter, "you cannot have the first idea how much I approve of this turn of events. I had wondered where we were going… Lord Hamill, consider yourself engaged to my daughter, see me in the morning and we'll have our people work out the details of the contract."

The earl let out a sigh and leaned back.

Rupert got the distinct idea that the earl had lived in a sort of terror that he would awake to find Mr. Roundbat as a son-in-law one day.

"Miss Mayton," the earl said, "I do not know how you do it, but everything always seems to come right in the end."

"Careful management, Lord Westmont," Miss Mayton said, "it is all in the careful management."

Rupert pressed his lips tightly together to stop them from smiling. About the last thing Miss Mayton seemed to ever employ was careful management.

Lady Juliet crossed over to the other side of the carriage,

squeezed next to Miss Mayton, and hugged her father. "You are such a dear, Papa," she said, kissing him on the cheek. "You never do throw any of our ideas back at us when we realize we've been foolish and have changed our minds."

The earl laughed. "So far, the mind-changing has seemed to work in my favor."

"Now, I do not wish you to stay away longer from your card game," Lady Juliet said, patting the earl's hand, "and, since I am engaged, I suppose a carriage ride with my intended is not out of the question."

"No, of course not, my dear. Assuming Miss Mayton is agreeable."

"You can count on me, Earl," Miss Mayton said.

"As I always do, Miss Mayton," the earl said. "Well! What an evening, eh? Lord Hamill, come by on the morrow at eleven and we'll put the thing together formally."

Rupert nodded. "Eleven, promptly."

"He will be prompt, Papa," Lady Juliet said, smiling at him. "He is a Corinthian, a man of action."

Lord Westmont nodded genially. "And he is not Mr. Round-bat," he said, "which I find myself inordinately cheered about."

The earl then left the carriage and waved them off, after Rupert had given Davis the order to take a leisurely carriage ride round the town.

Lady Juliet flew to Rupert's side and snuggled into the crook of his arm again.

"A carriage ride was an excellent idea," he whispered into her hair.

"A most excellent idea," Miss Mayton said from the other side of the carriage. "All my girls are so very clever. And really, what I find so interesting about a carriage ride at night is looking out the window at the passing houses. Sometimes, somebody fails to close a curtain and one might see a family going about their lives. I get entirely engrossed by the view, I am positively glued to it and almost forget who else is around me."

Miss Mayton then very determinedly stared out the window. It seemed they were to be subject to Miss Mayton's careful management and Rupert was beginning to grow rather fond of it.

An hour passed and Rupert could not have said where they went. They might have gone in circles for all he knew of it.

Lady Juliet was in his arms and kissing him with abandon—they might drive in circles the rest of their lives and he'd be happy to do it.

Miss Mayton, though her careful management was delightfully lax, did finally yawn and suggest the evening was coming to its natural close.

⟫⟩⟨⟪

FOR ONCE IN what seemed years, not even a deranged rooster could put a damp on Tattleton's feelings. That ill-omened avian was as usual sitting atop Mrs. Huffson's sewing basket.

But after all, was that not Mrs. Huffson's problem?

"I suppose the earl was delighted with the match," Mrs. Huffson said.

Tattleton nodded, as he was certain that must have been the case.

What a scene he had just witnessed!

He'd heard a carriage pull up outside, as he was always listening for one of the family to arrive home.

Opening the door, he'd found it was not one of the family's carriages at all. It was Lord Hamill's. As a further surprise, Miss Mayton and Lady Juliet had descended from it.

At first, he had quite naturally thought the worst. Some calamity engineered by Miss Mayton had either happened or was in the offing.

Perhaps they were intending to set off for Gretna Green and had come by for traveling bags. Perhaps there had been some sort of disgrace they were attempting to wiggle out of. Perhaps Miss

Mayton had set somebody's house on fire and they'd sprinted off before it was noticed.

His mind, so stretched with stress over the past few years, had even gone to the worst. Perhaps Lord Hamill had murdered Mr. Roundbat and they were in the midst of a cover up.

Though, had that been the case, Tattleton would have likely helped them do it.

But none of those disasters had come to pass! They were engaged. It was like a miracle—they were engaged, society was not set ablaze with gossip, no house was afire, and nobody was on the verge of a duel.

It was all so regular he'd almost been felled by the news.

"After what we have been through these past years, Mrs. Huffson," he said, "it almost feels alarming that we are not thrown topsy-turvy. Do you suppose we are missing something?"

"I daresay not," Mrs. Huffson said. "Lady Juliet, for all her high-flying sentiments about poetry, simply came to her senses and decided on Lord Hamill."

Yes, he supposed that must be it. Though, it seemed so improbable that one of the earl's daughters should just suddenly become rational. Not with Miss Mayton manning their ship.

He sighed a long and contented sigh. He supposed he would sleep very well this night.

"Just think, Mrs. Huffson," Tattleton said, "Lady Juliet is the last of them. Five daughters, all settled. Next year shall be one of calm regularity, and that is if we even bother to come to Town for the season. Perhaps we will not even come and will just stay quiet in the country."

These ideas were like a long-anticipated dream finally coming to pass.

"Well, there is still Lord Darden to get married," Mrs. Huffson pointed out.

"Oh that is quite different though," he said. "Lord Darden does not need to come out in society, he's been out for years. When the time is right, he will inform the earl of his choice of bride."

"At the rate he's going, we'll all be dead and buried by the time it's right for Lord Darden," Mrs. Huffson said. "I wouldn't be at all surprised to find there is some concerted effort made next year to hurry him along."

Tattleton dismissed the idea. The notion that anybody could manage Lord Darden and press him into wedlock was ridiculous.

He ignored the very slight sinking feeling that settled upon him.

Certainly, that idea could be handily dismissed.

Certainly.

⚜

JULIET HAD LAID abed until ten in the morning, marveling at the events of the last evening. Her aunt had very considerately had a tray prepared and sent up for her breakfast. It was as if she were a married lady already.

She did hop out of bed at ten though, as Hamill would come at eleven to see her father and she knew her Corinthian would not be late.

Lynette had been instructed to do her hair in a manner that would be suitable for a lady patiently waiting in a drawing room while her fiancé negotiated terms with her father.

Lynette had muttered, "That's a style, is it?" But then she'd cheerfully set about the task. Juliet could not say it looked much different than it ever did, but as she'd had no clear idea of what she was after she was satisfied enough.

Now, she was in the drawing room with Miss Mayton, kneeling on the window seat, eyes out for Lord Hamill.

Of course, he was not late but came trotting down Portland Place on his magnificent beast of a horse. He threw the reins to a groom and spotted her at the window.

She pried it open and stuck her head out.

He tipped his hat and called, "Wish me luck!"

"You will not need it!" she called back.

Miss Mayton had hurried to the window. "God speed, Lord Hamill!"

He laughed as Tattleton passed them on the way to the doors. Their butler attempted to frown at these goings-on, but he could not much manage it.

Juliet had left the drawing room doors open purposefully, so she could see Hamill as he was led to her father's library. He noted it and smiled as he passed, looking remarkably glorious in his morning coat. As glorious as he always had been, now that she could properly take it in.

He, Lord Hamill, was in the library with her father. It was happening. The stage had been set for her life to unfold. She would not wed a poet, but there was something of poetry in her feelings for Lord Hamill.

Juliet barely noticed as Johnny jogged to the front doors to answer another knock. The important knock had already occurred, and the important knocker was in the library.

Not a moment later, Beatrice flew into the room.

"I could not help but notice that Lord Hamill arrived, and that you were hanging out the window—is he…"

"He is with Father now, Bea," Juliet said.

Beatrice raced to her side. "Ah, the inevitable bricks have fallen."

"They did fall," she said. "They fell very hard upon me."

"I could not be more pleased for you, really I could not."

"I daresay you are relieved at my choice," Juliet said ruefully.

"I would have accepted any gentleman you chose…over time and as best I could. Just as you have done with Van Doren."

Juliet giggled. "I suppose even Van Doren will approve of Hamill."

Beatrice sighed. "Rather a lot, I am sure. The last thing he said on the matter of Juliet Bennington's heart was that if we were to be forced to listen to poetry in the Japanese style over dinner, he would throw his napkin on the table and go home."

"That would be very like him," Miss Mayton said, not appearing at all disturbed to envision Van Doren throwing his napkin around.

They ordered tea and Juliet recounted every moment of the prior evening to Beatrice's amazement.

"I will say one thing, Jules," Beatrice said, "you have rather broken with Bennington tradition by clearing up the confusion so fast. We've had a history of dragging things out, and I am relieved this particular misunderstanding did not go on for days and weeks."

"Oh, I could not wait once I realized my mistake. I had to chase after him, and then he was coming back to demand an explanation…"

"Which you readily gave him," Beatrice said.

"Just so. Right after flinging myself into his arms. A weaker man might have fallen over from the force of it."

Lord Hamill strode into the room and Juliet launched herself off the sofa and was by his side in a moment.

"All is well," Lord Hamill said, "we have an agreement."

"I knew it should be so," Juliet said. "My father is too dear of a man to drive a hard bargain."

Lord Hamill laughed. "I did not wait to find that out," he said. "I threw everything in your direction and there was nothing left to bargain for. He was astonished by your pin money, jointure, and jewelry fund, among other things."

"My jewelry fund?"

"A yearly amount that should afford you an entire dress made of diamonds, if you so please."

"You see, Bea?" Juliet said. "He is a *romantic* Corinthian."

"I rather do see," Beatrice said, laughing.

"Lady Van Doren," Lord Hamill said. "Miss Mayton." He bowed elegantly to the two ladies. "The earl was so good as to invite me to dine this evening, and mentioned he would send out a note to all the family. Miss Mayton, I know I can count on you.

I do hope I see you here this evening, Lady Van Doren."

"Goodness, we would not miss it," Beatrice said. "Van Doren will be very pleased to celebrate this engagement."

"Van Doren was dreading having to listen to poetry in the Japanese style over dinner," Juliet said. "He planned to throw down his napkin and storm out."

"As any rational person would," Lord Hamill said.

"Your timing in this matter, Lord Hamill," Miss Mayton said, "is both lucky and unlucky. I am in the habit of reading interesting literature after dinner, but we have just finished a story. His Grace, the Duke of Conbatten was rather bowled over by it."

"Was he?"

"Practically speechless." Miss Mayton tapped her chin with her forefinger. "Although, perhaps we might begin a new story? Yes, indeed, why not? *The Dire Desperations of Deadwood Dale* is itching to be read."

"That sounds very dire and desperate," Lord Hamill said.

"Exceedingly so, I can assure you," Miss Mayton said nodding.

"I look forward to it, Miss Mayton," Lord Hamill said. "Now, I suppose I might take my fiancée walking up and down the street?"

"Just as both you and Mr. Roundbat once did," Juliet said.

Lord Hamill nodded. "I should like to repeat the operation sans Mr. Roundbat. You can recite me some of your poetry that rhymes and we will not be assaulted by anything that does not. Naturally, Miss Mayton, Lady Van Doren, we would welcome your company."

"I cannot imagine why," Miss Mayton said.

"I thank you for the invitation, Lord Hamill," Beatrice said, "but I'd best get back to my husband. He was left on tenterhooks regarding your arrival to the house, and I will give him the happy news that there is to be no Japanese style poetry at dinner."

Juliet ran to fetch her tippet and bonnet, Lynette hurriedly securing her hat with well placed pins, and they set off walking the avenue.

Hamill put out his arm and Juliet rested her hand upon it. That arm was as strong and steady as a stone house and would never let her down.

"We have so much to talk about, I think," Juliet said. She wished to speak about one thing in particular that had been on her mind. "How do you feel about roosters, Hamill?"

Hamill appeared pensive, as if he thought there might be a right or wrong answer, which of course there was.

"I cannot claim to have thought deeply about them," he admitted. "But I am generally in favor of all the creatures of the earth, but for the deadly kind. Even those have their place, though."

"I suppose when you hear that I rescued a poor dear rooster from being killed in a cruel cockfight, you will think I ought to keep him. I am exceedingly fond of him."

Lord Hamill laughed as they reached the end of the street. The end of glorious Portland Place was conveniently peppered with mature trees and had no cross street where curious onlookers might be located.

He pulled her behind a tree and kissed her. He tipped her chin and said, "If you are fond of a rooster then I suppose you must have him."

"His name is Marvelous Marvin and he lives in the house." She really did want to get that last point across before she was too distracted by kissing Hamill. Juliet was all too aware that it was not altogether usual to keep a rooster in the house.

"May I ask why he lives in the house?" Hamill said, laughing at the notion.

"Well, he adores the garden, but only during the day. At sunset, he gets frantic to come indoors."

"He has not a coop then?"

"No, do you suppose that is why? Gracious, I am surprised I did not think of it. I guessed easily enough that he was frightened of predators, but did not think to have a coop built. He's been very happy sleeping on Mrs. Huffson's sewing basket in the servants' hall."

"Perhaps we ought to allow Marvin to decide for himself where he prefers to be. I will have a marvelous coop built and put some female companions in there and we'll see if he still prefers a sewing basket. I suspect he will rather have companions who understand him—a rooster is built to protect his flock."

"As you are built for me, it seems."

"I will protect my adorable little chicken always."

"Now that is a fine idea."

"And here is a finer idea," Hamill said, lifting her chin to kiss her.

And so they lingered behind the trees for nearly an hour. If Miss Mayton was keeping track of the time, she would have been shocked to her shoes. At least, any rational matron would have been. As it were, she had not the first idea of how long the couple was missing—she was entirely too engrossed in the contemplation of beginning a new book that evening, to the delight of her listeners.

Her listeners' delight, except, perhaps, Van Doren. That notion, though, was unlikely to trouble the lady. Everybody in the world knew Van Doren could only be pleased with two things—Beatrice, and his young daughter, Lily.

As for the rest of her listeners, she would presume they would be bowled over, as they always were.

CHAPTER TWENTY

AFTER SETTLING WITH her father and his delightful interlude walking Lady Juliet up and down the street and mostly hidden behind the trees, Rupert leapt on his horse and trotted away as Juliet waved from a window.

He had a full day ahead before he would return to dine. First, he must see Conbatten, who had sent him a note that morning. Then, he would return to his house and relay the happy news of his success with the earl to his family.

He hoped Conbatten was not putting together some plan to take place this evening, as he would have to refuse. He would not stand up Juliet at dinner. Although, he would be glad to see the duke. On the subject of the activities of the Queen's Knights, he wished for some advice from Conbatten.

Conbatten had been honest with his bride. However, Rupert's father never had, and his mother and sister remained unaware of such activities. His father claimed it was the duty of a husband to make very sure guesses about what one's wife would and would not like to know and he'd been certain Rupert's mother would not care to know.

His father had blamed all his late-night excursions on Rowndale's father, also a knight for the queen. As far as the duchess knew it, the senior Rowndale was prone to bouts of madness brought on by gin and must be sat with until the madness subsided. His mother had thought the duke a very good friend to do it.

What would Juliet prefer to know? Or not to know? It was a worry that lingered in the back of his mind. Even distracted by her company, it had been there. He could not make a mistake about which way to go.

He arrived to Grosvenor Square and was shown into the drawing room. Conbatten was not there, but the duchess was. As was her ever-present physician, sitting in a corner of the room and appearing stoic.

She rose and came forward. "Lord Hamill, I have heard the happy news from my father; we are all to dine together this evening."

"I am exceedingly fortunate to have had my suit succeed."

"Do sit, yes, I think we all view it as fortunate. That Mr. Roundbat fellow was…a bit of a trial. And now Conbatten has told me all of what he'd involved himself in. Juliet would have been very wretched if she'd gone that direction."

"Fortunately for me, Roundbat decided to have a dinner."

The duchess laughed. "My duke will be down shortly. He will be just getting out of his bath. I was in the habit of joining him in it, but in my condition I have quite gone off it for now."

Rupert nodded, but he did not reply. He hardly knew what he would say as comment on the duchess and Conbatten in a bath together.

The butler brought in a tea tray. It was an odd sort of tray. There were biscuits, which was very usual. But there were also small bowls of pickled vegetables, each with its own tiny fork.

"I am obsessed with vinegar these days, I suppose the baby likes things pickled. We can offer you something strong to drink if you like," the duchess said.

"No, I thank you," Rupert said. "There is too much to do today. In fact, I did wonder if Conbatten wrote me this morning because he might…have a plan in mind?"

Rupert's eyes drifted to the physician, not wishing to be explicit lest the man overhear the conversation.

The duchess seemed to understand the hint. She said, "You may speak freely in front of Mr. Laurelton. As he is to be with us night and day, obfuscation did not seem practical. We took him to the queen, and she gave him direct orders to never reveal any of it."

Mr. Laurelton nodded gravely.

"Excellent. Well, I only wondered if there was something that needed doing this evening. I will not miss dinner at the earl's house, regardless of what it is."

"Of course you must not," the duchess said. "We will see what he says, but of course you must not miss dinner. Juliet would be too terribly disappointed."

"Yes, as to Lady Juliet," Rupert said, "I wonder how much, if anything, she would wish to know of the Queen's Knights."

"Ah, I see. While it is all well and good for me to know it, as I do so highly approve my husband rushing off in courageous action, perhaps it will be different for my sister."

"Yes, that is what I wondered. My own mother and sister have never known a thing about it."

The duchess was pensive. "I really am not altogether certain. On the one hand, I should like you to be honest, but on the other, perhaps not if the honesty were to make her unhappy."

"That is just what I am wrestling with," Rupert said. "I do not wish to make a mistake about it. Once I say it, it cannot be unsaid."

"Then perhaps the most sensible course is to say nothing for now. Give it a moment, get to know one another as husband and wife. I am sure that over time, the right answer must come to you."

"I have thought the very same, but then wondered if I were just putting the whole thing off for my own comfort and convenience."

"I consider you very justified in waiting," the duchess said. "Although, if you do not tell her, you must think of a very good reason to go rushing off late at night. I will not have my sister worrying that you are some kind of philanderer."

"Certainly not."

"And, if she asks me about it directly, I will not lie to her."

"No, of course you must not."

"Well then, we will see how it unfolds."

Just then, Conbatten came in, looking as smartly dressed as he always did. Rupert had given up inquiring into his tailor, as apparently the duke would take that secret to his grave.

"Hamill," the duke said, "I understand you had the very good sense to engage yourself to a Bennington. All the best gentlemen do."

He kissed his wife on the cheek and glanced at the physician, who nodded as if to say that all was well.

"I have been exceedingly fortunate to be accepted," Rupert said.

"We will see you at dinner, I think you know," the duke said.

"Yes, and I was hoping the note you sent this morning was not regarding something that must be done tonight regarding the moneylenders."

The duke shook his head. "Their regular meeting will be on the morrow, and we will see what they have to say for themselves. They may already know by now that Roundbat has escaped them, at least for the time being. He packed up and left Town early this morning, no doubt to smooth things over with his baron."

"Good riddance," Rupert said, cheered by the idea that London was to see no more of that reprobate. He had not liked to think of Juliet being made uncomfortable, should Roundbat retain his favor with Lady Jersey and keep turning up everywhere.

"The moneylenders also will not have the first idea of where their muscle men have got off to, as we have them safely locked away in Brighton. I understand those three men are eating and drinking everything within their grasp, so they will not be in a hurry to set off anywhere."

"No, I suppose not," Rupert said.

"The moneylenders will not know the details of what occurred at Roundbat's dinner, nor how the baron replied to the ransom demand. In time, I will tell those fellows we've got residing in Brighton that the moneylenders believe they've absconded with the money. That will sever relations between them forever."

"And we will inform the moneylenders that we are on to their game and it must stop," Rupert said.

"Precisely. I am not unsympathetic to their cause, they ought to be paid what they are owed. However, they must devise another less violent method."

Rupert nodded. As much as the moneylenders must be stopped, he also found himself grateful for their ridiculous idea. Had they not gone after Roundbat as they had, on the night they had, he might not be just now engaged to wed Lady Juliet.

For that, he would always silently thank them.

Suddenly, there were sounds of a scuffle out in the hall. A voice cried, "I got a right to be let in the drawing room."

Conbatten's valet cried, "You most certainly do not, English heathen!"

The doors were thrown open and Petey, the boy from the Rats' Castle, ran in.

Henri was close on his heels. "Your Grace! I did everything to stop him!"

"Everything was not enough, apparently," the duke said drily.

The duchess appeared entirely diverted by the interruption.

Petey pulled off his cap and swept into a low bow. "Your Grace, and Your Grace, and my lord, and…mister," he said. He stood and appeared pleased that he had satisfactorily greeted all in the room.

"The little devil has been trying to be shown into the drawing room ever since he began arriving to this house!" Henri said. "I informed him it was not possible!"

"And yet, he has done the impossible," the duke said. He

turned to stare down Petey. "What is it you want?"

"I just wanted to have a look round is all."

"A look round. I see," the duke said. "If you have any plans to return with friends to relieve me of any of my possessions, I assure you that you would not leave with them. Nor would you leave alive."

"I'm no housebreaker!" Petey cried, appearing mortally offended by the idea. "I just wanted to see what I could 'spect when I'm workin' here."

"You are still set on that, are you?" Conbatten asked.

The duchess stifled a giggle, which it seemed Petey took to be a very good sign.

The boy leaned confidentially on the edge of the sofa. "Mayhap you've not noticed it, but your valet is crackin' into pieces. You're gonna need a body to step in when he collapses altogether."

"Henri does not crack to pieces!" the valet shouted, as if shouting would confirm his particular brand of sanity.

"So," the duchess said, barely concealing her mirth, "you anticipate that the duke's current valet will crack to pieces, and you will step in as the new valet?"

"That's the size of it," Petey said. He hooked his thumb toward the duchess and said, "See? She gets it."

"The nerve, the audacity," Henri muttered, "the English madness!"

Petey glanced at Henri and said, "I got a new set a clothes to look the part and I know what looks good, and I reckon I can tie up a neckcloth just fine."

"The duke does not countenance *just fine*," Henri said, rather incredulous over the idea.

"Also," Petey barreled on, "I done memorized that sheet of letters you gave me, Your Grace. I can write 'em and all I need now is a tutor to 'splain how to say 'em, read 'em, and put 'em into words."

"Is that all?" the duke asked.

Petey nodded. "A'fore you know it, I'll be right as rain on the readin' and writin' front."

"I will throw this scoundrel from the house!" Henri said.

"Ya see what I mean?" Petey said, glancing at Henri. "How long can he carry on like that?"

"No one knows," the duke said. "He has been carrying on like that since he first began his employment here."

Henri appeared suitably affronted, but did not answer the charge as everybody knew the truth of it.

"Now, young man," the duchess said, "you have been very bold in thinking you could stroll in and become the duke's valet. Henri is right when he tells you a just fine neckcloth would not do for my duke."

"Your Grace," Henri said gratefully, seemingly relieved that somebody finally understood the matter.

"What you really need," the duchess went on, "is an apprenticeship to learn the skills of a valet. Conbatten? What do you think?"

The duke did not look particularly enthusiastic, however Rupert was all but certain that Conbatten never denied his duchess anything.

"I suppose that might be arranged," the duke said. He leaned over Petey threateningly. "Assuming, though, you do not make any concerted effort to drive my valet mad for your own gain. Is that understood?"

As Petey was not looking particularly threatened, but rather nodding his head enthusiastically, Henri was entirely stricken.

"He is to stay? To work with Henri?" the valet cried. "I will throw us both in the Thames and be done with it!"

Another young boy might have been alarmed by the threat. Petey said, "I bet I'm a better swimmer than you are. I bet I make it to the bank and pull myself out."

"It is settled then," the duke said. "At least for now."

Henri was so overcome by the future that faced him that he dropped into a chair.

Petey said, "Now, there is the one other little matter of my ma. It's my dream that she ought to be a lady of leisure. Wages wise, how easy is that going to be?"

Conbatten glanced at his duchess. "His mother works at night. Late."

The duchess nodded knowingly. "I see. Well, young man, wages for an apprentice are not going to keep anybody in leisure. Perhaps in future, when you are a full-fledged valet to some lord, you might manage it. For now, I am sure we can find your mother work in the house, if she so wishes."

"She'll wish it. She's said to me sometimes, she's said, 'Petey, what I wouldn't do to get further away from the Seven Dials and breathe some clean air.' Anyway, she takes in laundry when she can find the work. You got any laundry that needs doin'?"

"Our housekeeper would say plenty and always," the duchess said. "Though, perhaps your mother might forgo speaking to the other servants about…her prior circumstances."

Petey winked. "I ken the idea. No reason to get anybody's back up regardin' anybody else's mode of living."

"Just so," the duchess said.

Petey walked over to Henri and patted his shoulder. "You've had a rough day, Henri. Ya ought not take things so hard and be threatenin' to drown a fella. Have ya tried deep breaths? Or gin?"

Henri narrowed his eyes but did not issue a further threat.

"All right, out with you two," the duke said. "Henri, the sooner you whip this lad into shape, the sooner he's out of your sight and placed as a valet to some unsuspecting lord we'll dig up somewhere."

This news was the first that struck Henri cheerfully. He hopped up. "This is true! He cannot stay forever. Come, we begin at once. Pay close attention lest I box your ears. You must learn fast. Very fast! Très vite!"

Henri grabbed Petey by the collar and dragged him from the room.

"So," Conbatten said to Rupert, "we will see you this evening. Your timing is fortunate, Miss Mayton has finally concluded a rather dreadful novel she was reading aloud—you will be spared this time, at least."

The duke seemed so cheerful over that idea that Rupert did not have the heart to inform him that *The Dire Desperations of Deadwood Dale* was shortly to come his way.

Rupert left the duke, his duchess, and the ever-vigilant physician and set off for his own house.

He laughed when he saw three faces looking eagerly out the windows of the drawing room. Handing off his horse, he jogged up the steps and went in.

"Well?" Theo cried.

"It was all done satisfactorily. The earl was a prince about it and it is official, I am formally engaged."

The duchess kissed him on the cheek. "I am delighted. We like her very well."

"Excellent news, my boy. I had wondered how that awful poem we concocted would go over, but it seems to have done the trick."

"She seems such a jolly lady," Theo said.

"Oh yes, we did talk about that amongst ourselves," the duke said, nodding. "There was always the chance you'd bring home some prim little miss and we shouldn't know what to do with her. I believe we can entertain Lady Juliet well enough."

"And she can entertain us with her poems," the duchess said. "One can only approve of a girl who writes poetry and very sensibly keeps it to just four lines."

"Yes," the duke said, laughing heartily, "four lines, that is the real ticket of the thing. I could listen to anything that short. It beats listening to some long and drawn-out thing on the pianoforte."

They went happily on, discussing the delights of Lady Juliet. Rupert ordered a second breakfast to be brought to the drawing room. The duke and duchess did not linger, though. They were active people and were determined to take their horses out for a gallop after assuring themselves that their son was satisfactorily settled.

After they'd gone, Theo said, "We really are so very pleased for you. In the country, I think I will move rooms and that way you and Lady Juliet will have that wing to yourselves."

"Very good notion, Theo, if you do not mind it."

"I certainly do not."

"Well, you'll be making a more permanent move out of the house some day soon, in any case."

For some reason, that idea seemed to strike his sister in a surprising manner. She almost looked stricken.

Sensing the cause, he said, "Now, you are not to worry that you did not encounter anybody interesting this season. Next season will do just as well. Perhaps you will be struck by Darden, that would be good fun, would it not? We ought to both marry Benningtons."

Theo did not immediately answer. Quietly, she said, "I was struck by someone long ago and he is not here. He is at home. I only came along for this season to show Mama and Papa that I was reasonable and had an open mind. Before I spring the news on them."

"The news? What news? Wait, do you mean Hemsworth?"

Theo nodded.

Rupert should have known. They'd grown up with Hemsworth, a neighboring baron, and he and Theo were as thick as thieves. Hemsworth was every bit the gentleman, though his prospects did not run exceedingly high. His house was sufficient, his land was not extensive but large enough. He was everything respectable, though nobody thought he would reach so high as a duke's daughter.

"And you do not know what our duke and duchess will think of the match," Rupert said.

"I do not." Her chin up she said, "But I will have him. Mark me."

Noting her resolve, Rupert said, "I do not doubt it, and consider me in your corner, just as you have been in mine."

On that hopeful note, Rupert's second and very extensive breakfast was wheeled in. He was absolutely starving.

CHAPTER TWENTY-ONE

JULIET LOOKED ROUND the table, positively beaming. Everybody was here—Conbatten and Rosalind, Viola and Baderston, Cordy and Harveston, and even Beatrice and Van Doren. But most especially, Hamill was here.

He did stack up so well next to the other gentlemen.

"Lord Hamill," the earl said, "you have come through a trial by fire at my dining table this evening. Our butler is below stairs entertaining my granddaughter and that's left Benny and Johnny to run the table. They are practicing at it, you see."

"I would have hardly noticed anything unusual, Earl," Lord Hamill said.

Juliet beamed at him. He was so generous! Of course he would not mention the various missteps of the service. Soup served with no soup spoons, a roast with no carving knife, and perhaps most startling, a wine poured that turned out to be Batavia Arrack.

It was not as if the two footmen didn't know what they were doing. It seemed to Juliet that their nerves had got to them, and once they forgot the soup spoons it was like a boulder rolling down a hill, impossible to stop.

The two young men were just now red faced and sweating at the sideboard, having served the dessert course.

"The important thing, to my mind," the earl said, "is that one learns from one's mistakes and those mistakes need not be dwelled upon. Nor mentioned to the butler just now downstairs."

This seemed to come as a great relief to Benny and Johnny. Though, the relief was rather short-lived as their gazes drifted to the doors.

Marvin strutted through and made his way under the table.

The earl quietly sighed. "Though I find I can make no particular excuse for why we have a rooster in the house, I'm afraid."

"Lady Juliet and I have discussed Marvin's situation thoroughly and of course he must come with us," Lord Hamill said.

"Must he? Jolly good!" the earl said, seeming very enthusiastic that Marvin was not to remain a permanent fixture of his household.

Van Doren let out a small yelp. "The blasted thing just pecked my leg."

"He doesn't like men," Juliet said.

At that announcement, all the men at the table leaned back and peered under the cloth to determine which way Marvin would go next.

"If that bird put even one mark on Lily, I'll wring its neck," Van Doren said.

"Tattleton would never allow harm to come to my granddaughter," the earl said.

"Get off," Van Doren said, shaking his leg under the table. "Go somewhere else."

"He adores Lily," Juliet said, "he just does not like men. Especially men who want to wring his poor neck. I am highly confident that Marvin will adore Hamill, who does not wish to wring his neck."

"Hopefully," Hamill said, "he understands my feelings on the matter."

At this opportune time, Johnny dove under the table between Miss Mayton and Van Doren. After a brief struggle, he emerged triumphant with Marvin in his arms.

The earl nodded approvingly and this small victory seemed to buoy up the two footmen. Benny hooked his thumb toward the door and Johnny sprinted off with the rooster.

"I suppose," Miss Mayton said, "this might be an opportune time to retreat to the drawing room? Lord Hamill, in this house the men often take their port in, rather than linger here alone."

Lord Hamill nodded at the idea.

"Now, Your Grace," Miss Mayton said to Conbatten, "I know how bowled over you were at the conclusion of *The Ghastly Goings-on of Gallowing Glen.*"

"Positively staggered," the duke said.

"Do not fear that the fun is over!" Miss Mayton said. "You will be delighted to understand that this night we begin a new book—*The Dire Desperations of Deadwood Dale.*"

"My delight knows no bounds, Miss Mayton," the duke said.

"I am with you there, Duke," the earl said. "Each one is better than the last!"

The party rose and exited the dining room. Juliet took Hamill by the hand and pulled him ahead. She wished to get him to the sofa so they could sit very close together.

HAMILL HAD ALWAYS wondered if his family were not just a little bit eccentric. They were not over-formal for a ducal house, for one thing. For another, except for Theo they were always running about and rarely sitting down. He'd supposed it was not every family who found themselves so full of energy after a day of riding and sailing that they must take candles out for nighttime lawn bowling.

If they were at all eccentric, they were entirely outclassed by the Benningtons.

Who ever heard of leaving two inexperienced footmen to run a table because the butler was fond of a visiting toddler down-stairs? The Batavia Arrack served as the wine had been particularly hilarious.

And then, while he was well aware of the rooster in the house, as it was to shortly relocate into his own, he'd not expected to see it march into the dining room and go right for Van Doren.

Now, they were to hear Miss Mayton read, and from Conbatten's prior descriptions, it was certain to be eccentric. The earl looked upon all the goings-on in supreme equanimity. Rupert adored them all.

He adored Juliet most of all, and just now she sat very close and used the folds of her dress to hide their entwined hands.

Miss Mayton opened her book and said, "I will set the scene from what we are told in the description. The very put-upon duke owns *Deadwood Dale*. It used to be named *Glorious Wood Dale* and had been a lush green woodland full of mature trees, birds, small animals, deer, mushrooms, and berries. That is all gone now. Nobody can say how, but all the trees are dead, and nothing lives there more.

"The poor duchess died some years ago—she'd been lighting a fire and the wood in the dale is so terribly dry that it sprung up and burnt her to a crisp. Naturally, our duke is entranced by the gentle governess, but what does he have to offer but this wasteland? Our gentle governess feels there is some foul play at work, but she is having trouble pinpointing the cause. So now we are left to wonder—will the gentle governess be able to love a man who lives in a dale full of dead trees?"

Rupert pressed his lips together very hard and expressly ignored Conbatten attempting to catch his eye, lest he roar with laughter. The duke must certainly be besotted with his wife if he'd managed to sit through several of these stories.

For that matter, Rupert was besotted himself and could see how it could be so.

"On tenterhooks, as always, Miss Mayton," the earl said.

Miss Mayton nodded graciously. "Chapter One."

What unfolded next was the sort of absurdity Rupert could only have dreamt of. Though the duke of the story had a very unpleasant brother who was bitter over not having the title, and though that brother was forever lurking round the dead wood and sprinkling powder round tree trunks, nobody but the gentle governess seemed to think anything of it.

Miss Mayton closed the book. "Now we are left to wonder, what is that brother up to? Is the powder he's putting round the dale really an attempted cure, as he claims? Or is it something more sinister?"

It is lye powder, Miss Mayton. The brother is killing all the trees with lye while that bonehead of a duke watches him do it.

"I'd really like to know what that fellow is up to!" the earl said. "Ah, but we'll never know until we come to the end of the story."

Conbatten did catch Rupert's eye this time and raised a brow.

Juliet leaned against him and whispered, "You'll want to come every night to hear how it unfolds."

Rupert nodded. He did not give a toss how it would unfold, but he would be pleased to come every night and hold Juliet's hand under cover of the folds of her skirt.

These Benningtons were delightful, and his fiancée was the most delightful of all.

THOUGH THERE WOULD be many nights in the Benningtons' drawing room, listening to the bumbling duke fail to realize he would have his glorious wood back if he simply got rid of his brother, there were other matters that demanded attention.

A visit was paid to the Rats' Castle on the night the money-lenders were to meet.

Rupert, Conbatten, and Rowndale found them there, speaking in raised voices. None of them were happy that their plan had not come off. None of them knew why. None of them knew what had happened to their hired men, though they all were in agreement that they must have made off with the money.

Conbatten explained that their money was gone, Roundbat was gone, and their unorthodox activities had come to the notice of the queen and must stop now and forever.

The moneylenders were not made any happier by that news, but they did agree. The last thing a moneylender wished for was to come to someone's notice. Particularly not a someone who was Queen of England.

For their future endeavors, they took to merely telling one slow-to-pay gentleman some terrifying story of what had allegedly happened to another slow-to-pay fellow.

They ended satisfied with the strategy, as it seemed threats were just as effective as actions and they were far easier to arrange. Some of their stories were as creative as Miss Mayton's dreadful books. Had there really been a fellow who'd lost all the fingernails of his right hand? Had another gentleman set off in a small boat from Brighton to escape them, only to capsize and drown? Who could say, but many a debtor did not wish to test out the veracity of the tales.

Rupert and Juliet were married in St. George's and the union was very well attended. The *ton* had been most approving of the match, as Lady Juliet had been often seen in the company of the odd Mr. Roundbat and all but Lady Jersey had viewed it unfortunate.

As Rupert's duke and duchess remained in Town and the country estate was left empty, they set off there. It was not a usual wedding trip, but neither cared where they went as long as they could be alone.

The first time Juliet saw her husband striding round the bedchamber without a stitch on, she was nearly woozy over it. She did think, once or twice, of what it would have been had she seen Roundbat in such a state. It sent a cold shiver through her and she considered it no more.

There was no poetry that could be written that could describe the glories of Hamill.

When he dove on the bed in that charming state, well...she

had made the right choice. The right choice, indeed.

During the long warm days, in which England's sun must have known they had just married and came out more often than was her habit, Hamill took her sailing or riding or on a long walk in the wood.

In the evenings, they would forgo the dining table and have comfortable trays in the small drawing room. Juliet would recite the poem she had composed that day, which Rupert was always very approving of, as they were generally titled *Ode to Hamill.*

As they were to have the whole east wing of the house to themselves, they explored it thoroughly. On occasion, Hamill would wake and discover his bride gone, just a note left on her pillow. She had hidden herself away and he might find her if he could.

Then would set off a merry chase in and out of rooms until she was located, thrown over his shoulder, and taken back to bed. Never was it so thrilling to be caught.

At those moments, Hamill called her Jules. In other moments, when he had been particularly struck by her, he called her "the jewel."

As Hamill had promised, Marvin had been sent along and given his choice of nighttime accommodation. After spending the day with his new flock, the rooster found no motivation to leave his chickens behind for a sewing basket and happily settled into his coop. He would stay a rather rangy and scraggily creature, but he had the spirit of a king and kept his place at the top of the pecking order with the ruthless claws he had sharpened in the ring.

Petey worked hard to learn the duties of a valet, and probably equally hard at driving Henri mad. If Henri declared he would throw himself into the Arno, Petey would point out that the Thames was closer. Once Petey learned how to say "You are insane" in French, he used it with abandon. His knot wasn't right? Tu es fou. There is a wrinkle left on that shirt? Tu es fou. You'd like to kill Petey? Tu es fou.

One evening, after having tied thousands of neckcloths round first a post and then a footman as practice, he was permitted to try one on the duke. Henri could not be forced to admit that it was equal in skill to his own, but the duke was satisfied with it.

As Conbatten was only satisfied with the highest of standards, Petey was deemed as having a future as a valet.

After that, he was no longer called Petey, but Peter Harris. He was taught to read, and had his accent refined. Peter Harris took to imitating everything he saw around him and delighted in sniffing at anything he did not find up to snuff. As most of what he saw around him was Conbatten, he became maddeningly discerning.

His standards for what he deemed acceptable rose so high they might suit a king. His French phrase for when he denounced a thing substandard—de mauvaise qualité—became a signature of sorts. He had transformed himself into a new person and he figured he might as well go all the way with it.

When a young viscount came to Town that next season who happened to need a valet, well, what else could Lord Townson do when the great Conbatten suggested he hire Peter Harris? Peter Harris was, Conbatten said, only second to his own valet.

Lord Townson might have even done some bragging about his new valet when he was questioned about his knot, though he was often frightened by his man's lofty standards. One never knew when Harris would pronounce a thing de mauvaise qualité.

Petey's ma, having lived a hard scrabble life in the Rats' Castle, had been brought in as a washerwoman in the duke's house. However, Rosalind had seen at once that her life had worn her down and she would not last long at such physical work.

The lady was retired to a cottage on the duke's estate, her only duty being to keep a small herb garden for the kitchens. It would turn out the woman had some education as a child and knew how to read, though she'd never had a moment in her hard existence to teach Petey. She became friends with the estate's librarian and spent many comfortable evenings with a book before her hearth, never forgetting the blessing of not needing to go out and search for her bread.

When Peter Harris, otherwise known as Petey, would inform Lord Townson that he planned to take a trip, he never did inform the lord as to where he was going. Townson was always afraid to ask, or to inquire what he was to do without his valet for a week, so Petey's trips to see his ma remained a mystery.

Petey enjoyed those sojourns, as he'd been determined to see his ma living a life of leisure and now she was. It was also very comfortable to occasionally drop the mask of Peter Harris and be Petey once more.

His mother found his way of going on just as hilarious as he did himself. They both laughed into the night over the idea that Lord Townson was terrified of having Petey denounce something as being de mauvaise qualité. They were near hysterical over the idea that Lord Townson would drop dead in a faint were he ever to view their small room in the Rats' Castle.

As that season closed and Hamill's family returned to the estate, Juliet settled into her new family life. The duke was a jolly old fellow, the duchess everything agreeable, and Theo became like a sister.

Juliet was free to suit herself most days, sometimes going out with Hamill, the duke, and the duchess on horseback or running around in the dark, lawn bowling by candlelight. She particularly took to sailing the lake, thrilling at the speed when the wind was up. She had her own boat built and christened *The Poetess*.

Other days, she curled up with Theo in the library while Theo read and Juliet wrote odes. It was on those days that she slowly heard the details of Hemsworth, the baron next door, and how Theo was determined to have him.

They schemed and plotted for some months on how the news had best be broken. Juliet had even written Miss Mayton for advice. Juliet's aunt felt the only sensible course was a run to Gretna Green, but in the end they decided an elopement must be the last resort.

It was Hemsworth himself who finally took matters into his own hands. He had been frugal in his management of his estate, putting profit by year after year. When the opportunity arose, he bought out a neighbor's estate—it had a much larger house and twice the land. He might never rise higher than a baron, but he was now a very prosperous baron.

Hemsworth came calling one afternoon, closeted himself with the duke, and laid out his prospects.

The duke was not entirely against it, and then not at all against it when he heard from Theo that it was to be Hemsworth or nobody. His daughter was more reserved than the rest of them, but they all knew she had a will of iron.

In the end, the duke and duchess were rather pleased that Theo would always live nearby. Others would lose daughters to marriage half across England and be fortunate to see them in Town during the season.

When Juliet was presented with her jewelry fund that first year, it brought back all the ideas that had come to her when she'd ventured into Mr. Roundbat's house.

It brought back the shame she'd felt when she'd realized she had lied to herself that creature comforts meant nothing. And, the bigger shame of realizing that so many went without, through no choice of their own. It was embarrassing to think she had been so naïve as to imagine she would be happy starving in a garret and living on poetry.

There were so many people starving in garrets, and they certainly could not be happy, with or without poetry.

She was determined to never allow the lesson to be forgotten.

She was determined to do something about it.

It had taken her some time to devise a plan, but then Rosalind had written her a delightful description of a boy named Petey who Conbatten had plucked from the neighborhood of the Seven Dials and had trained as a valet for a viscount.

With the duke and duchess's blessing, and Hamill too, she set aside that jewelry fund and used it very intentionally. She could not solve all the world's problems in one swoop, but she could go boy by boy and girl by girl. One or two at a time, they were sent to her, usually by Conbatten, though Juliet did not have the first idea where he kept meeting all these wastrels.

Depending on their nature and skills, a boy might be trained as a valet or a footman looking to work his way up to butler, or be apprenticed to a trade he had an interest in. One of the boys even became a well-respected farrier on the racing circuit.

A girl might like to be a lady's maid, or she might like to be a teacher or a seamstress. One girl dreamed of running a boarding house, and so she did.

If any of them were trained for a trade, Juliet would back their loan to open up their own shop.

None of them would remain starving in a garret, no matter how romantic that idea had once struck the now Marchioness of Hamill.

When she and Hamill began to return to Town for the seasons, for a few years Juliet was rather in the dark about why her husband would suddenly need to go out at midnight. She was, rather delightfully, in the belief that Hamill had engaged with a very knowledgeable but irascible professor of poetry who was educating him so he could better appreciate Juliet's poems. This professor was a confirmed night owl and would not see Hamill until late at night.

However, with time came wisdom. By the second season, these nighttime excursions began to seem very strange to Juliet. Especially since Hamill never had anything particularly new to say about her odes. He loved them all, as he always had.

The story entirely fell apart when Hamill was brought home with a broken arm and tried to claim the professor had gone mad and done it. He was forced to explain his involvement in the Queen's Knights.

Juliet stood up to it rather well. After all, there was a certain romance to it. She would kiss him goodbye and then write an ode about it, leaving it on his pillow to read when he returned. She did not fear too very much for his safety—he was a brick of a man, a real Corinthian, and he had Conbatten at his side.

So many odes piled up that Juliet decided to have them bound in a book and given out as Christmas presents. What the recipients did with twenty-five pages of odes to Hamill, one could not say. At least, one could not say, but for the Duke of Conbatten. Juliet's book, along with all the other dreadful things the Bennington ladies produced, went straight into his specially built family room, hidden from the world forevermore.

Tattleton left that season assuring himself that the hijinks and shenanigans that came along with seeing five young ladies wed had blessedly come to a close. His life was to go forward in calm regularity and he looked forward to noticing that he was bored.

There were glories to be had in boredom.

Even with nutty Miss Mayton still on the premises, glorious boredom must set in. After all, Miss Mayton would remain as eccentric and unreliable as ever, but with no daughters to lead astray she was turned harmless.

There would be no more stray cats, pregnant dogs, kid goats, surly parrots, or devilish roosters coming in. There would be no more arranged kidnappings or strange carriage rides or duels at dawn.

There would be only glorious boredom.

Quite naturally, Tattleton had no way to know of the letters that began flying between houses. He remained unaware of the plan that was slowly taking shape.

It was just as well. A butler must hold on to any peace he can find, while he can find it.

As for the Earl of Westmont, he viewed it a very fine thing that all of his daughters were married. There was, however, one outstanding question—when would Darden ever get around to it?

Lord Darden himself could not answer that question, as he was having far too much fun as a single gentleman about the town and was perennially busy leading the Young Bucks Club.

Fortunately, his sisters *had* given it a deal of thought, and then discussed the matter thoroughly with their husbands. Some of these husbands were amused, others alarmed, and Van Doren dismissive.

But then, what was a man to do when one's very pretty and entirely adored wife had devised a plan to help her brother on his way to wedded bliss?

Miss Mayton was of course all enthusiasm, ready to bring her practiced hand to the case.

There was another club forming, eleven members strong, and it was not one that Lord Darden would be very happy to know about. Or join.

The End

About the Author

By the time I was eleven, my Irish Nana and I had formed a book club of sorts. On a timetable only known to herself, Nana would grab her blackthorn walking stick and steam down to the local Woolworth's. There, she would buy the latest Barbara Cartland romance, hurry home to read it accompanied by viciously strong wine, (Wild Irish Rose, if you're wondering) and then pass the book on to me. Though I was not particularly interested in real boys yet, I was *very* interested in the gentlemen in those stories—daring, bold, and often enraging and unaccountable. After my Barbara Cartland phase, I went on to Georgette Heyer, Jane Austen and so many other gifted authors blessed with the ability to bring the Georgian and Regency eras to life.

I would like nothing more than to time travel back to the Regency (and time travel back to my twenties as long as we're going somewhere) to take my chances at a ball. Who would take the first? Who would escort me into supper? What sort of meaningful looks would be exchanged? I would hope, having made the trip, to encounter a gentleman who would give me a very hard time. He ought to be vexatious in the extreme, and *worth* every vexation, to make the journey worthwhile.

I most likely won't be able to work out the time travel gambit, so I will content myself with writing stories of adventure and romance in my beloved time period. There are lives to be created, marvelous gowns to wear, jewels to don, instant attractions that inevitably come with a difficulty, and hearts to break before putting them back together again. In traditional Regency fashion, my stories are clean—the action happens in a drawing room, rather than a bedroom.

As I muse over what will happen next to my H and h, and

wish I were there with them, I will occasionally remind myself that it's also nice to have a microwave, Netflix, cheese popcorn, and steaming hot showers.

Come see me on Facebook! @KateArcherAuthor